CRAVEN'S WAR: BATTLE OF THE NATIONS

By Nick S. Thomas

All rights reserved. Without limiting the rights under copyright reserved above, no part of this publication may be reproduced, stored in or introduced into a retrieval system, or transmitted, in any form, or by any means (electronic, mechanical, photocopying, recording, or otherwise) without the prior written permission of both the copyright owner and the above publisher of this book.

This is a work of fiction. Names, characters, places, brands, media, and incidents are either the product of the author's imagination or are used fictitiously. The author acknowledges the trademarked status and trademark owners of various products referenced in this work of fiction, which have been used without permission. The publication/use of these trademarks is not authorized, associated with, or sponsored by the trademark owners.

GET IN TOUCH

If you'd like to receive my latest news, special offers and free books then please sign up for the Swordworks Books newsletter. It's a great way of keeping up to date with my latest projects, as well as getting samples and free books from my friends at Swordworks throughout the year. You can also visit the official website here:

Official website: swordworksbooks.com

PROLOGUE

Napoleon marches across Europe to conquer all before him once and for all. Yet a surprising new coalition now stands against him, made possible by who was once one of Napoleon's best and most loyal marshals. Marshal Bernadotte, now the Crown Prince Charles John of Sweden. The Prince swore to Napoleon that his loyalty would be to Sweden from the day he joined their Royal family, and that is precisely what he has done to the surprise of many. The Prince has settled disputes between former enemies and allied them together for one final attempt to stop Napoleon before he can conquer all of Northern Europe. For should resistance from the German states, Prussia, and Russia waver, Wellington and the British Army in Spain would have no choice but to withdraw to England and accept Napoleon as the Emperor of all Europe.

Into this chaos steps Major James Craven, who was sent to Germany to assist the modest British contingent there, comprising of only one hundred and forty-two soldiers of the Rocket Troop. An experimental and unpopular new form of artillery, which many perceive to be a token gesture to the war effort in Germany rather than any meaningful or useful asset. In spite of this, the Rocket Troop proved that they were more than parade ground soldiers and a publicity stunt when they engaged the enemy at the Battle of Göhrde, where they lay down a terrifying salvo of fire upon the French infantry squares. This cemented their legacy in the history books as they contributed to a great victory amongst the first victories against Napoleon since his new campaign had begun.

But the Coalition stands on wobbly legs, for distrust and animosity continues to plague the collective, and Napoleon continues to undermine it at every stage so that he might divide and conquer. Craven was sent to Germany by Lord Wellington to help maintain the bonds of the Coalition by any and all means. So far, the alliance has held true, and some small successes bode well, but a great battle is on the horizon. A monumental threat that looms like a black cloud over all of Europe. The Battle of Dennewitz had given the French a bloody nose, but to achieve success the Coalition armies must meet Napoleon himself in open battle. A battle that is both feared and anticipated in equal measure, for it will surely be the defining battle of the war. Victory could drive Napoleon back to France, but defeat could mean the end of the Coalition, and with it any hope of victory against the Emperor.

CHAPTER 1

"Cavalry scouts," declared Paget as he looked through his spyglass and gazed upon the unsuspecting enemy. The breath he exhaled rose like a cloud of vapour in the brisk morning chill. It was late in September, and the temperatures were dropping rapidly just as they experienced back home in England. After so many years in the milder winters in Spain it was a little unsettling. Paget looked as pale as ice, despite his greatcoat being buttoned up around him. It was a foreboding sign of what was to come, for the winter would bring far more adverse conditions. Although it was not at the forefronts of any of their minds at present, for Napoleon had claimed that spot. He was the looming threat that hung over all of them. For it was a rare thing for Napoleon to see defeat, and that knowledge weighed heavily upon them all as they seemingly moved ever closer to a monumental clash with the French Emperor.

Craven turned back and gave a nod to Moxy who in turn passed news on to the rest of the Salford Rifles who were waiting in a well concealed position behind a shallow ridge. The ground was wet, and they had clearly been on it for some time, as their clothing was soaked through and they looked most miserable for it, but nobody protested. Craven looked to Timmerman who was above them on a higher ridge that reached up for the clouds. He knew what he had to do, as he took out a small mirror and rotated it into the morning sunshine to refract the light as a signal. Craven went to his own spyglass and observed the enemy cavalry for himself. There were more than fifty of them, a sizeable party for a scouting detail, and there could be more obscured from his view. He watched as one of their scouts eagerly pointed towards the origin of the gleaming light, which appeared as a beacon.

"You really think this will work, Sir?" Paget asked.

"Like flies to honey," smirked Craven.

"But why would they come, Sir? Will they not avoid an engagement?"

"Those who use these signals are of great value but have little defence, which is why they must use such methods to begin with. They will not be able to resist such an opportunity."

"But are you sure, Sir?"

Craven sighed as he put down his spyglass and pointed towards the enemy. Paget watched with great anticipation as the cavalry advanced on their position, but just as he had feared, their number near doubled. Others who had been concealed from view joined the formation.

"And if this signal attracts more attention than we can manage, Sir?" Paget asked wearily, knowing it was already true.

"You let me worry about that," replied Craven

confidently. He put away his spyglass and hunkered down a little lower so that he would not risk being spotted by the enemy.

Paget did the same, taking one last look at their position. The embankment approaching their position was too steep for cavalrymen to advance, but there was a shallower climb just to the West of their position. Cart and horse tracks on this gentle climb proved the viability of the path, and Paget gasped as he imagined their fate if the cavalry could make a swift advance upon them. He hurried to prepare himself for action, checking his rifle lock thrice over. Craven smiled at the scene.

"All is well."

But Paget did not look so sure. Their horses were nowhere to be seen, and so there was no hope of a quick escape should the French cavalry prove too much for them to hold back. Craven nodded to the others along the line, giving them the signal to ready their weapons. Moxy unravelled a rag from around the lock of his rifle, a simple and effective means to protect against the moisture all around them. Their flintlock rifles and muskets were far more reliable in adverse weather than the muskets of old, but they were far from impervious to its effects, and Moxy would never risk the personal embarrassment of a snap, where the lock fired but not even a flash in the pan was achieved.

The French cavalry was approaching quickly and eagerly now, as if they were enthusiastically giving chase during the hunt. Many drew their swords as they veered off onto the shallow climb and began their ascent.

"Now!" Craven roared.

He shot up and out of cover and took aim, shooting down the closest cavalryman with perfect aim.

Moxy couldn't help but laugh, for he imagined it could only have been luck. Craven had never been much of a marksman. The Welshman took the second shot, and a sporadic volley erupted almost immediately afterward. The fresh and crisp air around them was replaced with the acrid smell of powder smoke as a number of the cavalrymen were shot from their saddles.

"Fire at will!" Craven ordered as they all hurried to reload. The French cavalry was advancing even more quickly, eager to get their revenge. For skirmishing infantry were no match for cavalry if they could close the distance and run amok with sabres slashing in all directions.

Craven and most of the others were still only half loaded when the cavalry made their final approach. Paget hurried to slam his ramrod down the barrel and drive the cartridge home in a panic, but he looked in amazement as Craven gave up in his attempts. He expected the Major to reach for his sword in a desperate attempt to fend off the cavalry, but instead he reached into his tunic and took out a whistle, which he placed to his lips and blew loudly. The bushes along a hedgerow just off to their flank rustled as more than one hundred black-clad soldiers rose up from where they had been concealed and took aim.

"The Lützow Free Corps," Paget gasped in amazement.

The Prussian volunteer force unleashed a volley before the French cavalry could react to this new threat, and they took the full force of the blow. Many were shot out of the saddle as a cloud of black powder smoke wafted through the air. The situation for the cavalry was only made worse as Craven's Salford Rifles loosed off a second volley of their own. Those of the Frenchmen still in the saddle turned and fled at the gallop whilst others who were now on the ground ran or hobbled away as best they could. An order to charge was roared, and the Prussian soldiers stormed down the slope to put any who remained to the bayonet. It was a brutal sight, but nobody protested, not even Paget, for there would be no stopping them.

A cheer rang out from the triumphant Germans as they watched the French survivors flee in a panic. Meanwhile, the looting of the dead was already well underway.

"You knew, Sir?"

"You thought I would have brought the cavalry to our door without a plan?"

Paget shrugged, for he had seen far more reckless actions by the Major, and so nothing would surprise him.

"I'm more surprised at the fact that you asked for help," replied Paget as he looked to the black uniformed Germans.

"This war is bigger than any of us. It is their war.

We are just here to do what we can," replied Craven pragmatically.

"A fine plan," admitted Timmerman.

"Let's be on our way shall we, before they return in greater number."

"How could they? We smashed them at every turn," insisted Paget.

"We win small victories, but the real test is yet to come. One day we will see Napoleon himself before us, marching at the head of a great army, and it will not be a pretty sight."

"You think he will finally march upon us, Sir?"

"Yes, or he will force us to march upon him, for these great armies cannot stay in the field indefinitely. A victor must be decided."

"We cannot force Napoleon to submit?"

"Do you really believe he would? Whilst he has an army at his side, he will never stop," replied Timmerman.

"He still thinks he can win?"

"He knows he can, and so does every man in this army. Do not forget the shaky ground upon which we stand," explained Craven.

"But you believe we can win also, do you not, Sir?"

"Believe we can, of course, but will we?"

Paget was looking for a confidence boost, and he did not get it as Craven strode onwards.

"I've never seen him so uncertain of achieving victory," muttered Paget.

"He is not in control. We can fight our very best, and we can overcome ten times, even one hundred times our number, and it would not make a difference to the outcome of this campaign."

"I don't believe that, for I know we can do more!"

"There is a battle coming, the likes of which none of us has ever seen. Hundreds of thousands of soldiers, half a million perhaps all told. Thousands of cannons and cavalry formations so large they will reach beyond all comprehension and stretch further than a man's eye can see. What can the great Major Craven do in the face of such a vast force?"

"Napoleon is only one man, and the world fears him."

"You would have a second Napoleon?" Timmerman asked.

Paget shrugged. "Do you think we can win?"

"I never thought there was much chance against Napoleon, but he does." Timmerman gestured towards Craven as he left their sight.

"I always imagined we would be successful, but I fear that was little more than hopeless optimism and the dreams of a boy, but what about him? Is he right to believe in victory?"

"I have bet against Craven many times and been wrong, and so I would not bet against him again. He has achieved the seemingly impossible more times than I care to remember."

"Even against Napoleon?" Paget asked in a worried tone, for the Emperor cast a long and dark shadow over them all.

"Napoleon is feared, and fear makes him far more dangerous a foe than he ever would be with just his skills and armies alone."

"And so what is to be done?"

"Stop fearing him. Stop letting him have that hold over you, or Craven has. Craven believes in victory and hope even in the most dire of situations. Because he knows that believing you can win is half the battle."

"Yes, he has told me as such many a time," smiled Paget.

"Then you must believe."

Paget groaned as that was easier said than done with Napoleon and his vast French army looming on the horizon. Craven thanked the Lützow Free Corps for their help before he and the Salfords left the Germans to go on their looting of the enemy, of which nobody thought lesser of them for. For they were half equipped with captured French equipment, and it was difficult to feel sympathy for the invaders. Paget was soon back in the saddle atop his loyal and close friend Augustus as they rode on. It was a triumphant day, and they were all anticipating the warm welcome and celebratory food and drink. They had been riding for only thirty minutes when Moxy and Ellis who were ahead of their small column came to a halt, as if the Welshman had caught a scent.

"What is it, Sir?" Paget asked Craven,

"Shhh," insisted Craven as he watched and listened intently.

They could hear the thundering vibrations of the ground around them, and that meant only one thing,

"Cavalry," whispered Paget in horror.

A moment later they caught their first glimpse as

dozens of horsemen stormed up and over the ridge ahead of them. Craven turned back to try and double back on themselves, but more cavalry appeared in the distance, a bloodied and weary lot, the same ones they had ambushed earlier.

"They have come for payback," said Timmerman.

"What do we do, Sir?" Paget asked.

Craven's head snapped back and forth as he studied their options.

"Back track, they're weaker there," declared Bunce.

"I won't lead them back into the Free Corps," insisted Craven as he imagined the chaos of the cavalry force catching the infantrymen by surprise on the march.

"If we don't move, we will be no better off!" Timmerman insisted.

"I fear it is so," agreed Paget.

Craven quickly scanned the ground all around for an escape route when finally, he caught a glimpse of a narrow opening between the dense trees. Cart tracks led into the small road barely wide enough for two horses to travel side by side.

"There!"

None of them knew where it led, but it was better than the other options facing them. They were now outnumbered significantly, as more and more French cavalry galloped into view to hunt them down.

"Come on!" Craven dug in his heels and held firmly onto the reins of his horse, not even attempting to reach for a weapon. It was uncharacteristic for him, a fact which only served to highlight how grave their situation was, for Craven was notorious for standing his ground against impossible odds. Nobody questioned him, for none of them wanted to be left at the mercy of the vengeful French cavalry. They soared on towards the tiny opening, hoping that it would lead them to safety or at least not be what they feared most, a dead end. It was a gamble, but when the rest of the options were so bleak, it was the best hand to be played. and they all knew it. The narrow opening of which they were approaching would at least funnel the enemy into a bottleneck to even the odds.

"What are they doing out here?" Paget asked as he looked back at the two cavalry forces converging on their position.

"The whole area is a mess," replied Timmerman.

Craven nodded in agreement, for the vast armies of both sides continued to manoeuvre, often with little information or understanding of the other side's intentions and location. It was reminiscent of some of the frontier actions on the border of Portugal and Spain years before, but that was territory Craven and his comrades had come to know as well as their homelands, whereas here they were the fish out of water. The thunder of the French horses roared out as though the devil himself was chasing them.

"Can we outrun them?" Bunce asked.

"If the road remains open!" Craven answered him.

That did not give them much of a confidence boost, seeing as nobody knew what ground ahead of them was. However, with so few horses they soared into the narrow track with ease and no hold ups, as they began to put a bit of ground between them and the enemy, stretching out the French advance. They galloped on down the narrow track with dense trees on either side of them. Deep wagon tracks along the route proved it was a well-used road despite its modest width. They soon burst out into a small opening and a single rural farmhouse, though there was no sign of life. And with woods and a steep climb surrounding the residence, they soon spotted a similarly narrow track on the far side of the clearing. It brought some relief. They had all feared a dead end, especially as they could still hear the thunder of the French cavalry, which caused the ground beneath them to shake.

No order needed to be given as the party followed Craven on to the second path. Once again, they entered a track with tall and dense trees on either side. The foliage was not so close that they could not navigate it, but it would be slow going, and the enemy would soon catch up. So the open road was their only option. They rode on as quickly as they dared, driving their horses without exhausting them. Craven could see more daylight ahead, which gave some hope, but as they rode out into the open ground, they could see a river before them. He pulled back on his reins and brought them to a standstill as he looked down to the fast-flowing water. It was clearly quite deep, but as his gaze followed the water, he spotted a small bridge ahead.

"There!" He galloped on towards the crossing. The

bridge was a very old wooden one and too narrow for most carts to cross. It looked to be hundreds of years old and creaked menacingly as Craven led his horse onto the planks. And yet nobody hesitated to make the crossing, knowing that if they could not make it, death or capture by the enemy was the only option remaining. The planks of the bridge clattered loosely under their horses' hooves as they stormed across it. On the far side were several rural dwellings with a dozen of the inhabitants working nearby. A panicked cry quickly ran out from several of them in a way that only those who had seen the plights of war would react. For it was common for civilians to gather about and cheer for soldiers as they approached, but after years of theft, pillaging, and brutality by soldiers, these people fled in terror. It broke Paget's heart to cause such a horrified reaction to their arrival, but there was nothing to be done about it now. The locals threw down everything and fled for their lives empty handed.

"The French have been through here before?"

Nobody replied to Bunce, for they feared their own allies might not have treated the locals much better than the enemy. Craven brought them to a halt on the far side of the bridge and looked back. The first of the enemy emerged from the woods and gazed upon the deep river with their own eyes. They hesitated in the same manner as he had, but they soon caught a glimpse of the Salford Rifles and the crossing they had used to get over the obstacle.

"What are we doing?" Timmerman demanded.

"We aren't going to find a better place to fight," replied Craven.

"You want to protect these peasants who run from us?" Birback groaned.

"When have you ever shied away from a fight?" Paget snapped back at him.

Birback shrugged and brushed it off as if his manhood was being called into question.

"We don't know if the road is open for us to keep on running, but we do know that this is the perfect place to hold them back."

"Craven's right. We need to deter them now whilst we have a chance," replied Matthys.

It was surprising to hear it from him, the soldier who avoided battle and bloodshed until it was absolutely necessary.

"Joze, Paget, Bunce, take the horses out of sight and ensure they are secure. Birback, you are with me. The rest of you get to whatever cover you can find and be ready to repel these bastards," ordered Craven.

"Let us fight them at the bridge with cold steel," pleaded Timmerman.

"I wish that we could, but with pistols and carbines they would shoot down anyone who was standing against them."

Timmerman did not argue, for he knew it was true, and the prospect of being shot dead before having a chance to fight back was not appealing to any of them. The party hurried to take up positions in the doors and windows of the houses, as Craven and Birback hauled an old cart towards the bridge to seal it off and slow the enemy advance. They grabbed anything in sight and tossed it into the cart once it was in position, driving farm tools through the spokes of the wheels so that it could not easily be pulled away. Craven began to lash a rope from the obstacle and tie it around a support beam of the bridge, but a musket ball landed beside him, which showered him with wood splinters.

"That will have to do!" He hurried away as more shots rang out from several of the French cavalrymen who shot at them from the saddle on the other side of the river. Their companions hurried to reach the bridge, and yet as the first man led his horse onto the rickety old crossing, he hesitated, fearful that it would collapse under the weight of his horse. Moxy seized his opportunity and shot the Frenchman from his saddle as he remained stationary, frozen by indecisiveness. Ferreira fired the next shot and hit the next Frenchman in line, and it soon spurred the rest of them on to cast away their fears and rush onto the old crossing.

In spite of the speed at which the cavalry was moving, they were travelling in a straight line for the Salford Riflemen. Along a very narrow track, it made them an easy mark for the sharpshooters. Ellis fired next and sporadic fire continued. They did not fire volleys, but each in turn fired one after the other, so that by the time the cavalry had reached the cart barricade, Moxy was loaded once more and able to fire, keeping up a continuous well-aimed fire. One man leapt from his horse to try and clear the obstacle but was shot dead by Ferreira. Another took his place, whilst the rest took up their pistols and carbines to lay down fire on those entrenched in the houses beyond. Although firing from the saddle against those in cover they did little but make a great deal of noise and empty their weapons.

Timmerman looked to Craven, seeing their opportunity. Craven did not need to share any words as he drew his sword, and the two hurried on out of the house and made a rush for the cart. They leapt atop it, and Craven thrust his sword into the chest of the Frenchman working to remove the obstacles from the wheels so that they might move it aside. Another of the cavalrymen rushed up along the bridge to engage them, but Timmerman took up a pitchfork from the cart, using it like a trident in his offhand whilst wielding his sword in his right. The Frenchman swung his long sabre, but Timmerman caught it on the prongs of the pitchfork and quickly followed it with a huge cut from his sabre. His opponent was powerless to defend against it. Rifle fire flashed past them as their companions continued to keep up a well-aimed fire.

The cavalry could not move now for all the riderless horses and dead and wounded blocking their path. Several dismounted and tried to force their way through. One leapt up onto the sidewall of the bridge, only to be shot and fall into the water below. Two others managed to reach the cart, but Craven parried one away and ran him through whilst Timmerman launched the pitchfork like a javelin, skewering the other.

Several of the cavalrymen at the back were now loaded and took aim at those on the cart. Craven grabbed hold of Timmerman as the two leapt behind the cart for cover as the shots rang out. They were soon answered by those dug in amongst the houses. Wood splintered as shots struck the cart at their backs as Craven and Timmerman hunkered down from the fire, but a cheer soon rang out from their companions. They got up to see for themselves that the enemy had abandoned the fight and were retreating in complete chaos. Craven took a deep breath and sighed in relief, but Timmerman was grinning like a fool, as if he had revelled in every moment of the frenetic action.

"That was close, too close."

"A damned good time is what it was," smirked Timmerman.

CHAPTER 2

Craven sat down upon a rock placed as a stool beside a fire, with a bowl of steaming hot stew in his hands. It was so hot it nearly burnt his flesh, and yet that was a most welcome sensation following the chilling day. The sun was going down over their camp, with canvas tents stretching as far as they could see to the North. Though Craven and his Salford Rifles were on the Southern edge, with only the pickets between them and the frontier, which could be quite inhospitable and very dangerous as they had discovered earlier that day.

"We were lucky today," declared Ferreira as he thought back over their near disastrous return journey.

"If it was merely luck that saw us through, we'd all have been dead long ago," replied Timmerman.

Craven nodded in agreement.

"And if we had not found that bridge, no amount of skill and determination would have seen us through," insisted Ferreira.

"We'd have found a way, we always do," replied Craven.

Ferreira groaned, for he was not convinced.

Timmerman slapped him on the back and laughed.

"Cheer up, my dear man, for you will have plenty more opportunities to die in the coming weeks," he joked.

But Ferreira didn't see the funny side.

General Sir Charles Stewart casually stepped up beside them, looking jovial and most relaxed, as if excited to see them.

"You had a brush with French cavalry, I hear?"

"We did," admitted Craven.

"What a shame to have missed it. I should have liked to have been there."

"I am afraid you would not have tipped the balance. It was not by the sword that the battle was won, but with the rifle."

"I am afraid that is the way of the world. Perhaps one day the army will no longer have use of the sabre, but it will not be in this war."

"No, it will not," agreed Craven.

"It was a great honour to ride with you into battle, Craven, but I would hope it will not be the last time."

Craven looked uncomfortable.

"It was?" Sir Charles pressed him.

"You should not risk your life at the front lines, Sir, and should any ill come to you, Wellington would have my head for it."

"Do you know how many generals this war has claimed?"

"As leaders upon the battlefield, Sir, but that is not your duty here."

"No, it is not, and it is all very tedious. I crave

action, Major, and I will have it. I will not hear otherwise, not from you, not from Wellington, and not even from the King. I am lousy at a great many things, but being a cavalryman is not one of them, and nobody shall take that away from me."

"They cannot take away your achievements, Sir. Those will remain with you until the day you die."

"I could say the same about you, Major, but you do not sit idle and let others do the real soldiering, do you?"

Craven shrugged.

"Indeed, you know of what I speak. Whatever we achieve it is never enough. So long as the body and mind are strong, they hunger for action. I will not sit out this war in meetings and dances and making idle pleasantries. I was born to fight with a sword in hand and a saddle between my legs, and no man will stop me, do you hear?"

"Of course," admitted Craven, for he felt just the same, "I travelled the land to fight all comers before there was even a war to fight," he smiled in agreement.

"I wish I could have done the same, but for gentlemen there is only the fencing with foils and duelling with pistols. What sort of fools duel with pistols?"

Craven rolled his eyes and nodded in agreement once more, but he could feel Paget judging him from the sidelines, he himself having fought several pistol duels in recent memory.

"I must be on my way, Major, but do not forget me the next time you ride into battle."

"Unless you want to join the Salfords, I am afraid that will be inevitable, for we see more action than any of these lads." Craven gestured towards the encampment.

Sir Charles groaned in frustration.

"Then I shall look for you when my duties are done and I have some room to breathe, for I am not cut out for this work that is asked of me."

"I once thought that about leading soldiers in battle, but if you have what it takes to succeed with a sword in hand, everything else is achievable."

Sir Charles laughed.

"I am not sure that is true, but I appreciate it, nonetheless. Yes, I shall borrow that I think, for it has a good ring to it, even if it is complete bollocks."

Craven was stunned by the General's crude language, and yet even so he laughed along with him.

Sir Charles tapped him on the shoulder in a friendly fashion before going on. Craven went back to his bowl of stew that was still steaming. It was a beautiful sight to behold, and he was just about to enjoy a mouthful when his peace was disrupted once more.

"Major Craven?"

It certainly was not Sir Charles, and he instantly recognised the French accent. No one else sounded like the former French Marshal Bernadotte, now Crown Prince of Sweden.

"Yes?" Craven casually got up to face the Prince but took his mouthful of stew whilst doing so.

All in Craven's company knew who the Prince

was, but they were too cold and hungry to react to his presence and arrival, with a general distrust of the Frenchman still lingering on as it did for many in the Coalition.

"Don't let me keep you from your meal, for it is well earned after a good day's soldiering." Good evening to you, Major."

But Craven shrugged as if he had no intention of doing otherwise.

"Good evening to you, Major."

An intentional and unsubtle cough from a man beside the General kept him from doing so. He could see Sir Charles had returned and had more to say on behalf of his associate.

"You remember Mr Edward Solly?"

"We met briefly," replied Craven as he remembered the man from his first meeting with Sir Charles upon arriving in Germany. The man wore no military uniform but was well dressed as a gentleman walking upmarket streets of London might be, with a broad topped top hat and beautifully tailored coat to match.

"A pleasure to meet you again Mr Craven," declared Solly.

Craven groaned in response whilst quickly taking another sip of his food, hoping they would leave him in peace, but it was clear now that he was not going to be left in peace.

"Mr Solly is an English merchant with many dealings in Berlin, but he fancies himself an adventurer and perhaps even a journalist. He would much like to hear tales of your adventures so that he might take them back to England."

Craven groaned once more.

"Mr Craven, would you have me believe that a former prize fighter does not wish for fame and mention in the English newspapers?"

"Former prize fighter?" Craven smirked.

"You are a soldier now, are you not?"

"A soldier fights for pay."

"Fair enough. Well, I would love to hear of your exploits when you have some spare moments."

"I do not have many of those."

"Let us not harass the Major any further, for he has had a long day and we should not hound him further this day."

"Quite, but please do not forget me, Major Craven, for there are a great many back home who would love to hear of your adventures," insisted Solly.

"I'll tell you what. When Napoleon is defeated in open battle, then you may ask me all the questions you like."

"You believe it will happen, then? The great battle that is on everyone's minds? That time has finally come?" Solly asked excitedly.

"These vast armies have not gathered for nothing, and it will cost a great fortune to keep them in the field. Winter approaches and the cost will be even greater still. A battle must be forced, either by us or by Napoleon, but one way or another it must be done."

Solly looked bewildered.

"What is it?"

"I think Mr Solly expected to find a bounding brute, and not another Wellington," smiled Sir Charles.

"I am no Wellington, but if you expected a simple brained brawler, then you know nothing of war and fighting, Mr Solly. For the greatest asset a fighting man has is his brain. A simple brute might thrive under an intelligent leader, but under a foolish one he is destined for an early grave."

"Most poetic, you are a mighty surprise indeed, Major."

"I think you read too much into my words."

"And I think you are too modest, Sir. If you want to get ahead on your return to London, you must tell the world of your exploits. Loudly announce your presence and all of your achievements."

"He is right. A modest man will get nowhere," insisted Captain Harris, one of Sir Charles' aide-de-camps.

"I'll worry about London when this war is done."

"When this war is done, the people will not want to hear about soldiers anymore. You must take what you can get now whilst you are the talk of the city."

"Is this what soldiering has become?" Craven groaned.

"Spoken like a true soldier," smiled Solly.

"Let us leave the Major in peace. You will have plenty to write about in the coming weeks," insisted Sir Charles.

"It is coming, then, the great battle?" Craven

asked the General, wondering if he had some information or insight that the rest of them did not.

"Like you said, this vast army was not assembled for nothing. The great battle of our time is on the horizon."

"Then we must ensure we are ready when it comes."

"When are you not ready for battle, Major?" replied the General in jovial manner as he walked away with his companions.

"Sir?"

Craven turned about to find Paget waiting to address him.

"What is it?"

The young man lifted an object he had been concealing by his side until the moment was right. He held it out before him in both hands as if it were the gift of a sword, but it was not a sword, but merely a polished iron scabbard. He held it aloft as a mighty gift, and to Craven it was, for he knew exactly what it was and why it was being given.

"For the cavalry sabre which General Le Marchant gave you, Sir. It is only a trooper's scabbard, but it should do until we can find the one that Rocca stole from you, Sir. I noticed you carrying the sabre rolled up in a blanket, and that will not do at all, Sir."

Craven looked in disbelief and pleasant surprise, for he could not remember ever having received such a thoughtful gift.

"Where did you find it?" Craven asked as he took the gift into his hands.

"I purchased it from some of our German allies, Sir. Many of their cavalry sabres were made and sent from England, and so it should fit correctly."

"How much did it cost you?" Craven reached for his purse to pay the bill.

"No, Sir, it is a gift, and you do not pay for a gift."

Craven was stunned, for not only was it thoughtful, but it was no small gift from a man who was once rich but now survived on only a soldier's pay since being disowned by his father.

"A mighty gift, thank you."

"Hardly, Sir."

But Craven meant it, for the effort and thought meant as much to him as when Gaspard had first given him the sabre for which the scabbard was destined. He did not know what more to say, but he could see the exhaustion in Paget's eyes and the chill in his cheeks.

"Go and get yourself some hot food. You deserve it."

"Yes, Sir, thank you, Sir," he replied as he went to do precisely that as though he had been given marching orders.

"All these years and he is still trying to impress you," declared Ferreira with a smile.

"You've got it wrong. Paget does what he does for love," replied Charlie, who had been lurking unseen behind them.

"You think so?" Ferreira asked.

"I know it. He stopped trying to impress others a long time ago, and so did you," replied Charlie as she looked to Craven.

"You think I ever cared for what people thought?" he smirked.

"Of course, you did. You fight for fame, or at least you used to. Many an officer fights for his name and reputation, and you are little different. You just go about it a different way, or again, you used to. These days you are what many of those men always aspired to be."

"What are you saying?"

"That you have become a proper officer, but one of the good ones, one of those many others aspire to be but never reach."

"Is that a compliment I hear?" Ferreira smiled.

Craven laughed in agreement, for such words were most incongruous coming from her mouth.

"Mr Craven, Sir," declared a new arrival.

It was the General's aide-de-camp Captain Harris.

"With Sir Charles' compliments," he explained as he pointed to two servants behind him, each carrying two unmarked crates, one stacked upon the other. They placed them down before hurrying away with Harris. Canvas sheets covered the top of crates loosely. Craven approached with suspicion and curiosity. He lifted one of the sheets to reveal six bottles inside. He pulled one out and great smile stretched across his face.

"What is it, Sir?" Paget had come over to see what was happening.

"Wine, compliments of Sir Charles and the French," he smirked as he tossed the bottle into the

Captain's hands so that he could see for himself.

"A mighty gift," replied Paget in amazement. The French supply lines were stretched far and thin, and such a treasure would be rare and most valuable indeed. Craven ripped the cork from the first bottle and offered him the first taste. Paget looked amazed to be given such an honour. He took a small sip straight from the bottle, setting aside the crudeness of the gesture in appreciation of the honour which has been bestowed upon him.

"Well?" Timmerman licked his lips as he eagerly awaiting his turn.

"It is fit for Napoleon himself!" Paget roared.

"I'll be the judge of that." Timmerman took the bottle and sniffed it before taking a mouthful, which he proceeded to swill about his mouth as if tasting like a gentleman of high society. Craven could not help but laugh.

"Come on, you would drink anything."

"Yes, I would, but I still know what the good stuff tastes like, and that is as smooth as a whore's bosom."

Craven laughed, but Paget did not see the funny side, and yet Charlie did and glared at him as if to encourage him to lighten up.

"And what did we do to earn such a reward?" Ferreira asked.

"Do not question it," replied Craven.

"If not a reward, then it is bribe, is it not, Sir?"

"No doubt. Sir Charles wants to ride beside us in battle, and probably as many other actions as he may have time for."

"And is that a good idea, Sir?"

"Not particularly, but his mistakes are his own to make."

"Is it not our duty to protect him from such mistakes, Sir?"

Craven laughed at Paget.

"Try and tell any general of any army that, and you will be drummed out quicker than you can imagine."

"Then what will we do, Sir?"

"They call him Fighting Charlie, Sir Charles that is, did you know that?"

"I did, Sir."

"Well, if Fighting Charlie wants to ride with us, then so be it. We are so few that a competent rider and a hard fighter is most welcome."

Paget groaned for he knew it was a bad idea, and yet he was getting nowhere in raising the issue with Craven. And when he looked around at the cheerful faces of their companions, all of his worries began to fade away. Charlie thrust a cup of wine into his hands and the changeover was complete as he took a sip and a page from Craven's book, letting go of his fears so that bridge might be crossed another day.

"It's a good day, is it not?" Charlie asked him with a great smile upon her face.

"How could it not be? We are alive and we are victorious, what more could we ask for?"

"Wine, Mr Paget, and you have that, too!" Craven insisted.

Fires raged all about the camp, for the winter was

quickly approaching, and battle must be made soon. If it was delayed until the worst of the weather, they all knew what a nightmare scenario it would be. They had all lived through the winter in the Peninsula and even marched and fought in it, but it was obvious to them all that the conditions could be so much worse this far North. Paget took another sip when he noticed Holck standing alone whilst the others made merry. He approached the huge Dane, feeling uneasy that one of their companions was left out.

"You are still with us?" Paget asked him.

"I could ask the same of many of your companions."

"Our companions," insisted Paget in a friendly tone.

"Yes, I suppose that is true," admitted Holck.

"You are surprised that we follow him?" Paget gestured towards the Major.

"No, I can see why, and it is the reason I am still here."

"And what reason is that?"

"Because he makes this life worth living. There is never a boring day under the command of Major Craven."

Paget nodded in agreement.

"And so you will stay with us, even when we march against Napoleon himself?"

"Of course, how could I miss such an opportunity?"

"And if we cannot beat him? As Englishmen we may retreat across the channel, but for you, you will remain on Napoleon's doorstep."

"We must be victorious. There have been many coalitions against Napoleon, and this if the best chance we have of defeating him."

"And you really want that?"

"France would have dominion over all of Europe. England might have bombarded my city, but under Napoleon the French would do far worse."

"Then it is settled, and almost all the world stands with us against him," smiled Paget.

"And when he is defeated, will the leaders of the Coalition let Europe be at peace? Or will they walk in Napoleon's footsteps?"

"I cannot speak for all men and all nations, but I can promise you that we as Englishmen will not."

"You have an Empire about the world, and you want me to believe that is true?"

"We do not march across Europe to conquer the lands of our neighbours. What was done to Denmark was horrific, and I wish it was not necessary, but it was. And yet England did not invade your country, overthrow your government, and force your population into fighting our war."

"I believe you, but I am not sure you would find many men in my country who would."

"You believe me because of actions, not words, and in time, so will they."

Holck nodded in agreement.

"Will you drink with me?" Paget reached for another cup and offered it to Holck.

"I would not refuse wine, even from my enemy,"

he smiled and took the cup, holding it aloft before Paget, downing it in one.

"You truly are one of us, you know that?"

"I might have doubted it once, but it did not take long for me to realise it, for I would not sleep at night amongst you if I imagined you meant me harm."

Paget nodded in agreement.

"This might be a coalition of a great many nations, but Craven has assembled such a mix of people to his side long before. We might make unusual bedfellows, but the results we achieve speak for themselves. It is an honour to have you with us."

Holck reached for a bottle of wine and topped Paget's to the brim before doing his own.

"To Major Craven, and to victory," he toasted.

CHAPTER 3

"It is really quite beautiful here, isn't it?" Ellis asked as he sat opposite Moxy about the fire in the early hours of the morning. Heavy snoring rumbled from the tents nearby from the drunken soldiers who were still deeply asleep. Moxy took a gulp of the fresh morning air and sighed as he nodded in agreement.

"It reminds me of home," he admitted, for it was some relief to be back amongst luscious green lands that resembled his native Wales, as opposed to the sun-drenched lands they had battled over for the past few years, "Do you think we will ever see it again?"

"This war cannot last forever, and so long as we make it through, then yes, I am sure you will," replied Ellis.

"Me? What about you?"

"I am not sure that is my home anymore. My wife is in Spain."

"You would not bring her home with us when this is all over?"

"You think a Spanish woman would be welcomed with open arms back in England?"

"The soldiers welcome them well enough whilst we have been out here at war."

"Because that is all they could get, and hungry men will eat anything."

Moxy groaned for he knew there was some truth to it.

"Spaniards have never been very welcome back home, and I do not see how that could have changed."

"Because when this war began, we were enemies. England and Spain against one another as they always have been, but that has all changed now. United we have fought together as one."

"Maybe that matters to the folks out here that have fought alongside one another. Loved one another, but back home my wife would be called a Spanish whore and worse."

Moxy said nothing, knowing it was likely true, but as he thought back to their days in England together, he smiled.

"Before we came out to fight this war, when we travelled about Britain with Craven. We were called worse, and what did it matter? You will go home a hero, and an officer, no less."

"I was an officer before, and I didn't much like it then, and I never wanted to return to such a position."

"But for your wife it will mean everything. She will be the wife of a gentleman."

"And so what, we mingle with polite society, what will they think of my Spanish wife there?"

"None of us has a good plan for what we will do when this is all over, least of all Craven, but we shall deal with that problem the same as any other, when the time is right that we must."

Paget climbed out from his tent looking rather worse for wear, earning himself an amused smirk from Ellis and Moxy, but they all looked to the sound of horses. The Swedish Crown Prince was approaching. He had with him only two companions, and he was looking right at them, as if he was looking for them.

"Where is Major Craven?" the Prince demanded before Paget could get a word out to greet the future King of Sweden.

"He has not risen from his bed yet, Your Grace," declared Paget as he hurried to button his tunic and make himself look somewhat presentable, but Craven staggered out as he did so, a blanket wrapped about his shoulders like an improvised cloak.

"What can we do for you, Sir?" Craven croaked in a dry and weary voice.

"It sounds as though you have been doing rather a lot already from the reports I have received."

Craven shrugged. "I didn't come all this way to sit idly by," he admitted.

"Was it not your orders to advise and assist, and not to fight?"

"Actually, Lord Wellington asked me to do whatever I thought necessary to ensure victory here for you and this coalition."

"Good, then, for I have a task for you in pursuit of those ends."

"Oh?"

It was clear that the Prince's companions did not appreciate how casually Craven addressed the Prince, and yet they were in no position to speak up about it.

"In the armies of France, a sword master is attached to every regiment to train the men in the use of the swords they wear, but I am astounded to see and learn that this is not the practice in most other armies, not even in your own."

"Indeed," groaned Craven.

"That is a practice you should like to change, I would imagine?"

"Of course, any man who carries a sword should be well training in its use, or it is little more than decoration."

"I am glad that we agree on this issue, Major. I am sending you some of the men under my command. Officers and sergeants who you will ensure are capable in the use of the sword."

"Have they had any training with them?"

"I could not say."

"Sir, training men to be competent swordsmen is not achieved in a few hours or days. A great battle will surely soon be upon us, and there is not enough time."

"I do not ask that you make of them the finest swordsmen in all the world, Major. Only that you ensure they are better than they were yesterday, can you do that?"

It was still so incongruous to be taking orders from a French native and former enemy of Britain and her allies, and yet he nodded in agreement.

"Yes, Sir."

"These Swedish are well trained and disciplined with the musket, Major, and I would ensure their skill with the blade is at least somewhat matched. I am sending you fifty men. Fifty men who might benefit from your training and go back to their regiments and instruct those under their command in the same drill and knowledge. They will report to you within the hour."

"I will do all that I can."

"Very good."

"And, Sir, a great battle is coming, is it not?"

"It must, so long as the Coalition stays loyal to one another, it must."

The Prince tipped his hat to Craven before riding on without any more explanation, but it was not needed, for his fears and concerns where the same as felt by all those in command.

"I thought time was on our side, Sir, that Napoleon was running out of it, but it is us, isn't it?" Paget asked.

"I fear it is so. For whatever setbacks Napoleon has faced, he has his whole country united behind him, for as long as he needs them."

"Why will the people in the nations of this coalition not do the same?"

"Because they are not behind one man and one cause, but many. It is a fragile alliance, and the Crown Prince knows it. Wellington knows it, and so does Napoleon, and he will do everything in his power to drag this out until the alliance crumbles. If he does not pick it apart before that day comes."

"We have to make this battle happen before the year is up, don't we, Sir?"

"Yes, we do, and we will."

"But how, Sir? How can we make that happen?"

"I don't know, but I am going to find a way."

"But what about the Prince, Sir, and the men he would have us instruct?"

"I said we would give them some training, but not how much or for how long. We will give them the morning, work them until they have had enough, and then we will be on our way."

"On our way where, Sir?"

Craven shrugged.

"I don't know yet, but I will," insisted Craven cryptically.

"What are you orders, Sir?"

"Get 'em up, all of them. Dressed and ready to begin training in twenty minutes."

"Twenty?"

"We are not practicing with one another. We are teaching others. Let us get a plan together so that there is not a minute wasted."

"Yes, Sir."

Paget hurried away to see it done, eager to see what the rest of the day would bring.

Craven went to his tent and pulled back the flap of the door and cast it out onto the side of the tent to illuminate the inside by the daylight. His saddle lay beside his bed, and he reached into the bags resting atop it, pulling them back to reveal the two singlesticks he kept with him at all times for the purpose of training. Beside them was the scabbard, which Paget had so kindly gifted him, and the sabre still wrapped in a sheet beside it.

"It doesn't fit, does it?" asked a voice from over his shoulder.

It was Charlie, and he did not need to look with his own eyes for her voice was unmistakable.

"No, it doesn't," he sighed.

Charlie couldn't help but laugh.

"I don't have the heart to tell him," whispered Craven as he took the scabbard in his hands. It was a modest piece of equipment and to many it would be a worthless gift, but the thought and effort behind it meant the world to him.

"Tell him, he is stronger than you think."

Craven nodded in agreement just as the Captain himself rushed up to join them. He looked most pleased with himself as the rest of the Salford Rifles' officers and sergeants barked their orders that he had delegated to them. He noticed the scabbard in Craven's hands and at first looked most excited to see it, but then he noticed the sabre still wrapped up in his saddlebags.

"It does not fit?"

Craven hesitated, but that answered the question for the young man.

"No matter, give it here and the sabre, and I shall find another."

Craven looked to Charlie in surprise, but she merely smiled in response, confirming what she had asserted about the Captain.

"Thank you, but it can wait. We have a job to do, and I would not delay for even a minute."

"Yes, Sir," Paget grumbled in a deflated and disappointed tone.

"Do not feel bad for this, for it is not your mistake."

"Then whose is it, Sir?"

"The fools who make the damned swords and scabbards for the army. A sword made by pattern should fit any scabbard made for it, or what is the purpose of such industrial scale manufacture?"

"I admit it does not make sense to me, Sir, but your sabre was no ordinary sword manufactured for the army and ordnance stamped and tested. It was an officer's sword purchased by the man who designed the weapon himself. Perhaps the swords made for the army are merely a pale imitation of the masterpiece which General Le Marchant created?"

"I am sure that you are correct," smiled Craven.

"I will see that it is replaced with one which fits at least well enough to use just as soon as I have a moment to do so."

"Thank you, truly."

"It is my duty and my pleasure, Sir." He then reached for Craven's singlesticks to hurry on with his preparations.

"Paget?"

"Yes, Sir?" he paused.

"You're a good man, and a good friend, more than one could ever hope for."

"I thank you for saying so, Sir, but it is the very least I would expect of myself, and I should be terribly upset if I could not uphold such a standard," he replied before going on his way.

Craven chuckled. "He has no idea how special he is, does he?" he asked Charlie.

"None at all, for in his eyes he has so much more to prove."

"You look after him, for you are good for one another," replied Craven as he confirmed openly that he knew of their relationship, which was very much an open secret amongst their companions.

"I shall, right up until the day that I cannot."

"And what day would that be?"

"The day we go back to England, for then we are not comrades fighting side by side, but men and women in levels of society which do not mingle," she groaned as she imagined what that future might look like.

"Do not be so sure that is our future. This war has changed a great many things. Paget might have come to us as a spoilt rich boy and not a clue about life for the rest of us, but he is one of us now, and so are you."

"I truly hope that is true. One day we will return to England, and I hope that is not where we part ways."

"The end of this war will not be the end of this story. I will make sure of it."

"I believe your sentiments, but I am not sure that it will be your choice to make."

"A great many people thought they held power over my story, and time and time again I have proven them wrong." Craven then rushed on to join Paget and the force he had assembled.

"This war has moulded him into a real soldier, and still he thinks he is in command of his own destiny," smiled Charlie.

Craven reached the assembled Salford Rifles to find them in a beleaguered state, yawning and groaning at having been dragged from their beds whilst they still nursed sore heads from the volume of French wine the night before. Craven was in better shape than many of them, but only because he had weathered this storm enough times to be more resilient against its effects. And yet somehow the same did not ring true for Timmerman who was keeled over atop a barrel beside them, looking ghostly pale.

"Listen up," Craven declared to the unenthusiastic crowd of his companions, "The Crown Prince is sending us fifty officers and sergeants from his army of Sweden. We are to instruct them in the sword."

"For how long?" Moxy groaned.

"That much was not made clear, but I want to be on our way this afternoon. I want you to sweat these men. We will train them well, but we will exhaust them until they want no more and can do no more."

"And if it us who breaks first?" Timmerman croaked.

"Even in this state you could outfight the devil himself," replied Craven.

The rest of them laughed in agreement and even Timmerman himself got a chuckle from it as he got to his feet, motivated by the compliment and eager to live up to his reputation.

"They are here, Sir." Paget gestured towards the party of Swedish soldiers approaching in their blue coats.

"That was quick," replied Charlie.

"Good, the sooner we start the better," replied Craven.

The Swedes stopped before them, looking most casual and even a little bit resentful of having to receive training from an Englishman.

"How many of you have received any training in the use of the sword?"

There was no response and a look of confusion at Craven's question.

"Sword practice, have you had any training with the sword?"

Still there was no response.

"I don't think they understand you, Sir," Paget whispered.

"Don't understand me?" he recoiled in amazement. "How many of you speak English?"

There was not a single acknowledgement.

"Jesus Christ," sighed Timmerman.

"How can we train men who do not understand us?" demanded Craven in frustration.

Holck suddenly spoke out in a language, which was entirely incomprehensible to every other member of the Salford Rifles. Eight of the men raised their hands, clearly answering the question that Craven had asked them and Holck had translated for him.

"Eight? Eight men out of fifty have any

understanding of the art of fencing?" he gasped.

"I am afraid the state of affairs in our own army is little better," replied Paget.

Craven shook his head in despair.

"The army is about black powder these days, Major. Fossils like you and I are merely relics of a bygone era," replied Timmerman.

"People keep telling me the age of the sword is over, and yet here we are still winning," smirked Craven.

"How are we going to do this, Sir? One translator and fifty students?"

"They don't need to hear what we say, Mr Paget, only copy what we do."

"And you believe we can train these men in the sword in a few short hours?"

"We can make them better than they are now."

"That is not saying much," grumbled Timmerman.

"We don't need to make these Swedes the finest duellists in all the land, just capable enough in a brawl."

Timmerman smirked at the idea, for what was just the sort of fight he liked.

"And how do we do that?"

"We will train them in the simplest of ways, Mr Paget, just like a ship's crew. They need to be able to deliver a blow and stop anything on a hanging guard, and with those powers they will hold their own upon the battlefield."

"An officer should never really have to use their

sword. It is merely a symbol of authority, but to give these some men the confidence in their own arm will make them twice the soldier they are now," insisted Ellis.

"If only the army followed such a philosophy," Paget lamented.

"When we go back to England, we will ensure that they do."

"And they will listen?"

"We will make them listen, with the same fervour that we have used against the French," insisted Craven he replied before studying the faces of those who had come to train with him, or at least had been sent for that purpose. They were proud men, and not one amongst them was scruffy or poorly turned out. He drew out his sword and held it before him.

"Tell them we are going to give them the training to use those swords they wear."

Holck quickly translated. Many of them smiled and giggled. Craven targeted the loudest and most unrestrained of them, a young officer about the age of Paget, though he was a little taller than Craven.

"Ask him what he finds so amusing?"

But the man spoke before Holck could even ask the question.

"He says any fool can swing a sword."

"Really?" Craven asked with a big smile.

He looked across at the faces of the Swede's companions to see they were very much in agreement and had no respect for the training they had been sent to receive. Craven was amused but could find no words. He turned away and began to look about the camp as if he was searching for something. The Swedish soldiers looked confused, gazing upon one another, and whispering amongst themselves as if they had achieved a victory and gotten themselves out of having to put in a morning's work. Craven suddenly sprang into action, storming away as if he had given up, but Paget knew that was an impossibility.

"What's going on?" Joze asked.

"Just watch," replied Paget confidently.

Craven approached two cooks in their aprons who were butchering a horse carcass ready to be cooked later that day. He paced right up to them and grabbed hold of a large hunk of meat, which the men did not dare protest considering he wore the uniform of an officer, no matter which army it was from. Craven walked up to Joze and drew the knife he wore on his belt. He then paced with purpose over to a tree where he placed the hunk of horse meat, driving the knife into it with one vigorous punch to nail the meat in place upon the tree. He admired his work for just a moment before pacing back over to the man who had questioned the reason for them being there and the value of swords and swordsmanship in a modern industrial war.

"Tell him to draw his sword."

The young Swedish officer looked uncomfortable as if he had been challenged merely by Craven's tone, and doubly so after Holck had translated his order.

"Draw your sword!" Craven roared.

The man sprang into action and took out his weapon, as if fearful that he might be struck by Craven who still had his own bare blade in hand and ready to use.

"Tell him to cut the meat."

The officer relaxed, realising he was not in danger of harm and looked sheepishly at the hunk of horse meat nailed crudely to the tree as if it was beneath him.

"Tell him that if he can slice that cut of meat in half in a single swing, I will accept that these men are competent in the use of the sword, and they can leave now and never have to see me again."

"What is the Major doing?" Joze whispered to Paget.

"Betting on the ineptitude of arrogant men."

"But is the Major not a terrible gambler?"

"In all matters, except those which involve the sword, yes."

The Swedish officer looked to his comrades in disbelief, as if he had been given the easiest challenge in the world. They cheered him on, eager to prove the Englishman wrong and save them all a morning of work. The young Swede stormed confidently towards the target he had been given, as if he was a cavalry squadron that had been unleashed upon the enemy. He did not even slow to check his distance or practice the cutting motion before throwing all his body into a great big cut, which hit the target dead centre. But in all his haste and an equal lack of experience, he had not aligned the cutting edge to the target and slapped the slab of meet with the flat side of his sword. The blade flexed around the target with such force t it snapped in two, leaving the dumbfounded officer holding the hilt with only a few inches of the blade remaining. The crowd was silence for several moments until Birback let out a cackling laugh, soon joined by Timmerman and then the rest of the Salford Rifles.

Craven paced up to the embarrassed Swedish officer and took a close look at the dangling haunch of horse meat. The attack had left an imprint the width of the Swede's blade but not cut into the flesh at all.

"You will not kill a Frenchman like that, nor defend your own life when it matters."

Holck translated, but he needn't have for the demonstration had spelt out his message with overwhelming clarity.

"Soon you will march to do battle with Napoleon himself and his army, and when the time comes that you have to fight beside the soldiers under your command, would you have them see you fail like this? Or would you like to fight like your Viking ancestors and make them proud to follow you?"

Holck quickly translated, and a cheer rang out from the Swedes, eager now to learn the lessons which he had ready for them. Craven looked to the young man who had humiliated himself in the cutting challenge.

"Are you ready to begin?"

CHAPTER 4

"Not a bad morning's work?" Craven asked, as he looked at how Paget marvelled at the lines of Swedish soldiers practicing their partnered drills back and forth with remarkably finesse for beginners. Even the young officer, who had been humbled and humiliated when breaking his sword and failing the challenge he had so confidently accepted, was now smoothly and calmly lunging and recovering with careful motions of a singlestick he had been loaned by the Major in lieu of his broken sword.

"Will it be enough if they have to do battle against the enemy?"

"How good they are as swordsmen is less important than what they believe in their hearts. If they believe they can fight and be worthy of leading the soldiers under their command, that will count for a lot."

"Because believing you can win is half the battle?" Paget smiled, repeating a line Craven had often repeated.

"That's right. For many of these soldiers Napoleon is some great monster, a legend almost, and it will be most unnerving to face him. Giving these men that courage and belief is the first step."

"And for us, too, for it is a test we have never had to endure," replied Paget as he envisaged what it might feel like to face Napoleon in battle after so many years of anticipation, excitement, and dread at such a day finally arriving.

Timmerman approached with purpose as though he had news.

"The party we worked with have gone on to Dannenberg."

"Dannenberg?" Craven asked.

"Indeed."

Paget looked confused, for he had no idea what they spoke of, but Craven was happy to explain and not leave the ever-curious young officer guessing.

"The Lützow Free Corps, I believe they have some information which could be useful to us, or so I have been led to believe by Sir Charles and his associates."

Timmerman went on to fill in the blanks.

"With the lull in action here, many of the Corps has gone on to Dannenberg to visit the wounded Eleonore Prochaska, or August Renz as we knew her. Dannenberg is her home, and she rests there in hope of recovery, or perhaps a peaceful end."

Craven took out his map of the area of Northern Germany, but Timmerman already knew what he was looking for.

"It is two days' ride from here."

Paget remembered the horrifying bloodied state in which they had found Eleonore after she was struck down by the enemy, and the horrified looks upon the faces of those who finally realised her true identity. It was an image burnt into his memory, particularly as he could not stop imagining Charlie in a similar situation, her identity revealed by surgeons after suffering a similar fate.

"Two days there and two days back, that takes us out of the field for a long time," declared Paget.

"The Free Corps members have something which could be most valuable to us. Wellington asked me to do everything in my power to help the war effort here, and that is just what we will do. We are not line infantry. We do not sit around and wait for the big battles. We will go in search of..."

"Trouble, Sir?" Paget interrupted him.

"You are damned right," smirked Timmerman.

"We have done what the Prince asked of us. Let's wrap this up and be on our way. I want to cover as much ground as we can today."

"I will see to the horses and provisions, Sir," replied Paget.

Craven whistled loudly to bring his new students to a halt and direct their attention to him. Holck took up position beside him ready to translate.

"This training is complete, or as complete as it can be in the time that we have." He paused for Holck to explain it to them before we went on.

"I cannot teach you all that there is to know about the sword in one morning, but I can make you competent enough to face the enemy and feel confident in your own ability to inflict damage and defend your own lives. Now that you have the basic tools that you need, I cannot recommend enough that you practice them whenever and as frequently as you can. Practice making effective cuts and drill with the partners. The men under your command train to load and fire their muskets with competence and efficiency, and it is your duty to put as least as much work into the training of the weapon you yourselves carry. Good luck, gentlemen, and may we all together be victorious in the coming days and weeks."

Holck translated quickly before a cheer rang out, led by the young man who had failed at his cutting challenge only a few hours earlier. As the Swedish soldiers sheathed their swords, many came forward to shake the hand of Craven and his associates before going on their way with a spring in their step. They excitedly chatted with one another in stark contrast to the bleak and dismissive manner in which they had arrived.

"Well said," declared Timmerman.

"I'm not new to this, you know," he snapped back.

"That was good and noble work," declared Matthys.

"It was. Refreshing in fact to be actually doing what I was born to do."

"You keep saying that, but it has been a long time since you have been only a swordsman, a great many years in fact," replied Matthys.

"What am I now, then?"

"A leader."

Craven laughed, but Matthys nodded along confidently with Timmerman's statement.

"If we were merely swordsmen, we would still be battling one another until the end of our days," added Timmerman.

Craven grumbled, as deep down he knew it was true. He had made a life out of his commitment to the sword, and yet that commitment was now entirely focused on the army and the leadership of those under his command. It was a role he had been fulfilling for so long now he had not even realised how far he had come.

"This war has made good men of more than just myself," he replied, looking to Timmerman.

"I don't deny it. I'd be dead and buried if it wasn't for these past few years."

"We have all been given a second chance, and we have embraced it," explained Matthys.

"And when it is all over, and if we are still alive to see that day?"

"There is no going back to what we were. You cannot undo all that we have seen, and all that we have achieved. We are not the men we were five years ago, none of us."

"Five years, is that how long it has been?" Craven mused.

"More since that fateful meeting with Wellington and the day Mr Paget came into our lives," replied Matthys.

"That you associate those two things is…well, it is something," Craven smiled.

"Are they not as important as one another?"

"Maybe you are right."

"He absolutely is. You were a bastard when you left England, and when I caught up with you in Portugal, you were not the same man. It just took me a long time to see it. I thought I was fighting the Craven of old, the rogue I once knew, but that man no longer exists," added Timmerman.

Once again Matthys nodded in agreement. Craven sighed and then smiled, for the unlikely set of friends before him were right.

"What is this information we go in search of?" Matthys asked.

"Honestly, I am not entirely sure, but there are some contacts which Sir Charles believes could be most valuable to us, and at least it gives us something to aim for. And I promised we would find Eleonore when the time was right."

"And you think that it is?" asked Timmerman.

"Fate is carrying us to that town, is it not?"

Soon they were in the saddle and on their way. Everyone knew where they were going, but seemingly only Craven knew why, and to visit Eleonore was a thinly veiled cover story.

"So, are you going to tell us what this is about?" Paget asked Timmerman.

"I wish that I knew, but I only learnt from Sir Charles what I shared with you." Timmerman looked to Craven for answers the same as Paget did.

"There is nothing to know, and even if I did know it, it would not be for you to know."

"This must be quite the secret, but I am sure that if this was putting us in danger the Major would share it with us," replied Paget.

"Do you think Wellington shares information with those under his command merely for the sake of their safety?"

Paget shrugged at Timmerman.

"For now there is nothing to say and there is no threat to any of us, no more than any other day," insisted Craven sternly to silence the arguments.

They took the message, but Paget did not look comfortable to be left in the dark, and yet Timmerman was basking in the sense of mystery and danger. They rode on until complete darkness before stopping by the roadside and quickly assembling a fire. It was a long day on the road, but as soon as the horses were seen to, Paget reached for Craven's singlesticks and began looking for a sparring partner.

"A morning spent on practice, and you still want more?" Bunce groaned.

"A morning of teaching novices. I want a challenge."

"Why not!" Timmerman roared.

Nearly all amongst the party watched with great curiosity and more than a little concern. Timmerman had tried to kill Paget several times in years gone by, and whilst they now trusted him as an ally, this challenge seemed to be a powder keg about to explode.

"Excellent!" Paget responded with excitement.

Craven could not tell if the Captain was oblivious to the apparent danger or that he embraced it. For Paget was not the naive boy he once was, but he was not always the most street wise or savvy.

"This should be good," grunted Birback who gleefully watched on in the hope of blood being spilt, despite the use of wooden singlesticks. For whilst they may not cleave like a sword, the ash staves were still quite capable in their ability to bludgeon an opponent, to break limbs, fracture skulls and more; particularly when they were played with so loosely and with so few rules and accepted practices.

The two men saluted, a sign of respect not many would expect from Timmerman, even after all they had been through together. They came on guard with the baskets of their singlesticks extended before them towards their opponent.

"Don't go easy on me now."

"I would not dream of it," smiled Paget.

He leapt forward in a surprise turn of aggression, for there is not one amongst the crowd would not have bet on Timmerman to have made the first move, for his hot temper and lack of patience so often got the better of him. Timmerman parried it with ease, but Paget leapt quickly to one side in a smoothly executed traverse. He launched a very quick circular cut from below towards the lead forearm of his opponent. Timmerman slipped his hand back out of the way and laughed.

"Your tricks might work on a Frenchman, but not here," he grunted.

"You're faster than I remember."

"Because he's not drunk!" Moxy called out.

The crowd cheered, for there was a lot of truth to the assessment in spite of it being made in jest. They got back into their guards before one another once more. They eyed one another up and down, seeking for any weakness in each other's guard or posture, or the slightest tell of the next motion. They crossed their blades in the inside position where the nails of their sword bearing hands were turned up. Paget smiled, for he knew the weakness of this position. That of under cuts from his left, and he waited for Timmerman to throw there as if he had set a trap. Timmerman obliged and lowered his blade. Paget smirked just a little, thinking his opponent had fallen right into his trap, but Timmerman flicked his blade quickly up on the other side of Paget's and gave a quick snapping beat against what would be the back edge of Paget's sword. The singlestick was ripped from the young man's hands and thrown ten feet away.

Paget was unarmed and helpless, and Timmerman looked on with glee that he might now strike his opponent unopposed. He had no scruples over striking an unarmed man, let alone one which he was doing battle with. Timmerman rushed forward and swung a huge blow to strike Paget down in one, but Paget leapt to the side and under the blow, rolling across the cold hard ground until he landed on one knee beside the singlestick that had been cast from his grip. A cheer rang out from Charlie as others clapped along at the last-minute save. None was more impressed than Amyn, for the athletic demonstration was much to his liking, and yet he did not erupt into celebration like many of the others. He was far too calm and well-mannered for such a brash display. And yet Paget caught a glimpse of the subtle smile on the Mameluke's face and felt proud at achieving such an accolade.

Timmerman nodded along in appreciation as he watched his opponent get back to his feet, ready to continue the fight.

"Come on, Paget!" Bunce roared.

The two men clashed once more. Cut after cut was thrown back and forth and parried in kind without any blow striking either man until Timmerman threw a sneaky strike to the leg after multiple high feints. The stick struck Paget's lead leg and wobbled it, but his hand was fast enough to respond, and he lashed a cut into Timmerman's face, striking his nose firmly. He staggered back as Paget limped away also. Timmerman cupped his bloodied nose and then looked at the palm full of blood in his hand. The crowd was silent, expecting a turbulent response from the famously ill-tempered officer, and yet he began to roar with laughter deep down from within his belly. He threw his singlestick over to the feet of Craven and stormed towards Paget, wrapping his arms about in friendship.

"A damned good showing!"

The small audience clapped and cheered at the wholesome and friendly display, with both men bearing the wounds of the affair and gladly accepting a draw. Timmerman hunched down a little and allowed Paget to rest an arm over his shoulder to help him limp back to the campfire.

"That will swell up plenty, and you will feel it in

every stride of the ride tomorrow," declared Charlie.

"What is a little pain?" replied Paget defiantly, groaning further as he sat down.

The next day they were on the road at first light, and Paget was doing everything he could to hide that pain, which made Charlie smile. For he had gained some of Craven's stubbornness. The group was in good spirits, and by the end of the day they reached the town sign for Dannenberg. It looked to be a peaceful town of a few thousand people. Oil lamps hung from many of the houses. Two men of the watch approached Craven's party as they arrived, but Holck soon spoke up for them, and they were allowed to pass without any hesitation. Although there was some intrigue over their uniforms, which they did not recognise.

"English?" asked one of the watchmen.

"We are indeed," replied Craven.

On they rode into the sleepy little town, for most of the inhabitants were in their homes or the taverns.

"Do we need some accommodations?" Holck asked.

"Let us find the Free Corps first, for I would not wait to speak with them, and with Eleonore," declared Craven, knowing that they only had one amongst them who spoke the language and could get anything done.

Holck asked one of the watchmen as he passed by, and they were soon on their way. They found two of the Lützow Free Corps smoking outside a house ahead of them. Their black mismatched uniforms were unmistakable. Craven rode up to them and dismounted before giving the reins to Joze.

"Eleonore Prochaska?" he asked the two men, who recognised him instantly, and pointed in through the door behind them.

"Charlie, Paget, Matthys, Holck, you are with me. The rest of you see to the horses and then see if you can sort some beds for us for the night."

"How do you propose we do that?" Timmerman asked.

"Find someone who speaks French, and if that fails, throw money at the problem."

"We will work it out," insisted Bunce.

Craven led the three others inside where they were guided on, for the men of the Corps knew exactly what they were there for, and many recognised them. They were taken to the largest room of the house with a roaring fire. It was evidently a lounge in everyday use, but a bed had been placed on one wall where Eleonore lay covered in sheets. She looked pale, and the half dozen of her companions standing about her bed looked little better. For a moment Craven wasn't sure if she was even still breathing, but after a few moments she stirred, though her breathing was pained and difficult. Her burnt and shrapnel riddled tunic had been cleaned as best as possible and now hung on the wall above the bed as a shrine, along with her musket and shako. One of the soldiers began talking with Holck, who passed on and translated their discussion.

"He says she does not have long now," he

whispered.

Charlie overheard and passed it on to Paget who shed a tear upon the news.

"Can we speak with her?"

The soldier clearly understood what he meant and gestured for them to come forward.

"Eleonore recognised Charlie instantly, for she knew she concealed her identity the in the same way.

"You fought with honour," declared Paget.

Eleonore nodded gently before addressing Charlie, speaking as freely as she could in a faint tone, knowing that Holck would translate for her, which he did.

"She asks for you to promise to keep on fighting for her country after she is gone."

"We will, I will, and you shall be in our hearts when we march upon the battlefield," replied Charlie.

"And the victory will belong to you also," added Paget.

Victory? Craven thought that much was not a certainty, and far from it, and yet he knew Paget was confident in the fact and did not merely blurt out what he thought a dying soldier might want to hear.

"We fought through Portugal and Spain as if they were our homelands, but they were not, and we will do the same here. Anywhere that Napoleon and his armies march we will oppose them until our last dying breath, or his," declared Craven.

Holck translated and a muted cheer in support of his words echoed about the room. Nobody dared raise their voice, as if they were in church. They fell silent as Eleonore spoke once more in little more than a whisper. It brought tears to her companions as Holck translated for the others.

"I have given everything to my country, and now it is time for you to do the same. Leave me now, but do not weep for me. Make merry together, and drink to our victories, and not to our losses."

"We will do so, you have my word," replied Craven.

She was entirely out of breath and falling in and out of consciousness, clearly needing some peace and some rest. Craven led his party out as her companions shared a last few words. An officer of the Corps soon joined Craven and his people, greeting them with near perfect English. He was evidently a well-educated man.

"We can offer you lodgings here in the houses nearby. You must share a room between six or eight, but it will be better than a night outside, as I am sure you are aware."

"Thank you, it is much appreciated."

"Eleonore, or August Renz as you knew her, she is very special to us, but you are part of her story also, and she would have us be friends."

"I agree."

"Then come with me where we might drink together and find you some food."

He led them on to a hall down the street and entered it to find dozens of the Free Corps members eating and drinking, though in a most sombre and quiet tone. The officer roared angrily at them, noting

Eleonore's name as he scolded them.

"He asks them if this is how she would want them to act, like sad little boys," translated Holck.

"She is a tough one," smiled Craven.

They were soon seated, and a number of Craven's companions began to arrive and join them, but it was the German officer he was most keen to converse with.

"Sir Charles sent me, and I believe you know of the matter why."

"I do, but there is nothing that need be said tonight which cannot be said in the morning. Tonight, we will do what Eleonore told us she wanted of us. She will live on as a symbol of this resistance against Napoleon, I am sure of it."

"I agree, what is your name?" Craven asked of the friendly and welcoming officer.

"I am Captain Edinger."

"Major Craven."

"We know. Stories of your adventures in Spain inspired many to join our ranks. A rogue collective of soldiers and rogues making life hell for the French. There are a great many here who would like to be just like you."

"That news reached this far?" Paget asked in amazement.

"Of course, that the Spanish and English and Portuguese could stand against Napoleon has given us all hope, for it seemed he was unbeatable only a year ago even. For when French armies marched across all of Northern Europe and all the way to Moscow, it seemed like the end was near, and yet still you and your countrymen and your allies kept fighting in Spain, and not just fighting, but winning."

"I am glad we could provide some inspiration, but it seems to me that whoever of your recruits wanted to be us, well they already are."

"It is an honour to hear it from you, Sir. But you are tired and hungry, and weary from the road. We are in little better a state than yourselves, having only arrived late last night. Let us show you some hospitality and leave all our troubles until the morning."

A plate of food and a tankard of beer was placed before Craven, and he could not help but appreciate the plan.

"To Eleonore," he declared.

"Eleonore!" the room roared in response.

CHAPTER 5

Craven awoke early with so much troubling his mind. A heavy snoring from Birback echoed about the small room where half of his party slept side by side, but through exhaustion it was not keeping the others from their sleep. Craven stepped carefully between them until he reached the door, where he scooped up his sword belt from the mass of weaponry propped there. He set out for the stairs, but as he reached the bottom of them, he found Captain Edinger waiting at a breakfast table enjoying a simple early meal. Though he looked rather solemn.

"She is at peace," he declared. "Eleonore," he added as if he needed to clarify to whom he spoke.

"Then it is fortunate that we arrived in time to see her one last time."

"Is that why you came?"

"A journey can have more than one purpose, and we are all at the mercy of the duties which are bound to us."

"At least you are honest about that fact. For a war cannot stop merely because of the injuries of a single soldier, no matter who they are."

He was very well spoken and clearly highly

intelligent. He spoke as a man who had been to a brilliant university, and yet at the same time with a more practical manner as a man who had lived a far rougher life than his accent would suggest.

"The Lützow Free Corps is said to be formed of students and academics. I cannot deny that I do nothing to change that perception, but the truth is most of the soldiers I fight beside are merely craftsmen and labourers, just like Eleonore. Real patriots who have given everything and risked everything to be here. Are you that kind of patriot, Major?"

Craven sat down opposite him so that they might speak as comrades and not be looming over him.

"I never was much of a patriot, but I think I have come to be over time. What matters more to me than anything is those under my command. The companions who fight beside me, and I know that in supporting them I am supporting my country, and so maybe yes, yes, I am. But not because someone told me I should be or that it was expected of me. I fight for what I believe in."

Edinger smiled and nodded in agreement.

"It is some relief to hear it, and you are in good company, then. For that is who we are also. In fact, had we been born in the same land, I think we might have served alongside one another."

"Do we not?"

"Why did you really come here to Germany?" he asked sincerely.

"To help win this war by any means necessary."

"And can you really make a difference?"

"I know that we can, for we already have in Portugal and Spain. The Iberian Peninsula may have been a distant land to me years past, but today it is as much a home to me as England, perhaps more so. I have spilt my blood all across those lands and battled as if it were my homeland."

"And you will do the same here?"

"I will, but what about the German people?" Craven smiled as he turned the argument on its head.

Edinger sighed.

"It is true that the German states are divided in this affair, but many are in Napoleon's pocket not through any choice, but by force."

"And if they are given a choice to join us?"

"They will take it."

"And you are sure of that?"

"I am. No German truly wants to be under the heel of a Frenchman."

"That much I can understand," smiled Craven.

Edinger fell silent, and Craven seized his opportunity.

"To the other matter of our presence here," he declared mysteriously.

"Come with me," replied Edinger, not wanting to talk about it amongst company, not even their own trusted comrades.

As they got up, Paget reached the bottom of the stairs, but Craven waved him off, for he needed privacy for what was to come next. They walked out into the crisp morning air and into the streets, but the

Captain did not speak a word until they passed a busy well and got a good thirty paces beyond anyone who might care to listen. It was quickly becoming apparent just how closely guarded a secret was about to be shared with him.

"You are in the trade of information as I am told?"

"I have long been told it can be the key to victory, and that a battle might be won or lost long before a shot is fired because of it."

"I believe it to be true also," sighed Edinger.

"Well, what have you got for me?"

"A contact who might provide most useful. A Prussian noblewoman and widow, who the French believe is a harmless witness to all that they do, if not a willing and active supporter of their ambitions."

"And you know that she is not?"

"For certain. She is a relative of mine, and I would swear by my life that she is loyal to Prussia and to this coalition we find ourselves in."

"What can she do for us?"

"Katarina Weiss is her name, and she spends time in the company of senior French officers. A great many a soldier talks openly before women, thinking they do not listen nor understand, nor really care for the topics of men and war."

"Then they are fools."

"Indeed, but they are French fools."

"How do we reach this Katarina?"

Edinger shrugged and looked a little pained by the prospect.

"You have no means of contact?"

"I am afraid not. We cannot risk sending a letter to her for fear of whose eyes might see it, and myself and many of my comrades cannot risk going near her. We would be recognised by many of our countrymen who work for the enemy, whether willingly or not."

"But we would not, for not a single one of your countrymen would recognise us?"

"Indeed."

"But the lady is located in lands where the French are a common sight?"

"Yes, that is correct."

"And you think a squadron of English cavalry could just ride on in without any questions?"

"No, but a French one could," smiled the Captain.

Craven looked confused, but he eagerly gestured for Craven to follow him. He was led down two streets and then to a small warehouse building opposite a cobbler and a haberdashery. Craven could not understand why he was being taken to this place, but he did not question it. For he was most intrigued as to how Edinger intended to see them safely through enemy lines. For as an English regiment they stood out as outsiders everywhere they went.

Captain Edinger hauled the door to the building open and ushered him inside. There was little light in the building, and it took a few moments for Craven's eyes to adjust to the darkness, but as he did so, he realised what he was looking at. Shelves stacked with piles of uniforms. Many were French but also German states also.

"Your supply of uniforms for your Corps?"

"Yes, we take whatever we can find. Old uniforms, others are captured from the enemy. Some are taken from the dead and wounded. We gather whatever we can from any and all sources, and then dye them into our black."

"You would have us dress as Frenchmen and merely walk through the enemy lines?"

"It would not be the first time you have done so, Major," Edinger smiled, proving he had indeed been following Craven's career with quite some focus and attention to detail.

"No, it wouldn't." Craven picked up the tunic of a French cavalry officer, "You think we can pass as the enemy and pull this off?"

"Just like us, the French armies are vast and encompass many different peoples and many different uniforms. As long as you look like you should be where you are, nobody will question a French colonel."

"Colonel?" Craven asked at the prospect of such a promotion, even if it was only an act.

Edinger pulled out a colonel's tunic of a French light cavalry regiment. It was quite remarkable and beautifully made. He handed it to Craven who first marvelled at the exquisite quality, but then at the size.

"I could not even button this about my body."

"Who do you know that would fit into this jacket? The ability to speak some French would help greatly, too. Do you know anybody like that?"

Craven laughed before nodding in agreement.

"Yes, indeed I do."

"Once you are upon the road you may share these plans with your companions, but remember, the more tongues who know Katarina Weiss's name and true intentions, the more danger you place her in."

"Understood."

"You will select your uniforms in this building, and you may bring your men in here to do so, but everything removed from this place will be covered and hidden. And it will not see the light of day until you are far from here, do you understand?"

"I do."

But Edinger did not look convinced, and he grabbed Craven by the shoulder.

"I believe in my countrymen, but not all can be trusted. I will help you in all the ways I can, but not if you endanger the lives of my people and the mission which we are undertaking, is that clear?"

"Absolutely, and you have my word, we will be most discreet, and I will ensure that no ill comes to the Lady Katarina."

"You ensure that it does not, for if you do not and any harm comes to her, I will hold you personally responsible, and no ability with the sword will save you from my wrath," declared Edinger sternly.

* * *

"What do you think they are discussing?" Paget asked impatiently whilst his comrades ate breakfast.

"If you need to know, then the Major will tell you."

"And if he does not?"

"Then you didn't need to know," smirked Timmerman.

"I can't bear it, to be in the dark."

"These men have lost Eleonore and you fret over not knowing what two men talk about?" Charlie questioned.

Paget shrugged and looked away in discomfort and a little shame.

"He is right to want to know, for the things we do not know can get us killed," replied Matthys.

"So, we should not mourn the passing of a great heroine?" Charlie asked.

"Of course, but we are capable of thinking about more than one thing at a time. We do not merely give up on our duties because of one death, no matter how important that person was to us."

"She is not even in the ground and yet we have moved on," grumbled Charlie.

"This is not what she would have wanted. Remember her words. She asked for us to go on fighting and to drink to our victories, not dwell on our losses," insisted Vicenta.

Her words struck deep, for she had a lot in common with the fallen German hero, and Charlie struggled to find an argument to use against her.

"Will we stay for her funeral at least?"

"We will go where our orders take us, Charlie," replied Matthys.

"Orders? What orders? We have no commander."

"Wrong, we have Craven. He is your leader and mine, and he is doing everything in his power to do what Eleonore would have wanted and what she asked of us," growled Timmerman.

"Of course, you would say that, for what would you care about her loss?" Charlie answered angrily.

"More than I ever thought I would. I will not deny I felt sorrow at the sight of her, for she was a tough fighter who is worthy of your admiration and mine, and I give it freely. But I have wasted too many years fretting over the wrong things, and I am not about to do that now. Fine soldiers die every day, and some of them are our comrades. I didn't used to care much for any of it, but now I do. But I will not let that compassion stand in the way of our duty. Not our duty to country, but to one another."

"He is right," agreed Amyn.

Charlie looked for support anywhere she could find it, but there was none to be found. She stormed off angrily and smashed the door open as she rushed on outside. Paget shot up to follow her, but a firm grasp of his arm by Vicenta held him in place.

"Unhand me," he ordered.

But she would not.

"Let her go, for there is nothing you can say to sooth her soul."

Paget looked to Matthys for assistance, but he shook his head in agreement with Vicenta. Paget huffed in frustration as he dropped back into his chair. Charlie stormed out from the building in a whirlwind of rage and frustration.

"Charlie!" a voice roared.

It was Craven, and she came to a standstill at the

sound of his voice.

"What is going on in there?" he demanded.

"We came here for Eleonore, but those ice hearted bastards we call friends have already swept her from their minds!"

Craven sighed.

"Not you, too?" she gasped.

"I am sorry for the loss of Eleonore. I truly am. I will mourn her the same as so many who have fallen before her, but she is gone now. We cannot save her, but we can save others if we keep on moving forward."

"You got what you came for, then?" she asked cynically.

"I did, and so did you. A few moments with Eleonore is a privilege that should not be overlooked."

"I know," she replied, holding back tears.

"I can understand why this hurts so much, or maybe I can't, but I can sympathise. But no matter how low you feel, I can guarantee you things can be a hundred times worse if we do not ensure a victory here."

"How can we? We are barely more than twenty soldiers in a land we do not understand," she replied in despair.

Craven took a deep breath as he realised the crisis she was suffering.

"The situation you describe, tell me, how is it any different to when we arrived back in Portugal a little over five years ago?"

She shrugged.

"Well, I'll tell you. There were even fewer of

us then. You were still mourning the loss of your husband and child. I was on the run. We had no money, no purpose and no future, and yet, look what we have made of ourselves."

She nodded in agreement as she remembered back to the bleak days of the retreat to Corunna and the bitterly sad times that followed.

"What do you fear? That you, too, will be wounded and discovered as she has been?" he whispered to her.

"Perhaps, I do not even know," she admitted.

"Would it be so bad a death? Eleonore will be remembered forever."

Charlie shrugged, for she was not even sure why she fretted so much now, for she was simply overwhelmed.

"I have gotten us this far, have I not?"

She nodded in agreement.

"Then will you trust me to keep us moving forward?"

"Of course, I will, it is not you or I or Paget or any one of them who is the problem. It is this damn war."

Craven was taken aback for a moment as he realised the bloodlust and desire for revenge had finally faded entirely from her heart and mind. But in doing so, the armour for which it gave her had also been lost. This had been a long time coming, but Craven had not understood what a pit of despair lay at the end of such a change.

"If you do not want to go on fighting, nobody will think less of you for it. There are limits for all of us.

Hawkshaw knew that, and he went home with his reputation firmly intact."

Charlie gave the proposal some genuine consideration for a few moments before shaking her head.

"No, I do not go on because I want to do harm, but because I want to protect those who I love from it, and I cannot do that if I go back to England."

Craven nodded in agreement.

"I am sorry. I am sorry that I let this strike at me so severely."

"You have seen the faces of the men who served with Eleonore. They are devastated by her loss, and there is no shame in it."

"Do you really believe we can make a difference here?"

"I know that we can, but first of all we have to give one young man a promotion, a rather large one," he smiled.

She had no concept of what he spoke, but it intrigued her and carried her mind away from the despair she had been feeling.

"Come on, the first part of our mission is complete, but there is so much more to do."

They walked back into the house together, leading to a look of relief on Paget's face. He could see she was not half as angry and unsettled as she had been when she had left. The room was silent as they waited for news from Craven.

"We came here for two reasons. I am most grateful that we arrived in time to see Eleonore before she passed, and let her death be a reminder of what we are fighting for here. This is not our land, but neither was Portugal nor Spain."

"Speak for yourself," snarled Ferreira.

"Indeed," added Vicenta.

Joze merely laughed and nodded along.

"You understand my meaning. Anywhere a people stand in defiance of Napoleon is as good as our home. And everywhere we do battle against him is fighting not just for that land and people but our own also. I cannot tell you what the second purpose of our journey here was, or not yet, for I have sworn I would not. But I can tell you this. We do not travel idly about. I am sorry that we cannot stay for the funeral of Eleonore, for I would not miss it, but we have pressing matters which she would not want us to miss, and that much I say with absolute certainty. Isn't that right, Charlie?"

"It is. She was a fighter, and she would have us go on fighting."

A cheer echoed about the room in support.

"Come with me," declared Craven mysteriously.

He turned and left leaving them wanting more, and they quickly leapt into motion to follow after him.

"Where are we going?" Paget asked Matthys, for he typically knew all of the goings on, and yet he shrugged as he was entirely in the dark.

"And you? What do you know of this?" Paget asked Timmerman as the man who had delivered the news to Craven from Sir Charles.

"I would tell you if I knew, but Craven has kept this one to himself."

"You're a damned good liar," declared Paget boldly.

Timmerman roared with laughter.

"Perhaps that is true, but in this case, I speak the truth, which is that there is nothing to say."

On they went as Craven led them to the same warehouse that Edinger had led him to, but he stopped outside the door to address them before they went inside.

"Listen to me very carefully," he whispered as they gathered around him.

"What you see inside you speak of to no one. You do not take any article from this building with it being entirely concealed from view, is that clear?"

Grumbles of agreement rang out, for they were all eager to unravel the mystery. Craven hauled the door open and remained there on guard as he ushered them all inside. He pulled the door shut, sealing it with an iron bolt. He turned back to see that they were in darkness as before, waiting for their vision to adjust, but it quickly became apparent what they were looking at. Ferreira nodded as he realised what was about to happen, for it was not the first time he had impersonated a Frenchman, but they all looked to Craven for answers and an explanation of what they were about to do.

"Listen to me very carefully. I cannot tell you where we are going or why, not yet, but I can tell you what is needed of us here. We must soon appear as a

French cavalry squadron in the most convincing way. Those who speak French, Timmerman, Paget, Bunce, you will play the part of our officers so that you might fool any Frenchmen we meet along the way." He picked up the petite cavalry officer's tunic which Edinger had showed to him.

"Congratulations, Colonel Paget," smiled Craven as he handed it to Paget.

Cackles of laughter erupted about the room as he took it.

"Colonel?" Paget stuttered, for it was a dream he had always wished to fulfil.

"In the French army, but Colonel, nonetheless," declared Craven.

CHAPTER 6

Craven firmly secured a sack full of equipment onto the rear of his saddle, checking all was held in place and concealed from view before looking to his companions to ensure they were doing the same. None of them had any inclination as to what their mission was, and so it was impossible to explain to them the importance of secrecy without giving too much away. Yet he soon spotted Joze wearing a French shako as he went about his preparations. Craven left his horse and went to the young man who was his loyal servant.

"Put that away, now," whispered Craven.

"It's just a little fun, Sir, and we are out of sight," declared Joze as he looked at the walls of the barn around them, although the door was tied open.

Craven grabbed him violently by the collar and hauled him in close before ripping the French hat from his head without letting go of his hold. Joze looked stunned and scared at the sudden aggression.

"I told you in no uncertain terms, this is not a game. Put it out of sight, now!" He stuffed the shako into Joze's hands before shoving him away.

"Yes, Sir." He then went to see it done.

"You didn't need to be so hard on him," declared Ellis.

"Yes, he did," replied Matthys in defence of his actions.

Ellis was stunned by the response.

"A slip up here could put many lives in danger, including our own," replied Matthys.

Ellis smirked as he looked to Craven as if it were being blown way out of proportions, but the Major's stern expression confirmed it was not.

"What are you getting us into here?" Ellis demanded.

"Not here," insisted Craven as he walked away.

Ellis looked to Matthys for answers.

"He never keeps things from us, why now?"

"Evidently it was necessary, for even after a simple warning that was easy to follow, an indiscretion occurred."

"He was just having a little fun, can you blame him?"

"Yes, I can. If this secrecy is required for the safety and success of our mission, then it shall be so," insisted Matthys.

Joze looked most crestfallen as he stuffed the shako into a sack and tied it shut before throwing it up and over his saddle. Many sympathetic eyes gazed upon him, but it was Ferreira who went to have some words with him.

"I hope you know there was no malice behind what Craven just did," he whispered to the young man.

Joze looked to be most put out and unnerved.

"He did not have to humiliate me in front of everyone."

Ferreira looked puzzled.

"What?"

"You were a ruthless child of the streets when we first met. You'd stab someone in the back if it got you anything worth having."

"Yes?"

"And yet this bothers you?"

"It does."

"Why?"

"Because respect is everything, and I thought I had earnt it."

"You have, and there is not one here amongst us who would deny that, and certainly not the Major. Look, I am no wiser to his plans here than you are, but if Craven says it is this important and must be done this way, then that is how it must be done."

But he didn't want to hear it and turned away to leave angrily but found Timmerman blocking his path. It was a troubling sight, for his reputation was fearsome.

"There are times for horseplay. Lord knows I have had my fair share, but this is not it. Craven needed something of you. A simple request which he believes is vital to our safety. This is not a time for horseplay."

Joze sighed as he hung his head in shame.

"Craven did not humiliate you. You humiliated yourself," added Ferreira.

Even Timmerman was surprised by the harsh

words, but he nodded in agreement.

"You can't change what you did, but you can choose what you do next," he added.

"I suppose if Craven can forgive you, he can forgive anything?" Joze smiled, trying to lift his spirits after realising he needed to accept that he had done wrong.

"Craven hasn't forgiven me. He has just learnt to live with me, and I him," admitted Timmerman.

"I can only say the same, for I was dragged into this ridiculous life of his kicking and screaming. All I ever wanted was a peaceful life, and instead I got the thunderstorm that is James Craven," Ferreira said.

They led their horses out of the stable and mounted up. They were heavily laden, but they doubted anyone would question it. Soldiers hauling all sorts of equipment was a common sight in these turbulent times. Craven stopped to look and listen. It was eerily quiet and made him feel most suspicious as he looked down at his sword, wondering if he would have need of it.

"Where is everyone, Sir?" Paget asked.

He had no answers and so he led them on, but soon enough they discovered where the all the town folk were, gathered en masse as members of the Free Corps carried the body of Eleonore to her final resting place. As her casket appeared, carried upon the shoulder of her comrades, a wail of cries and tears began to flow from those who had gathered. Craven looked to Charlie, expecting it to trigger some response.

"We can stay a little longer if you want to," he declared compassionately.

Charlie thought about it for only a second before shaking her head.

"We can honour her now by doing what she asked of us. Ride on," she insisted.

"They will write songs about her. She will never be forgotten," declared Moxy.

"Let us ensure she is remembered as a hero of a great victory, then," added Charlie.

Craven led them on. They travelled for several miles without any explanation, but most knew they were heading towards French positions, and the sense of danger grew with every step they took. They rode on all day still without any explanation from Craven at all, but nobody pressed for it any longer, knowing they would not learn of their plans until Craven was prepared and ready to tell them. He led them to an excluded clearing amongst a dense wood where they made camp for the night as the sun was going down. There was a small cabin there, which seemed to be of no surprise to Craven, who did not even investigate the modest and remote dwelling.

"Gather around!" Craven roared, though most were already warming themselves about the fire. All were silent as they waited on the news that Craven had kept so close to his chest since they left Dannenberg.

"The reason for the secrecy in what we do is that we ride to make contact with an ally living amongst the French. For the safety of that ally, I will not share their name or anything about their identity with you unless I absolutely must."

"And if some harm was to come to you or we become separated, Sir?" Paget asked.

"Better that we do not find this contact than risk the enemy discovering their identity and intentions."

"And you expect we can just put on French uniforms and march in amongst the enemy?" Bunce asked.

"Yes, for with a colonel at our head we will have the authority not to be stopped."

"And if we are discovered? We will be treated as spies," replied Paget.

"It would not be the first time," smiled Craven.

"I'd rather not die in a French uniform," added Timmerman.

"Then don't die," replied Birback.

"If the information I have been given about this contact is correct, we might be able to discover information from the enemy which could be highly valuable. Right now, the Coalition armies manoeuvre, and they bicker and argue as they try to come together to face Napoleon. The best way to achieve that goal is to know everything we can about our enemy."

"And there is something specific we go in search for, Sir?"

Craven shrugged towards Paget.

"I go in search of the things we do not know, and that we do not know that we do not know them," replied Craven in a tongue twister that had several of them sighing in frustration.

"It is a big risk for such an unknown," replied Paget.

"It is a leap of faith, and I for one am willing to make it," replied Matthys.

"Good, because I was not asking. You wanted me to lead this regiment and lead it I will do. That cabin there will store our uniforms and anything that might identify us as anything but Frenchmen. Use those sacks on your saddles to bag up everything which is to be left behind and place it there in that cabin where it will be dry and safe," he ordered.

"You knew it was here?" Paget was surprised that Craven had a plan and was not just winging it.

"Just because I do not tell you things, Mr Paget, it does not mean I do not know them," smirked Craven.

"Yes, Sir." Paget felt a little foolish for not knowing better.

"Everything off. From this night on we don the uniforms of the French, and whilst we are near both civilians and soldiers nobody is to speak except those who can speak French. And even they will keep any communication to a minimum. We must do everything we can do not draw attention ourselves."

"That will be rather difficult, Sir." Paget was pulling open his sack of French equipment and took out the dazzling colonel's tunic.

"In a sea of Frenchmen, we are merely more Frenchmen," replied Craven.

"What an unsettling thought," added Bunce.

Craven grabbed his own bag of equipment and began to strip off his gear and change into the costume that they had acquired. The breeches were tight and form fitting. The tunic was a bright green and looked most dashing as he pulled it on, for the uniforms were those of the outlandish hussar type fashion. He clipped a sword belt about his waist, a large and heavily curved French light cavalry sabre dangling from it.

"It quite suits you, Sir," smiled Paget.

"Enough of that," snapped Bunce.

But Paget rather appreciated the uniform and felt quite at home in it.

"Perhaps I should have been a cavalryman?"

"Aren't we?" Timmerman asked.

Paget stopped to think about it for a moment as he realised that they conducted much of the work of the light cavalry amongst their other duties.

"We do not have the uniforms for it, though. Perhaps it is a fortunate thing, for I am not sure I could afford the upkeep," he pondered. He looked at the finery he was wearing and imagined what it would cost for an officer to outfit himself in such an attire. For an officer must purchase all their own equipment, a fate which had never concerned Paget until he lost the financial backing of his father and had to live on Army pay alone. Craven finished fitting his new uniform before rolling up the sack of his own equipment and carrying it to the cabin. He placed it inside and stacked his rifle against one of the walls. He got outside to find Moxy gazing upon his own rifle, as if he was to never see it again.

"Come on, out with it."

"What if someone comes and steals them whilst we are away?"

"They won't."

"What about the moisture in this place? It could play merry hell with our rifles."

"They aren't staying here for the winter. When we return, a little cleaning will have them as good as we left them."

"What if we never make it back?"

"Well, it won't matter then will it, we'll be dead," smiled Craven.

"You are sure you can find this place again?"

"Just get in there." Craven grabbed the Welshman and shoved him inside.

Soon the door was shut with everything inside, and they gathered about the fire in their new uniforms with nothing but French sabres with which to defend themselves. The pistols and carbines many French cavalry carried had not been supplied to them, for such weaponry was more valuable than anything else.

"We could have waited until morning," grumbled Moxy.

"No, we must accustom ourselves to this equipment. We must live in it and look as though we own it. A little time wearing in, some wood smoke and sweat, and we will pass as what we are dressed as," insisted Timmerman.

"And if we are caught? We will be shot as spies, won't we?" asked Bunce.

"Then don't get caught," replied Timmerman as

he echoed Birback's earlier comments.

"This is now how a soldier conducts war," protested Bunce.

"Wrong, this is how war has always been conducted. It is not pretty, but nobody cares as long as you succeed," replied Craven.

Soon enough they had been sitting around the fire that their new uniforms felt like home, which was most unsettling to anyone who spent any time dwelling on the issue. Ellis noticed Moxy peering over at the cabin where his rifle was stored every few moments as if his long-lost love was locked away inside.

"She'll be fine," insisted Ellis.

"Will she? Left in some damp cabin in the middle of nowhere? Who else knows of this place? Any French soldiers passing by could take the lot."

"And how would they find it? Look at this place. Nobody is coming here unless they have a damned good reason," replied Ellis to try and calm his nerves.

"And if we are attacked on the road?"

"We have horses to carry us away at speed and swords should we need to defend our lives."

"If it has come to the need to draw swords, we are in a bigger hole than a few sabre swings will get us out of," grumbled Moxy.

"I wouldn't tell Craven that, for he would slap you for saying so," declared Matthys who had been looming in the darkness behind them.

"I would slap him for saying what?" Craven asked, having overheard him.

"Moxy believes we are defenceless with only our swords," declared Ellis.

Moxy sighed as he was dropped in it.

"Perhaps you might be," declared Craven.

The group had a good laugh at Moxy's expense, and he could hold his tongue no further.

"You'd be a dead man long ago if it wasn't for me and my rifle!"

The crowd cheered at his plucky and cheeky courage, and Craven laughed along with them. They awoke next day to gaze upon one another with confusion and disbelief, for it was a most unsettling sight to awake seemingly amongst the enemy.

"Let's go!" Craven ordered.

They readied their horses and straightened up their uniforms. In no time at all they were on the road once more, but this time as Frenchmen, in appearance at least. Craven led from the front as he typically did, but he soon stopped and waved for Paget to take the lead as the Colonel of which he now acted. He felt most awkward but did so. As he formed his position at the front of the column, he felt a great responsibility fall upon his shoulders, combined with a great excitement for fulfilling a lifelong dream, even if it was only an act. An hour later they came up and over a ridge to find almost fifty French cavalrymen resting at the roadside. Paget felt his heart almost stop at the sight.

"Do not hesitate. They are our allies, remember," whispered Craven.

"Yes, Sir," muttered Paget as he spurred Augustus

on.

He gazed down upon the French cavalrymen as if expecting to get a rise from them, and yet they were not interested in communicating at all, and many looked down and away as the apparent French colonel passed by. On they rode without any communication at all, but Paget could barely breathe until they had gotten a hundred paces past the enemy. He was pale and looked as though he was about to pass out.

"All is well," Timmerman said quietly but sincerely.

Finally, Paget took a deep breath of fresh air and began to pant heavily from the stress of the situation.

"Believe in yourself. Do not fear that you are an actor who is about to get discovered. Believe you are a French colonel. Believe that you are better than everyone around you and that they owe you their respect."

Paget coughed to clear his throat and sat up a little more upright in the saddle as he tried to embody the role which he had been given. They rode on, and as they passed through a small wood, they came out on the far side to find hundreds of military tents where a mass of French infantry was encamped.

"Keep moving forward. We have business to conduct, and we answer to nobody," whispered Timmerman.

Paget did so as he tried to hide his fear. The deeper they travelled into enemy held territory the lower the chances of escape would be if they were to be discovered. He gazed down at the infantrymen as they passed by the grid-like layout of tents. Some were older veterans who looked to have lived long and hard lives on campaign, but a great many were fresh faced uncertain recruits. On they rode along a dirt track which circled around the camp. A beautiful country estate home lay ahead on the edge of a town.

"That is it," declared Craven.

The vast three-storey brick manor house was surrounded by well-maintained gardens and manicured lawns. A long gravel pathway led to the house, which was positively luxurious compared to the well-trodden mud track they were leaving. Exquisitely trimmed hedges and decorative fountains completed the feel that they were entering a paradise. A lavish carriage waited outside the palatial home with several French cavalrymen waiting beside it as bodyguards to whomever travelled in the opulent transport.

"Those men could very well have questions for us," declared Paget with concern.

"Give them nothing. Our business is our own and we are not to be interfered with," replied Timmerman.

Craven nodded in approval, though without even seeing Paget's face, he knew how terrified the young man must be. It was a huge pressure to place upon his shoulders, and yet they had no other choice. They rode up to the front of the house with purpose. The cavalrymen about the carriage gave them only a cursory glance, but with their arrival they brought a cloud of dirt from the gallop of their horses' hooves, which set upon the magnificent carriage like a storm cloud. Paget's feet had only just touched the ground when a furious French officer burst out from the house and yelled profanities at them. Few of the Salford Rifles understood the language, but the intention was clear. The officer was furious at the disrespect which was being shown, as he then looked to the dirt-covered carriage of which he was evidently in part responsible for. He looked to Paget and began angrily raging at him, shaking his hands and blurting out profanities. Paget did not know what to do and so he remained calm and confident, unwavering even.

"Do not make a scene," Craven whispered from behind them.

But the French officer stormed up to Paget and placed an angry finger upon his chest. Timmerman sprang into action and slapped the hand away. He stormed forward, shoving the Frenchman back so that he stumbled several paces before tripping over and landing on his backside. Birback roared with laughter and several of the French cavalrymen about the carriage followed him.

"Oh, shit," Craven muttered.

The humiliated French officer got back to his feet and furiously drew out his sword. Timmerman happily obliged and did the same. Nobody attempted to interfere with the affair, as they watched on with great intrigue, perhaps just glad to witness a little excitement after a monotonous period of service.

"What is he doing?" Bunce murmured to Craven as an appeal for him to step in.

"Saving this in the only way he knows how."

"Will this not bring unwanted attention?"

"We are hiding in plain sight, and we must act the part of whom we are dressed."

But Bunce sighed with frustration and looked around the grounds, as if expecting trouble to be coming their way and for their identity to be discovered. He gazed around at the faces of the French soldiers who watched on. They were enthralled by the impromptu duel, and it was such a perfect distraction that they were thinking of nothing else. Not why the cavalry led by Paget were here, or if they truly were who they appeared to be. They were merely friendly competition.

Timmerman came to his guard, but not in his usual way. His sword arm was well extended forward and the point of his sword also, more like he was using a smallsword, or at least putting a great emphasis on the use of the point, as the French loved to do. He and his opponent shared some angry words in French before finally coming to blows. Timmerman was light on his feet, not fighting with the wild and drunken anger he so often had in past years.

But the Frenchman was furious and grew angrier with each pass. He thundered blows in as if he wanted to split Timmerman in half, but the Englishman remained uncharacteristically calm.

"What if he kills him?"

"He won't. He knows better than to endanger us like that."

"Are you sure, Sir?" Paget asked with uncertainty.

Craven shrugged for he was not entirely

confident. Timmerman had always been a wildcard, but there was nothing he could do now but watch and hope that his old adversary understood the risks.

Timmerman parried heavy blow after heavy blow with ease, but in a brief lull in the action as the two fighters separated, he looked to Craven, who nodded in return, a signal for him to finish the affair. The Frenchman screamed angrily as he rushed onwards once more, but Timmerman was waiting for him. He dropped his sword over his enemy's and rotated about it, the two blades locked together. The Frenchman was dumbfounded as he struggled to keep control of his weapon. Finally, the rotations stopped with Timmerman's blade rested on top of his, the tip just an inch from the man's face.

Paget gasped. The murder of a French officer would draw a great deal of attention to them, but Timmerman did not plunge the point home. Instead, he rested the edge of his sword over the Frenchman's sword hand and drew it back in a quick slicing action. A long but very shallow cut opened up along the back of the Frenchman's hand, causing him to drop his sword as he winced in pain, and his blood dripped from his hand onto the floor below. He looked furious and reached for the weapon once more, for despite the flow of blood there was little but superficial damage. He was quite willing and able to fight on, despite the fact that first blood would be enough to settle most disputes.

A musket shot erupted beside them, causing all to stop and look. A well-dressed lady was standing at the entrance to the house with a narrow barrelled and beautifully ornate fowling piece. A cloud of powder smoke circled above her where she had fired off a shot into the air. She spoke a few stern but calm words in French before turning about and leaving them to sort themselves out.

"Not on my land," translated Bunce.

The bloodied French officer sighed as he sheathed his sword and glared at Timmerman.

"This is your chance. Go," insisted Craven.

Paget shot forward to chase after the lady. Craven nodded for Timmerman to follow him. Together the two men stormed forward in a determined march as Craven turned back to those who remained.

"Bunce, you are in command now. You are the only one who can keep our secret safe if anyone comes our way."

"Yes, Sir," replied Bunce uneasily. He had not expected such pressure to fall upon his shoulders, having thought that had landed entirely on Paget's shoulders. Craven turned back to see their two companions vanish inside the manor house, not knowing who or what lay waiting for them inside.

"Good luck, and God speed," he muttered to himself.

CHAPTER 7

Paget took a deep breath as they stepped inside the palace-like home. He gazed around in all directions of the huge lobby. Two wealthy-looking civilian men chatted in one corner, but there was no sign of any soldiers, though they could hear the echo of a man walking with purpose down the staircase before them. Paget looked to Timmerman for advice, but neither dared speak as they waited and hoped whoever it might be would not endanger them. The man strode into view, wearing the uniform of a French general. Paget was horrified, but he summoned all his strength to not show it. The general paused a brief moment to look upon them and opened his mouth as if he was about to speak. Paget was barely able to stay conscious and breathing through the fear and tension, and yet the Frenchman simple sighed, as if he did not want to waste his time with them and continued on. Paget gasped in relief as he vanished from view, but the two other men in the room chuckled at the reaction. For to them it was merely an amusing scene of an intimidated younger officer in fear of his superiors. Timmerman led them on before any questions were asked of them.

"That was too close," whispered Paget.

"Not at all. We have given them no reason to think anything is amiss."

They passed several servants who dared not stop and question them. For their uniforms had granted them a great power, especially Paget's colonel's tunic. A rank which gave him authority over almost anyone they could hope to meet, except for such men as the general they had just stumbled into. They looked from room to room for the lady who had unleashed a shot outside her front door, not daring to ask anyone for help for fear of arising suspicion.

"Timmerman," whispered Paget to draw his attention.

He looked over to see Paget gazing towards the open doors of a library where the lady sat, gazing out of a window and looking most pensive.

"Remember, she does not know us, or whether we are friend or foe. We must tread carefully."

"You want me to do it?" Paget gasped.

"You are the Colonel," smiled Timmerman.

Paget took a deep breath as he tried to calm his nerves, for he looked even tenser than when the general had first appeared. Paget led them on and just a few paces into the library where he introduced himself in French, using his French colonel's rank but foolishly his own real name. The lady looked them up and down. She had a stern look about her and eyes that could look right through even the most steadfast soul. She was in her early fifties, her hair pale grey, but she appeared to be in very good and fit health, carrying herself with authority and grace. She did not reply to Paget and merely got up and went past them to shut the doors they had walked though before returning to her chair most casually.

"You are not Frenchmen," she declared in English.

Timmerman looked stunned.

"Who are you?" she asked calmly.

"Captain Berkeley Paget, Ma'am," replied Paget without hesitation.

Timmerman glared at the younger man, but it had not been a slip of the tongue this time.

"We cannot expect trust if we are not honest," he insisted.

"And you?"

"Major Alexander Vandertray Timmerman," he replied, following Paget's example.

"I have heard these names," mused the Prussian lady.

"We are men of the Salford Rifles, Ma'am," declared Paget.

"The Salford Rifles? Ah, yes, I have read of your exploits, but not here amongst the German states," she replied with some suspicion.

"We are recent arrivals," added Timmerman.

"And yet you wear French uniforms and travel here amongst your enemies?"

"So that we might visit you, Ma'am," insisted Paget.

"If you are discovered, you will be executed as spies."

"As you would be," replied Timmerman in a

slightly threatening tone.

"We were sent by Captain Edinger," added Paget.

The lady carefully studied their faces for a moment, as if trying to assess if they could be trusted, and finally, she smiled.

"How is he enjoying his time with the Schlesisches Regiment?"

"Schlesisches are cavalry. Captain Edinger is an infantryman of the Lützow Free Corps, but you knew that, didn't you?"

"Of course," she smiled at Timmerman. They'd passed her test, and she got up to greet them.

"I am Lady Katarina Weiss."

"Then you are who we have been looking for," replied Paget.

"You take a great risk coming here."

"As do you, fighting against the French even as you live amongst them."

"I have no choice. This is my home, and I will not abandon it, and I cannot resist the French openly, but I do what I can."

"It is very brave," replied Paget with great admiration.

"You have come here for information?" she replied bluntly.

"A great battle is coming, and even the smallest piece of information you may have gained from the French could help."

"You want to know about troop movements?"

"Yes," smiled Paget.

"I can tell you more than that. Napoleon moves all

his efforts and strength on Leipzig, and there he will make his stand."

Paget took out his map from his coat to check the landscape and what that might mean.

"You know this for certain?" Timmerman demanded.

"I have heard it from the mouth of three generals."

"A clever position. The city is surrounded by converging rivers and a great many bridges, a perfect place to make a stand against the armies which march against him," declared Paget, as he travelled along the roads from city to city with his finger. Leipzig was just one hundred miles Southwest of Berlin, which they had been sent to defend, "We move on the offensive, but I fear we march into a trap."

"Napoleon was always going to choose the ground on which he made his stand, all we can do is find a path to victory," replied Timmerman.

"You should not dwell here. French soldiers come and go regularly, and if I can see through those costumes, so too will the enemy soon enough."

Paget nodded in agreement.

"Drawing attention to yourselves like you did this morning does not help your cause," she added, looking to Timmerman as the culprit of the duel in front of her home.

"We are dressed as Frenchmen. We have to act like Frenchmen, too."

"I am afraid in this case he is right, for it was the best choice in a difficult situation," Paget explained in his defence.

"You might be right, but I do not have to like it. My home is no place for war."

"Napoleon brings war to wherever he marches, I am afraid."

"What have you seen of war?" she asked, for Paget looked even younger than his youthful age, seemingly not having seen enough years to have significant experience.

"He has been fighting this war since Talavera and before," snapped Timmerman in Paget's defence this time.

The lady looked both surprised and impressed, but not sure if she could trust a seemingly outrageous claim. It would not be the first time a soldier had made fantastical claims that were far beyond reality.

"I was there when Craven, just a Captain at the time, led the charge at Porto, and at Talavera, and so many battles since," stated Paget.

"Craven? Yes, of course, I remember the newspapers. They called you Craven's Blades?"

"That is correct."

"Then it is an honour to have you here in the North, and may you be as victorious as you were in Spain."

"And you, Ma'am, what will you do?"

"I will remain here and do all that I can."

There was a creak at the doors behind them, and Timmerman looked around with suspicion. He carefully went to them and drew them open to peer outside. A member of staff approached from the far end of the corridor, but there was no other sign of life. He closed to the doors once more but did not look entirely convinced of their safety and secrecy.

"It is a dangerous game you play here," he declared to the lady.

"And yours is not?"

"We are soldiers, it is our duty."

"I may not wear a uniform, Captain Paget, but it is my duty, too, to resist the enemy in all the ways that I can."

"You are very brave."

The lady smiled as if she was greatly amused by Paget's attitude.

"There is one more thing, a supply depot of significant size that is being assembled for Marshal Marmont, it is not far from here."

"Craven will want no know of it," smirked Timmerman, for that sounded like the perfect target for them.

***

Craven looked nervously over the shoulder of Bunce, keeping a keen but subtle eye on the French carriage as a general stormed out to climb aboard, though he stopped to rant and rave at the one Timmerman had done battle with. The general did not hold back as he slapped his man in the face and ridiculed him loudly enough for all to hear. Even Craven, not that he understood the language, found the intention was clear.

"The Major has brought this upon us, what am I to say if the general comes to me?" Bunce asked in fear.

"You will grovel and make your apologies."

"Bow down and cower? When Timmerman took a stand?"

"He did battle with a rambunctious and rude captain, but that man there is a general, and you will not risk angering such a man, just as you would if he was an English general, for the consequences could have us discovered."

They watched as the general climbed up into the carriage but then stuck his head through the curtain of the window on the far side so that he could shake his fist angrily at Craven's comrades. He raged at them as his carriage moved on. The captain with a bloodied hand who had battled with Timmerman gazed down from his saddle at Craven's friends with furious anger. Anger that he had both been beaten, but also that he had then been humiliated before them.

"My name is Captain Maline, and you will not forget it." Bunce translated as soon as he was out of ear shot.

The carriage stormed away from the lady's house with the escort riders almost at the gallop to keep up.

"That is a man on a mission and with little time," declared Matthys.

"Yes, it is coming to a head now, isn't it?"

"What is, Sir?" Bunce asked Craven.

"The battle we have all been waiting for and talking about every single day since we got here," replied Craven in amazement that it needed to be answered.

"Would Napoleon not retreat to France and make his stand there, Sir?"

Craven shook his head.

"Napoleon came here to win, and that is precisely what he intends to do. He means to break those before him, just like he did at Austerlitz and Borodino."

"I am afraid they are before my time, Sir."

"On both occasions Napoleon was outnumbered by a force who confidently sought to destroy him, and yet he turned the tables on them. He has done it countless times, and he will be confident of doing it once more."

"Look," gestured Charlie.

They turned back to find that Paget and Timmerman were approaching.

"Well, did you find her?" Craven asked.

"We did, Sir," replied Paget uneasily, as if not wanting to speak the news for all to hear.

"No more secrets now, not between our closest friends. Now we have come this far, there is nothing more to hide."

"Lady Katarina has been most useful, Sir."

"And you trust her?"

"I do, Sir," he replied sincerely, "She says Napoleon focuses everything on Leipzig."

Craven took out his map and took a quick cautious look around before studying it.

"Not a bad choice, and she is sure of this?"

"Absolutely, Sir, and not only from a single source."

"This is it, this is what we needed, to know the mind of the enemy," declared Craven with joy.

"There is more. Marmont has a depot not far from here where he assembles a great deal of equipment and powder," replied Timmerman with glee.

"Marmont?" Ferreira asked, relishing the chance to embarrass the French Marshal once more and make him pay for all he had done in Portugal and Spain.

But Paget was surprised to see Craven was not excited by the prospect.

"You are not tempted, Sir?"

Craven shook his head.

"On most other days I would be, but not here. We've got what we came for and we did so without being discovered. Let us take this victory for what it is and be on our way before the enemy discovers our true identity."

"You believe they will, Sir?"

"That Captain Maline will be eager for revenge to undo his humiliation. What happens when he starts asking around about who we are and where we came from?"

"Nobody will have any answers, Sir."

"Indeed, and that will only draw suspicion, and if a supply depot nearby was to be struck also, it would not take a military genius to connect us with those events."

"And that would bring all hell down upon Lady Katarina for associating with us," pondered Paget with concern.

"Indeed, let us not dwell in this place, no good can

come of it."

They leapt back into their saddles and Paget soon led them, stopping for only brief moment to notice Lady Katarina watching them from her library window.

"I had to fight, it was not a choice," declared Timmerman to Craven as if making an apology.

"You did the right thing under the circumstances. For now, all that Frenchman can think about is his bitter anger, clouded by humiliation. And in that blindness, he does not even pause to think that anything about us might be out of place."

"Good, then," added Timmerman in some relief that he was not thought ill of.

"This ruse cannot last forever. If the general had pressed upon us in any way this would all have come crashing down."

They rode on in column. Soon enough they were beside the French encampment once more, and it was a most unnerving sight to behold for even the most steadfast of them, for it was an entire army before their eyes. French cavalry rode about in the distance and were the identity of Craven's companions to be discovered, they would have a vast force descending upon them within moments.

"You could have killed that man," whispered Paget to Timmerman who rode beside him.

"Yes."

"And he could have killed you."

"Perhaps, but my death would have been of no consequence, but as the bodyguard of a general, his death would have brought all eyes upon you and Craven and everyone here."

"You would risk your life to protect us?"

"It surprises me also, but I have grown rather fond of you all," smirked Timmerman.

"You could have let me deal with Maline myself."

"A colonel would not stoop so low as to entertain such a thing. You are a colonel now, at least for a little while longer, and you need to act it."

"I am not sure it is a position I could enjoy. For it was once all I ever would have wanted, but now things are so different to what I imagined them to be."

"I can understand, and in this I understand you better than Craven ever will."

"You do?"

"Of course, we are not so different in where we came from. I will admit that our paths branched out very different in time, though they have converged once more. I, too, was once a lot like you and wanted all that you did. I was never the gentleman you are, but we had so much in common, even the expectations of our families."

"You were outcast also?"

"Yes, but in my case, I rather deserved it. Whereas you most certainly did not."

"How can you be so sure?"

"Because you are a great man, and any father not proud of you is a fool."

Craven's eyes twitched in amazement as he rode behind them and overheard the conversation.

"My father did not disown me. I did he."

"And you would abandon that fortune for the sake of principle?"

"Yes, and I would do the same ten times over."

"I am not sure that I could. You lost everything because you stood by your principles, but I lost all that I could have had because I abandoned mine."

"Then we shall be poor together," smiled Paget.

"There is more of value in life than only money. Many men would give up all they have to be here doing what we are."

They rode on for some time, passing other French troops without incident, and soon enough they were making the final few hundred yards back to the cabin where they had stashed their uniforms and any and all equipment which might mark them out as Coalition soldiers. Moxy suddenly soared forward at the gallop.

"Stop!" Craven roared.

But nothing would stop the Welshman as he spurred his horse on and galloped for the cabin as fast as he could. He leapt from the saddle as he reached the cabin and stormed up to the door which he tore open. Moxy vanished inside as the rest of them rode into the clearing, all eyes on the cabin, both fearful and intrigued to know if their equipment remained. They could hear Moxy furiously rummaging inside before he finally stormed out with his rifle held high as though it was a trophy he had one. He cried out in delight as many of the others clapped at his joy.

"Gather up four rifles for those on watch, but we stay in these uniforms until morning," declared

Craven.

There was at least three hours of light left, but he was wary of setting out upon the road with so little time to put distance between them and the enemy.

"You heard the Major. Let's get a fire going and settle in for the evening!" Matthys ordered.

They quickly set about re-igniting the fire pit they had used the night before. Craven watched and marvelled as Moxy cleaned his rifle on the step of the cabin. He paced up and sat down beside the Welshman.

"Be ready for anything, do you hear me?"

"You said nobody knew of this place?"[9]

"That we know of, but a French scouting troop could easily enough stumble across this place purely by accident."

Moxy recoiled.

"What?"

"That is not how you described this place yesterday. You said you were entirely sure our weapons and uniforms would be safe here," he protested.

"As safe as we could hope for them to be. We are in a land plagued by war on a scale we have never seen before. Nowhere is truly safe."

Moxy grumbled in agreement.

"Keep a keen watch, but do not fire your rifle unless it is a matter of life and death. We do not know who might be in the area and drawn to such a noise."

CHAPTER 8

Craven was shaken awake, his right hand forming a fist as he prepared to strike his attacker, but it was Moxy with rifle in hand.

"What is it?" croaked the sleepy Major.

"A rider approaches."

"You are certain?" Craven looked out around the clearing. Their fire still smouldered and emitted a lovely warmth, but it provided little light now in the darkness of night. He threw off his blanket and got to one knee with his sheathed sword in one hand ready to do battle. Moxy hurried over to the tree line to wait in concealment with his rifle trained on whoever approached. Ellis and Joze awoke the others one by one, and as the thunder of the approaching horses' hooves drew nearer, they were all ready to do battle. Several with swords were already drawn, but not Craven. He still did not know what to expect, but also trusted in Moxy and Ferreira to cover him with their rifles.

"Who is it?" Paget asked.

Craven shrugged for he had no idea, but it could only be one or two horses and so he was not overly concerned.

"It is Lady Katarina," declared Paget with his eagle eyes.

A figure soon came into view and Craven could see for himself that the Captain was correct.

"Captain Paget?"

"I am here, Ma'am." He stepped forward and sheathed his sword.

She was riding side saddle and slid off to the ground before anyone could help her, though she looked confident enough that she had clearly done it thousands of times before.

"You should not be here," insisted Paget.

"The same could be said of yourselves, but I have no choice."

"Why did you come here?" Craven stepped forward to address her directly.

The lady took the measure of him for a moment before smiling.

"It is really you, isn't it? James Craven?"

"Major James Craven," he snapped back.

"I should have known you would have come and not left it to others."

"What are you doing here in the middle of the night? Your behaviour will draw suspicion."

"I am afraid I am already exposed. I would not have come here if it were not a desperate situation."

"How did you even know where to find us?" Paget asked.

"My family have long used this place for hunting, and I have known it since childhood, just as Captain Edinger does."

"Are you compromised?"

"I believe I will be by noon tomorrow, Major."

"Tell me everything."

The lady nodded in agreement before noticing the fire still burning, and she went to it to warm her hands. Moxy placed several fresh logs onto the ashes to rekindle it for her, as Craven stepped up beside her, awaiting an explanation.

"One of my staff has become suspicious of me and has taken a letter of which I had written to one of my family members, which will cast doubt upon my loyalties if the French were to receive it."

"And you believe they will?"

"The man in my service means to set out at first light, and whilst I do now know the reason why for certain, I believe I am sure of it."

"Why did you not have one of your men or servants deal with this for you?"

"Because I do not know who I can trust, and the fewer of my staff who know of my actions against the French, the less risk for all of us."

"She's right. It is a dangerous game, and better that her staff know nothing of it," replied Vicenta.

"This is a lady you address," snapped Paget, displeased of the informal way she spoke of the Prussian lady.

But Vicenta shrugged, for she had no care for titles or niceties.

"It is of no consequence, I know little of your military ways either," Katarina responded, trying to defuse the situation.

"Somehow I doubt that," replied Timmerman, as he had already seen how astute she was around military men.

"Is this our problem?" Birback grumbled.

"Nobody asked you," Paget snapped at him. He was clearly eager to help the lady in distress.

"If she is discovered, then the information that we came for might become worthless. Those generals who shared it might quickly move to ensure Napoleon changes his plans," explained Craven.

"When has anyone convinced Napoleon to change his mind?" Paget asked.

"He is a tactician above all else, which explains his great successes. If information is taken to him that weakens his position and strengthens his opponent's, there is no telling what he might do, is there?"

"We must protect the lady's identity and the information we have gathered by all means necessary," insisted Matthys.

"And how do you propose we do that?" Ferreira asked.

"Kill this man, the German," stated Amyn coldly.

"Kill him?" Paget asked in disbelief.

"He is a traitor to his mistress and a threat to us all," he explained coldly.

"We are not murderers," protested Bunce.

"Are we not?" Birback smirked at him.

"Where is he now?"

"Amongst my household, Major."

"Then we go there and get the job done," insisted Timmerman.

"No, I will not have blood spilt in my home. It would only attract prying eyes, and that is the last thing we need."

Craven thought about it for a few moments as he tried to craft a plan.

"You know where this man travels?" asked Paget.

"Why does he not just go to the French army camped on your doorstep?" asked Birback.

"They have already marched on."

"Then where will your servant ride for?" Craven asked.

"The depot I told Captain Paget of."

Craven smiled, realising he had a chance to kill two birds with one stone. Paget was already shaking his head for he knew precisely what Craven was thinking.

"Sir, you said we had no time to spare, and that we would not attack and risk being discovered in these uniforms."

"We won't be wearing these uniforms," smiled Craven as he turned back to Moxy.

"Break out our equipment. We ride as the Salford Rifles!"

A cheer echoed out. Many around them began to strip away their French uniforms as they stormed towards the cabin to retrieve their beloved uniforms and weapons. But Paget remained behind, looking unconvinced.

"Sir, what of the news we carry? What of the haste of our mission?"

"That information and the source from which

it came is even more important now, for we should return to no avail if those two things cannot be protected."

"You play a French colonel well," declared Katarina appreciatively on the weary and uncertain Paget.

"He was born for it," replied Timmerman.

"That much I am sure of," replied Katarina.

They watched as Craven emerged from the cabin. He buttoned up his scarlet officer's tunic, pulled his greatcoat on top of that, and placed his shako atop his head. He was quite the striking figure to Katarina.

"Is it really him? Is that really James Craven?"

"It is."

"Then perhaps there is hope for me yet."

"If there is any way for you to come out of this safely, then Craven will see it done."

"I believe so, but you do not give yourself enough credit. It was not Craven who came to me under the nose of a French general. And it was not Craven who duelled with a French officer outside my home merely to keep up this façade," she added as she looked to Timmerman in appreciation.

"Go on, get your things," insisted Craven to the two officers who had stayed by the lady's side.

They hurried off, leaving Craven alone with the Prussian lady and widow.

"Thank you, for you owe me nothing."

"Any enemy of Napoleon is an ally of mine, and I will ensure we do everything in our power to assist. We came to you in secrecy, but now we are British soldiers once more."

Soon enough the group was gathering around and wearing their own uniforms, feeling much more comfortable for it, as well as far better armed.

"The French uniforms, Sir?"

"Leave them here, Moxy, for we move quickly. We shall collect them on our return."

"Is their purpose not complete, Sir?" asked Bunce.

"We were loaned this equipment by the grace of the Free Corps, and we shall see them returned, for with this equipment they can outfit and fight against the French."

"Your servant moves at first light?" Craven asked the lady once more.

"Yes."

"Then we travel by night."

"Upon daylight we will attract a great deal of attention, what of the French army, Sir?" Bunce asked.

"They have already moved on."

"We are sure of that?"

"As sure as we can be."

"And the next French column, what about them?"

"We cannot concern ourselves with speculation. We move quickly. We strike in the morning, and we shall be gone before the enemy may receive news of our presence. As far as the enemy knows, we're merely a raiding party, and the lady may return home to continue her work."

"We should move without any more delay," insisted Timmerman.

"Agreed, let's be on our way." Joze passed him

the reins of his horse. They rode on through the night without any light, but soon enough the first rays of sunshine appeared on the horizon. Craven increased the pace of his horse as they hurried to their position. Soon enough they came to a halt at a wood overlooking Katarina's home.

"This man who goes to betray you to the French, what is his name?" Craven asked.

"Carl Eisele."

"You will point him out, and once we have begun our pursuit, you will go back to your home."

"And if there are more like him amongst my staff?"

"Remind them where their loyalty lies, for it is not to France," he replied sternly.

"And if they do not stand with me?"

"Your business is none of theirs. Do not reveal to them your role in this, merely that they serve at your pleasure."

"Spoken like a true king," smiled Timmerman.

"Soon enough all this will be over. We will meet with Napoleon upon the battlefield and the future of all of Europe shall be decided. If we are victorious, then you may share in our glory."

"And if you are not?"

"Then you never met James Craven and the Salford Rifles, and you had no part to play in this war besides entertaining the soldiers of France in your home."

"You are a kind man."

Craven looked stunned, for it was not something

he was accustomed to hearing.

"He looks after those who need it," replied Paget.

"There."

They followed Moxy's gaze to see a man ride out from the stables upon a horse. He was alone and wore no uniform.

"Is it him?" Craven asked.

"It is," replied Katarina.

"He rides for Marmont's supply depot?"

"Yes."

"Go back to your home, I insist."

"Thank you, and may God be with you," she replied earnestly.

"Every man hopes it to be true, but I do not need God, only these devils," he smiled, looking around at his closest friends and comrades.

The lady led her horse away to head for another road as Craven climbed onto his horse.

"What is the plan?" Timmerman asked.

"Stop Eisele by any and all means necessary."

"And if he reaches the depot before us?"

"Then we burn it to the ground."

He rode on, leading his party after the German traitor.

"If he sees us, he will run," Paget sounded worried.

But Craven looked back at his party to see that all wore their greatcoats. He shook his head.

"Until anyone is within a few paces of us, no man would guess of where we come from, especially here."

Paget did not look convinced but made no protest

as he hoped it to be true. They rode on and soon reached a road at which they could see Eisele riding. He was travelling at quite some speed and great urgency.

"Do not lose sight of him," insisted Craven, confident that Paget was riding the fastest horse amongst them.

"He will get suspicious," insisted Paget.

"Let him," snapped Craven angrily.

They upped their pace greatly, and it was not long before Eisele peered back in fear that they might be in pursuit of him, and yet he could not know either way.

"What will you do with him?" Holck asked.

"He has betrayed his country and his people, let alone his employer, there is only one thing for it," replied Craven coldly.

"One could say the same about me."

"You do not fight against your country."

"And if you were ordered to do so and cross over into my lands?"

"Then I would not ask you to come with us."

After a mile of travelling at a significant pace, they watched as Eisele stopped before two French sentries, with a large camp beyond them. He spoke with them for a few minutes as he looked back upon Craven's party before going on. The two sentries carried muskets with bayonets affixed, as so many men on guard did so. To have to defend oneself and a position with only a single shot in the chamber of a musket left one very vulnerable. The two guards stepped up to the road, their muskets at the port and ready to deploy without yet posing a threat. One cried out to ask who they were and what was their business, simple language that even Craven understood. He looked past the men to see Eisele vanish inside the walls of a walled farmhouse that was stacked with crates and barrels and all sorts of supplies. Only a few soldiers were on duty, with one sitting on a birch of the roof of the farmhouse with a ladder leading to his crow's nest-like position.

Paget began to communicate with the two guards, but Craven merely grabbed the muzzle of one of the muskets with both his hands and ripped it away from the man holding it, smashing the butt into the man's face. He crumpled to a heap on the ground as the other hurried to reach for the lock of his musket to make it ready, but Joze appeared seemingly from nowhere and slit the Frenchman's throat without mercy.

Bunce looked disgusted by the feral scene, but nobody protested.

"Find Eisele!" Craven roared.

They soared on through the gatehouse, the gates of which were long gone. The few Frenchmen on duty did not react at first, assuming they were allies, for no shots had rung out to alert them to any danger.

"Craven!" Paget shouted.

He looked up just in time to see the Frenchman take aim with his musket, but Moxy's rifle erupted first and shot him dead. Craven nodded to him in appreciation.

"Don't ever take my rifle again," insisted Moxy

angrily.

Craven smirked before quickly surveying the scene as Birback and Amyn leapt from their saddles to chase on after Eisele. A French officer burst out from the farmhouse with sword in hand, but Timmerman drew a pistol and shot him dead. A bell suddenly rang out from the other side of the building as the alarm was raised. Moxy hurried to reload as Ferreira shot the next man out of the farmhouse door. Birback and Amyn rushed past the two bodies and leapt inside the building. A pistol was aimed at the two, and Amyn shoved Birback violently back out of the door as the weapon was fired, striking Amyn in the left shoulder. Birback got to his feet and briefly gazed upon the Mameluke, amazed that he had seemingly saved his life. He hauled him out of the doorway before storming in to go after their attackers. Matthys rushed to help Amyn as Caffy stormed through the door to help Birback, but he got inside to find Birback beating two French soldiers senseless with the butt of the pistol that had been fired at he and Amyn.

The two of them rushed on through into the next room to find a French officer with two of his sergeants and Eisele amongst them. The officer cried out at them in French, just as Timmerman shoved his way in between his comrades to translate. Eisele spat words out in support.

"He says we are too late. Katarina's secret is out."

"Not if no one lives to tell the tale," growled Birback.

The Frenchmen evidently understood his

meaning as they drew their swords in readiness to resist the intruders. He soared forward to hack the French officer down, but a quick disengage of his blade, and the Frenchman's blade was embedded in his chest. Caffy and Birback stormed onwards to engage the sergeants. Timmerman growled furiously at the wound that had been inflicted on him and merely took hold of the blade with his left hand where it had entered his body. He hacked down at the blade with his own, snapping it in half, leaving one part in his chest and the other still in the hands of his attacker. Timmerman yanked the blade from his body and held it defiantly as an offhand dagger. The Frenchman came at him, but with only half a sword he had so little reach, and Timmerman hacked at his head from a position of safety.

Caffy ran though his man, and Birback beat the other violently with his ward iron as Eisele tried to open a back door to make his escape. Timmerman launched the blade remnant in his hand as though it were a throwing knife. The broken blade which dripped with his own blood flashed across the room, embedding in Eisele's shoulder blade. He cried out as he dropped to one knee and failed to prise the door open. Timmerman grabbed him by the collar and hauled him back out towards the entrance of the house. They got outside to find Moxy splitting a powder keg open with the pommel of his sabre. He rolled it along the floor for fifty yards, the leaking barrel creating a long trail along the ground until it was all but empty. Vicenta and Ellis rolled other powder kegs across the yard of the farmhouse, tossing powder over anything that might burn, including several wagons and a large pile of firewood, and then into the house itself. Joze and Charlie looked after the horses outside the gatehouse.

Timmerman slammed Eisele against the farmhouse wall, causing the blade embedded in his shoulder to be hammered through until it burst out through his chest. He cried out in pain, but Timmerman had no sympathy at all for him. He gestured for Holck to join them.

"Tell him he is a traitor."

"I think these words will be lost on him."

"Tell him!" Timmerman roared.

Holck translated, but Eisele glared back at them in defiance.

"Fighting for the French against your own people, for shame," seethed Timmerman.

Eisele looked furious, but as he opened his mouth to respond, a musket shot erupted and the ball struck his chest, killing him instantly. Timmerman let his body slump lifelessly to the ground as he turned back to see a number of French troops gathering to resist them. They were in open order and with only a single older and campaign weary officer to lead them. Ferreira opened fire against them and shot one dead, as Craven soared towards the veteran officer, engaging him sword versus sword. He was too fast for the veteran as he bedazzled the Frenchman with a flurry of feints and quick attacks, landing a shallow thrust on the man's arm which caused him to drop his sword and back away. One of his men came rushing forward to his aid, but Moxy shot him dead. But Craven could see a tented camp of French soldiers in the distance was coming alive, and French soldiers hurried forward with weapons in hand.

"Light it up!" Craven roared to Moxy.

A sporadic but well aimed volley ripped out from the Salfords, knocking down nearly a dozen of the enemy and created a thick fog of powder smoke between them. Moxy hurried to the barrel of which he had emptied in a long fuse-like trail. He placed his rifle down beside the broken barrel and the last of the powder spilling from it. He primed the lock of his empty weapon and fired. The lock snapped to life and sparks flew as the flint hit the frizzen. The powder erupted before him in a great flash. Ellis grabbed him by the arm and hauled him away just in time as the powder smoke erupted into a great flash, singeing the Welshman's eyebrows. Ellis continued to draw him away until he scrambled to his feet as the powder trail burned violently. The French soldiers opposing them cried out in a panic as they fled from the impending inferno.

"Come on!"

Craven leapt into the saddle as the rest of them reached their position. They raced on just a few paces as the fiery powder trail reached a massive stack of powder kegs and a thunderous explosion ignited. The deafening explosion only spurred their terrified horses on to a faster pace as fire lashed at the backs of their riders, and a great mass of smoke and debris enveloped them. Craven finally came to a standstill as the debris began to settle around them, and they looked back. The roof had been blown off the farmhouse and two of the walls had collapsed also. They could not see any of the French soldiers for the vast powder fog between them.

"Yes!" Timmerman cried out excitedly.

A cheer rang out from the rest of them as they realised they had been successful.

"Eisele?" Paget asked.

"He is done," replied Timmerman.

"And so are we. Let us be on our way before the whole French army descends upon us," insisted Craven.

He looked back at the destructive scene one last time, relieved that they had buried Lady Katerina's secret amongst the burning ruins of one of Marmont's supply stores. He could only smile as he imagined the look upon the Marshal's face as he learnt of the news of such a blow to his powder stores.

CHAPTER 9

"I must speak with the Crown Prince immediately," insisted Craven to one of the Swedish soldiers keeping guard at the gatehouse leading to Charles John's headquarters. The guards evidentially recognised Craven at least somewhat but were reluctant to let him pass. Holck spoke up for him as he tried to negotiate in their own language, but they were having none of it. And Craven's rank gave him no authority to force them to step aside, for they were the guard of a member of the Swedish Royal family now, let alone a Commander of one of the Coalition armies. He sighed in frustration, for he could not think of a way to get their information to the right people unless he could reach the Prince.

"Craven?"

He looked through the metal railings beside the gatehouse to see Sir Charles approaching.

"Yes, I must see the Crown Prince, for I have information of the utmost importance."

"Let him through, you fools," declared Sir Charles as he approached the guards, but they would not move, and so he shoved one of them aside. The Swedish soldier looked bewildered but dared not oppose a general who was the guest of the Crown Prince to whom he served and owed his allegiance. Sir Charles gestured for Craven to step through the opening, with Holck and Timmerman following as his aides to help in any communication needs which might arise.

They approached the grand manor, which was even more decadent than that of Lady Katerina. Yet he had no idea to whom it belonged, for it was common for army commanders to commandeer a nobleman's estate for the use as a headquarters wherever they went. The great manor was built from stone and featured huge arched windows and lavish columns. Blue Swedish banners flew from flag poles before the manor, and dozens of soldiers came and went, some bringing news and others supplies. Messenger hurried back and forth.

"What is of such importance?" Sir Charles asked.

"I have discovered Napoleon's plans. I know where he intends to do battle."

"You are sure?"

"I am. Those fools at the gate should know better than to prevent me from seeing the Crown Prince, for I am attached to his army, am I not?"

Sir Charles shrugged with uncertainty.

"The Rocket Troop serve under the command of the Army of the North, and I am rightly here as a military attaché, but you, Craven? I am not sure even God knows what your role is here."

"I was sent by Wellington."

"I don't think that means anything at all to these

people. Wellington might fight the same adversary, but he does it in a different part of the world."

"And yet is France not the target for us all?"

"Yes, and yet after all these years, none of us have yet laid a foot into that country," lamented Sir Charles.

"When I left, we were merely weeks away."

"But you won't be if the armies here in the North are defeated, will you? If Napoleon can be victorious here, then he will turn South and march for Wellington. And there will be nothing that can stop him, not you or I or Wellington himself."

"That is why I was sent here, to ensure that does not happen."

"You truly believe Lord Wellington puts that much faith in you?"

"Begrudgingly, yes. He may not agree with my methods, but he knows that I get results."

"Then I wish you every luck, for we need it. If we can amass the Coalition armies here, we will have the advantage in numbers on Napoleon, but as history as shown us, that is no guarantee of success. Everyone is on edge. I can feel it everywhere I go. From the common soldier to the generals of our armies, we walk on a knife's edge to the path of victory and defeat."

"It is a path I know well," smiled Craven, for he embraced the chaos and always had done.

Sir Charles led the party on into the manor house and to a dining room that was being used as an operations room. Maps and messengers' notes were scattered about the table. Six senior officers deliberated with the Crown Prince around them. Sir Charles coughed loudly to draw the Prince's attention.

"You will want to hear this," he stated.

The Crown Prince was not so certain, and then he spotted Craven.

"Out, everyone!"

The officers looked most put out as they filed past Craven as he entered the room with Sir Charles, who shut the door behind them so that only the three of them remained.

"What is this about?" demanded the Crown Prince bluntly.

"I have information regarding Napoleon's intentions. Where he is marching all of his forces and where he intends to make battle."

"Show me."

Craven rushed forward to the large map spread out across the operations table.

"Here, at Leipzig."

The Crown Prince nodded in agreement.

"Yes, yes of course. Of course, that is where he would choose to fight," said the Prince to himself. "How sure are you of this information?" he demanded with great concern, for he knew how much would be at stake if they were to make a decision based upon it.

"I have it from a trustworthy source who heard it directly from multiple French generals," he declared boldly.

"I would love to hear how that came to be, and yet I am sure you have every need of protecting your source of intelligence."

"I am, and I would not share them with Wellington, nor the King of England himself."

The Prince studied his map, carefully tracing all the roads back and forth between all of the major towns and cities.

"I am not sure who is the hunter and who is the hunted anymore," he sighed.

"Time will show everything," replied Craven.

The Prince smiled.

"Yes, it will, and what we do here in these next weeks will be written into the history books as one of the greatest defining moments in the history of Europe, if not all the world."

"Napoleon knows it also."

"Yes, he does. You forget, Major, that I know the Emperor better than any of you."

"I had not forgotten, but he has been my enemy longer than yours," smiled Craven.

"What to do, what to do?" asked the Prince rhetorically.

"If the French amass to do battle, and we know the location upon which they take, then we should oblige them," insisted Craven.

"It is not my choice to make. I command the Army of the North, but Schwarzenberg is supreme commander of all operations on German lands."

"Then go to him and ensure that our armies march in the right direction," pleaded Craven.

"Our armies?" asked the Prince in surprise.

"Yes, I may not be a German, a Russian, or a Swede, but neither are you, and yet I am every bit as much a part of this army as you are now, Sir. That is what I have for you, but what you choose to do with it is none of my business." Craven turned to leave.

"No, Major, you are coming with me."

Craven stopped. A tingle went down his spine. For to have a Frenchman giving him orders felt most unsettling, but even Timmerman shook his head as if to signal that he should not pick a fight here.

"And where is that?" Craven asked wearily, knowing he was not going to like the response.

"To General Schwarzenberg, for information of this magnitude, he will want to hear it from the source."

"But I am not the source, merely the messenger."

"You went in search of this information and so you will deliver it. Come on!"

The Prince scooped up his sword and hooked the scabbard rings onto the two belts dangling from his waist. He led Craven out and to the stables where a stable hand had a horse ready and waiting for the Prince. He looked out to see the rest of the Salford Rifles a hundred paces away, waiting and watching for any sign of news.

"Go to them and get your horse, and bring your squadron with us, for they can ride as my escort once again," declared the Prince.

One of his aide-de-camps tried to protest and spoke furiously in French, which caused Timmerman to smile, but the Prince shrugged him off. Craven raced to fetch his horse as the Prince's staff struggled in a panic to try and make sure of the safety of their Commander and heir to the throne, a position of responsibility to which the former French Marshal seemed almost oblivious to. Craven jogged back to the others and leapt into the saddle.

"The Prince believed you, Sir?" Paget asked.

"Yes, but it is not he who we need to convince," grimaced Craven.

Paget was taken aback, but he had no time to query it further as the Crown Prince galloped up before them.

"On me!" he ordered as he rode onwards with Craven by his side.

Craven looked most out of sorts.

"You still don't trust me, do you?"

"It is not an easy task," admitted Craven.

"Those who serve as my closest aides treat me as the heir to my adopted country, but they forget something. That is my future, and all that I am today is a soldier. My job is to secure the safety and the future of Sweden, and that is precisely what I shall do."

"We have talked of this before, and I truly believe that I can trust in your words, but in my heart, I cannot deny that it is not so easy."

"Good, for if it was easy, I would question your character. For you should not trust a former enemy so easily."

"And you do now, Sir?"

"I know I can trust you to resist Napoleon and his armies until your dying breath, and that is what matters to me."

"You will be King one day, I cannot think of anything stranger in these days than a Frenchman wanting to be king," smiled Craven.

"Napoleon is a king only by a different name, and the world knows it. Only his subjects cannot see it, for they love him too much."

Craven was stunned to hear such a blunt assessment and could find no words to follow it. They galloped on for some time, not knowing what to talk about. They were from such vastly different backgrounds that it seemed the war was the only thing they had in common. Finally, they reached an encamped army in the grounds of a great manor house, not unlike the one used by the Crown Prince. And yet it was even better attended by senior officers who littered the lawns deep in conversation. The Crown Prince's arrival drew many eyes, and the company he kept certainly got many tongues moving.

"Let me speak and do nothing to cause trouble here. This coalition is as strong as one could hope for, but it would not take much to fracture it, do you understand?"

"Yes, Sir," replied Craven, continuing to address the Prince as a soldier and not royalty, but the former French Marshal did not mind, for it was far more comfortable and familiar to him. They rode right up to the front door of the house. Nobody dared say a word in the presence of the Crown Prince, even though they might have some colourful words they would love to share of Craven. The Prince leapt from his horse.

"Craven, come with me. The rest of your men can wait at the stables with my horse."

Craven did as ordered, as they passed the reins of their horses over to Joze and Paget. They stepped inside to find dozens of colonels and generals deep in conversation in the large atrium. Captains and majors hurried about as if they were house staff. Many paused their conversation at the sight of the newcomers. The Crown Prince received many suspicious glances, the same that Craven had given him and sometimes still did, but Craven himself received far worse.

"Follow me," insisted the Crown Prince.

The room erupted into conversation once more in all manner of languages, including French, German, Russian, and Swedish. But Craven did not understand any of them. On they went towards a large campaign room, though as they made their final approach the doors were sealed. The Prince stopped and looked to the end of the hall where a mass of officers was filing out of a doorway into a garden outside. They followed on with much intrigue where they found dozens of officers and their wives and mistresses watching races between the cavalry of many different nations. It was a flamboyant and opulent display, but it was the perfect way to pass the time as the army awaited its most terrifying test against Napoleon. Craven felt most out of place, and yet he was granted a pass by the nature of the company he kept. The Swedish Crown Prince was one of the most senior officers and commanders amongst them all, and yet even he reported to a higher power, to which they now approached.

Schwarzenberg was an imposing man. The tall Austrian was just a few years older than Craven but looked older still and carried himself with a great confidence and air of authority. His gleaming white tunic was adorned with a vast amount of gold braid befitting his station.

"Why do you bring me an Englishman?" he demanded of Prince Charles John.

Craven was surprised by his command of the English language and his recognition of his uniform.

"Major James Craven brings news which is of the utmost importance."

Schwarzenberg sighed in frustration that his time was being interrupted, but he groaned in acceptance as he led them back to the campaign room, where he gestured for his men to seal the door, leaving Craven in the company of two Princes.

"Speak," declared Schwarzenberg.

His dark eyes pierced into the back of Craven's head as if he was looking right through him.

"Napoleon assembles all his forces at Leipzig. He means to do battle there."

"And how would an Englishman know the mind of the Emperor of France?"

"From the words of his generals to a reliable source."

"And what source is that?"

"I cannot say."

Schwarzenberg sighed in frustration.

"Surely you understand, Sir, that I cannot

endanger someone who has risked everything to share this information with me."

Schwarzenberg was silent for a moment as he studied Craven and then the maps between them. He soon shook his head in a rejection of Craven's news.

"I do not know you, Major, nor do I have any reason to trust you, but you would have me command my armies based on your word? Not even your word but mere hearsay shared with you from another person who I have no reason to trust."

Craven was stunned but did not know how to respond.

"I trust the Major, and I am certain that what he says is true," insisted Prince Charles John.

But Schwarzenberg shook his head.

"It is not enough." He looked to Craven. "I do not know what you have come here for, Major, for your war is in Spain, but whilst you are here, you will serve at the grace of Prince Charles."

"I do, Sir."

"Good, then get back to your duties, and leave the conduct of this war to those who are conducting it."

He stormed away and ripped a door open before storming off angrily. Craven remained stunned as he looked to the Crown Prince for answers.

"I am sorry," declared the former French Marshal with genuine sympathy.

"Why will he not listen? We are on the knife's edge of the greatest battle of all our lives, and yet he will not listen to information that could tip the balance?"

"Do you know how many men come forward with information which could turn the tide of the war?"

Craven shook his head.

"More and more every day. For so many ambitious officers approach the command of our armies with news that they hope might gain them some step up in rank or reputation," lamented the Prince.

"I don't give a damn about any of that!"

"But how can Schwarzenberg tell the difference? Only one year ago he was forced to fight for Napoleon after years of resisting him upon the battlefield. This is the second chance he never imagined he might have gotten, and he will not let anything endanger it."

"He fought for Napoleon?" Craven asked in amazement, for he was still having trouble wrapping his head around the politics and toing and froing of the European powers.

"Austria was a vassal of France for many years. Then she was neutral, and finally a member of this coalition after it was proven that victory was a possibility."

Craven shrugged as it was a lot to understand.

"Austria has a complicated history with France, fighting alongside my old country, and then against it to restore the French monarchy, and then to the even more turbulent times which I mentioned previously. This is one of the many fragilities that I have tried to explain to you. As an Englishman it is a simple task to understand who your enemy is, for you have been fighting against France for centuries."

Craven smiled and nodded in agreement.

"And yet, you allied with Spain, perhaps an even more bitter rival for you than France," added the Prince.

Craven sighed in frustration. He was furious and wanted nothing more than to sweep everything off of the table beside them in a fit of rage, and yet he knew that was no way to endear himself to Schwarzenberg.

"What now? I went out to look for information that I thought could help in the war effort. I achieved that at great risk to myself and my men, and it was for nothing?"

He had no right to speak to a prince in such a way, and yet the Frenchman understood his frustrations and sympathised with him, and so made no issue of it.

"If you and I can find common ground, then why not between he and I?" sighed Craven.

"It takes time. You know this."

"Time is the one thing we have little of."

The Prince nodded in agreement.

"Does he distrust all Englishmen?"

"I do not know, but the Prince is correct to not chance his entire strategy based upon information that cannot be verified."

"Then you are with him?" Craven asked angrily.

"I am with you, and I am with the Prince. We are in this together. Find a way to prove this information is true, and Schwarzenberg will be with you."

Craven slammed his hand down furiously on the table, causing two large and heavy brass candlesticks to rock violently.

"If I went to Wellington with this, he would not

hesitate to act upon it," he groaned.

"Because you have spent years gaining Wellington's trust."

Craven nodded, for he knew it was true, but it made it no less frustrating. He could hear the cheer of the crowd of officers outside and the thunder of the hooves of the horses as they raced past. For a moment he felt powerless, as he knew for certain the information which he carried was legitimate, and yet instead of acting upon it, the Coalition armies were idle, enjoying sports and festivities whilst Napoleon loomed over them like a black cloud.

"A great battle is coming whether we want it or not. What I want to know is whether the Coalition really believes in victory. For it feels as though our commanders eat their final meal and make merry knowing they will die tomorrow. Have they accepted defeat before the first shot has been fired?"

"I am one of the leaders of the Coalition, and I do not accept defeat," he replied earnestly.

Craven nodded in appreciation.

"I never wanted to be involved at this level of a war, not this one or the one in Spain, nor Portugal. But now that I am, I feel shackled down as though a ball and chain is about my ankle. No matter how hard I try to move forward, I am held back."

"You are not the first man to feel it is so."

Craven looked stunned to hear it from a man who had risen so far in life to now be the de facto leader of a nation.

"These experiences you have today are no

different to my own for many years. Whether it be in the service of Schwarzenberg or Napoleon, this is the life of a soldier, until perhaps you reach the very top, and then you must battle an entirely new magnitude of problems. Do not fret over what you cannot change, Major. Save that energy for the things which you can."

Craven accepted that, for they were wise words, the sort which he would expect to hear from Matthys.

"Do you have orders for me?" he asked with that in mind.

"You do not answer to me, Major. I am not sure you truly answer to anyone. I do not know what is the best use for you, and this I share in common with Wellington, I believe. You have proven many a general wrong in the past. I am glad I am not against you, Major, for if there is one thing you truly excel at, it is fighting the French."

Craven chuckled in agreement.

"Go, go and do what you do best, Craven."

CHAPTER 10

Craven drank water from his canteen as he looked longingly out across the hills to the South and West, wondering what the enemy had in store for them. Though in his mind he already knew, for he knew what Napoleon's strategy was now. And that made it all the more frustrating that he could not convince the powers to be to do anything about it. He could only wait and watch as mistakes were made that were seemingly avoidable if his report was trusted and taken seriously.

"Schwarzenberg did not believe you, did he?" Timmerman joined him.

The rest of their companions were busy in the background, cleaning and maintaining their weapons and equipment.

"He did not," admitted Craven.

"I wouldn't have either."

Craven glared at him.

"What are you to this coalition? You have a reputation for fighting, but not here. To these people you are a foreigner, whose reputation and antics might well have been manufactured merely for the purposes of morale," explained Timmerman.

"But they were not," growled Craven.

"Would you believe all that you read in the newspapers? Would you gamble everything you have, and all of your companions on it?"

Craven sighed and shrugged, for he knew his old nemesis had a point.

"So, what are you going to do about it?"

"What is there to do?"

"I don't know, but I know James Craven wouldn't give up so easily."

"I had the backing of Prince Charles and still it was not enough, what more can I do? Schwarzenberg would not believe this information unless he heard it from a source he knows he can trust. How can that be achieved?"

Timmerman had no answers, but Craven turned around to gaze upon their friends when he spotted Sir Charles Stewart deep in conversation with Paget. Craven's face contorted, and Timmerman smiled as he could see a plan coming together in his mind. Craven suddenly sprang forward with a determined stride.

"That's the bastard I knew," smirked Timmerman.

"Do you have the ear of Prince Schwarzenberg?" Craven asked the British general bluntly.

"Why of course," came the response.

"You said you wanted danger and you wanted to ride with us again, do you still want it?"

"Both of those things!" Sir Charles roared.

"And if I told you there was a risk of being caught and hanged or shot as a spy?"

"Anything to leave this boredom behind," he replied without hesitation as he gestured back towards the camp. Craven thought back to the festivities to which Schwarzenberg attended and nodded in agreement.

"How do you look in a French uniform?"

Sir Charles looked most puzzled but also intrigued.

"Do you still have that spare uniform?" he asked Timmerman.

"I do."

"What is this about?" Sir Charles asked.

"Do you trust me?" Craven replied.

"I think so," replied Sir Charles with a little doubt.

"Then come with me."

Soon enough they were on the road once more, just Craven's small squadron and Sir Charles, with no further explanation. And yet they answered to nobody and so they did as they pleased whilst soldiers went about their duties in one of a great many camps scattered across the land. Sir Charles' curiosity soon faded away as he was merely overjoyed to be on the road and amongst fighting men once more, not wasting away in ballrooms and endless pointless conversation. After many miles, Craven brought them to a halt, ready to finally reveal to the former cavalryman just what they were up to. He nodded to Timmerman, who took out a French tunic and tossed it to the General. Sir Charles had no comprehension of what was to come next as he held it up before his eyes, looking most confused, but it suddenly dawned on him as he put the pieces together.

"We are going into the lion's den, dressed as one of them, aren't we?"

"Yes, we are," replied Craven with glee.

"When I joined you on this mission I imagined a daring attack on the enemy, not a deception which could get us all captured or killed without a fight," he groaned, although he still had a smile on his face, for in truth he was loving the sense of danger approaching. But Craven's thoughts veered to the larger picture after his meeting with Schwarzenberg.

"Do you think it can be done? All the armies amassed, all of the cavalry and all of the cannons, do you think it will be enough?" Craven asked the General.

"The armies we have assembled are truly vast, the likes of which Wellington could only dream of, but will it be enough? Who can say?"

"You can, is that not why you are here?"

Sir Charles laughed.

"I was sent here to get rid of me," he added.

"And yet that is no reason you cannot thrive here."

"And how do you propose I do that? I have no army. I have not even a regiment. I am a general without an army, and I am not a cavalryman anymore," he lamented.

"Then what do you call this?" Craven gestured around at the mounted squad they were leading, though it was a confusing sight, for they were all in the process of changing into the uniforms of

French cavalrymen, all but him. Sir Charles lifted the French tunic once more, shaking his head at the sight of it and the prospect of what they were about to do. He huffed one last time before accepting the circumstances as he unbuttoned his own ready to swap it.

"If I die in the uniform of a Frenchman, my spirit will haunt you for eternity," he declared playfully to Craven.

"Then don't die," joked Craven.

They buttoned up their French uniforms and bagged up all their equipment as before.

"Find a dry spot in there." Craven pointed to a dilapidated barn with barely half of its roof left. The slat walls were rotting under decades if not centuries of wear in the often-damp weather conditions. Moxy looked mortified and would not move.

"We aren't doing this again."

"We will do what must be done," growled Craven.

"Come on, we will return soon enough," insisted Matthys as he coaxed the Welshman along. He begrudgingly agreed as he found no sympathy amongst the others. Soon enough they were on the road disguised as French cavalry once more, only this time with a British general amongst them. They all knew the danger they were putting him under, but nobody spoke of it. Several hours passed before finally, they spotted a French cavalry squadron scouting the area.

"Do you speak French?" Craven asked Sir Charles.

"Of course."

"Can you pass as a Frenchman?"

"How dare you," he snapped, "But, yes," he added.

"Good. Don't speak to them unless you have to and just act like you are supposed to be where you are."

"This is a dangerous game you play, Craven."

"You and me both."

On they rode. To their surprise and relief, the cavalry ahead of them paid them no attention, which was a new experience for Sir Charles. He had never seen an enemy force and not get a reaction from them, typically of a most violent kind.

"They do not even check our identity?" Sir Charles asked in amazement.

"How often do we ever stop our allies to make conversation or investigate if they are who they appear to be?"

Sir Charles shrugged. "Perhaps we should more often," he admitted.

His mind began to wander as he considered just how many spies and enemy agents might move amongst them. It was especially easy amongst the Coalition, for there were so many different nations, uniforms, and languages spoken that few would even know what to look for in identifying an enemy agent.

"I am not sure I like this side of soldiering."

"This isn't soldiering. We are spies, and we will be treated as spies if we are caught," admitted Craven.

"What do you hope to achieve with this reckless mission?"

It was clear the dashing cavalryman felt some genuine fear at their situation.

"Napoleon gathers his forces at Leipzig, and that is where he will do battle with the armies of the Coalition."

"You know this?"

"I do, and I heard it from a source which I trust, but that is not enough for Schwarzenberg."

"That is why you brought me along, so that I might be a source which the Prince would trust on our return?"

Craven smiled, and that was enough to confirm it was true.

"What would you have me do?"

"Report all that you see and learn, and that is all."

"Keep me alive, and I will see it done."

"I think you can handle yourself," replied Craven, knowing that Fighting Charlie welcomed all challengers.

On they rode, passing several advanced French positions and camps, but it was not long before they were amongst the heart of the army, a point underlined by the vast baggage train they could see ahead. The sun was going down now, which was casting Craven's party into shadow and helping to disguise them further, but as they approached one position, a French captain stepped out to address them. He got out only a single word before Paget interrupted him and scolded the man for trying to interrupt their journey. Craven did not understand the words, but the meaning was clear, and he could not help but smile as they rode onwards without issue. They dared not search for accommodation. It was too great a risk to expose themselves to, and it seemed almost impossible anyway, for French soldiers and their allies had flooded every town and village for many miles all around.

They could hear many languages being spoken. Napoleon's army composed of soldiers from several German states, Poles, Italians, and more. The scenes were little different to what Craven and his comrades were accustomed to seeing amongst the Coalition armies. It felt comforting almost, and it was easy to forget that they were surrounded by their enemies who would strike them down in an instant if they knew their true identity. They went on to the edge of a wood and stopped as if to make camp.

"Get a fire going," Craven whispered to Moxy.

"You want to stay here amongst them?" he gasped.

"I don't know, but we will draw suspicion if we are idle."

The Welshman headed into the wood with several others to gather firewood, as Craven and the rest of officers gathered around to discuss their next step.

"What do we really want to achieve here?" Sir Charles asked.

"We need to hear of the enemy's plans from their own mouths."

"Then we will have to mingle with them," declared Timmerman.

"That is a dangerous game," said a worried Sir Charles.

"We did not come all this way to return empty-handed," replied Craven.

They could hear many French voices all around them. It was most discomforting, for that usually signalled the beginning of a battle, but they could not fight their way out of this situation, no matter how capable their skills with the sword.

"If it must be done, then we shall see it done," insisted Paget.

"Bunce, you stay with us so we have one amongst us who can speak French. Timmerman and Paget, you will go with Sir Charles and keep him safe. Stay together, for one man seemingly out of place will draw suspicion, but together you might just pass as the enemy," ordered Craven.

"And if any of us is discovered?" asked Sir Charles.

"There will be no fighting our way out of here, and I will not have any man sacrifice himself needlessly. If things go awry, it is every man's duty to get free of this place so that they may go on fighting."

Paget took a deep breath as he realised how much was at stake, and how quickly and easily it could all go wrong.

"We are in character from the moment we leave them. We speak only in French, and we discuss only matters which French officers would," insisted Paget.

The other two nodded in agreement, even though Sir Charles was taking orders from a mere captain, and yet he did not resist, for he was entirely out of his element here. Paget was little better off, though he had some little preparation from his adventures beside

Craven.

He watched the three men leave as they suddenly upped the volume of their communications with one another, but now in French.

Timmerman made crude jokes and shared stories as they walked, which soon lightened the mood and allowed them all to relax as they strolled into the lion's den. After a few minutes they spoke as calmly and naturally as if they were socialising amongst their own Coalition members. Craven watched from afar whilst most of those around him kept a keen eye on all comings and goings around them. Their saddles remained on their horses where they had been tied to the trees nearby so that they could flee at a moment's notice if it should come to it.

"Don't worry. If it can be done, they will see it done," insisted Charlie as she watched from Craven's side.

"I know," he agreed.

But that would not stop him impatiently watching as their three companions tried to draw information from a few dozen of Napoleon's officers as they mingled around several fires. Two hours went by, and finally, Paget led the group back to the camp. All the way back they chatted amongst themselves in French. They acted playful and relaxed, but Craven knew Paget was anything but. He knew when the young man truly felt fear, and yet he was doing an exceptional job of hiding it. Finally, they were reunited.

"Did you get what we need?" Craven demanded.

"A few of the men believe Leipzig is indeed Napoleon's plan," explained Paget.

"It is not enough. I cannot go to Schwarzenberg with the hearsay of junior officers," lamented Sir Charles.

"What do we do, Sir?" Paget asked.

Craven looked around at the area he had been studying all evening.

"Stay the night, and see what we might learn in the morning," added Timmerman.

It was the horrifying prospect which none of them wanted to entertain. They all looked to Craven now to make that decision, one which would massively increase their chances of being discovered.

"I won't go back empty handed."

"If we cannot achieve success, then perhaps we never will?" Paget questioned the decision to remain in such a precarious position.

"Riding out into the night at this hour will perhaps raise even more suspicion?" added Matthys. Timmerman agreed with him.

"This is a dangerous path you have led us down."

"Nobody forced you to walk it, Sir," replied Craven unsympathetically.

None of the others had anything to say.

"We make camp. If anyone asks, we are on duties given to us by Marshal Marmont himself and should not be interfered with," declared Craven.

"And when we cannot provide any proof of it?"

"Pray that they don't, Mr Paget."

It was not very comforting, but they did as

ordered. Birback tossed a number of thick logs onto two fires to keep them warm through the night as Moxy kept watch, in spite of having no rifle. He held onto his sheathed sword as if it was indeed his rifle, as though he was homesick. Matthys approached him after some time.

"I know what you are going to say," groaned the Welshman as though he had eyes in the back of his head.

"And what is that?"

"That I should relax."

"No," replied Matthys bluntly, which caught his attention and curiosity.

"We don't need you to be relaxed. We need you to look relaxed."

Moxy sighed as he knew it was true.

"Keep a keen eye and we will keep a watch all night, but it must not look as though we are."

Moxy grumbled in agreement as he got up to go and join the others beside the fire.

"This isn't my kind of work," he grumbled.

"Neither is it for Craven, for he is not a man known for his subtle and calm approaches to a problem, and yet he is doing just that."

They gathered about the fires to settle in for the night, watching over one another's shoulders to keep a keen eye on the enemy who were all around them. Word was soon passed for only French to be spoken now. Craven rested back against his saddle on the ground, his feet in front of the fire. He gazed up at the stars, for there was nothing else to do. He soon fell into a deep sleep, forgetting where they were and the danger that hung over them.

He awoke to find an officer upon a horse blocking out the morning sun and casting himself as a black shadow. Craven could not make out any features of the man except for his hat, a great bicorne worn side to side. He smiled for a moment, for only the Royal Navy wore them in such a way, and he was about to mock a sailor for trading his ship in for a force when he heard French voices echo out around him.

Paget towered over him and kicked him rather adeptly, yelling out at him in French. Craven obliged, for the young man was playing his part with great passion. He got to his feet and now the silhouetted rider came into view. He had never met the man, but he knew from artistic depictions precisely who he was, it was unmistakeable. It was none other than Napoleon Bonaparte himself. He sat up tall and proud in the saddle as he looked down at the seemingly idle soldiers who had slept through first light.

Napoleon called to Paget as the two began to exchange words. Craven turned away and looked to Matthys in despair. The danger they were in had now been elevated to levels they could never have imagined. And yet Sir Charles smiled back at him, amused by the absurdity of the interaction. They listened in as Paget pressed Napoleon for any information he could get whilst grovelling and worshipping at his feet. Craven heard Leipzig mentioned several times, and he looked to Sir Charles once again to see he was nodding in agreement. They had all that they needed, and now they only had to survive long enough to take the information back home to Schwarzenberg's headquarters.

A rider approached and stopped beside them to talk with Napoleon. A glimmer of morning sunshine reflected from the brass end cap of a pistol carried upon the saddle of the newly arrived officer. Craven's eye was drawn to it, and he recognised the weapon instantly. From only the brass cap and the holster in which it was carried, it was his stolen double-barrelled pistol, and as his eyes continued to study the rest of the newcomer, he realised it was his horse and saddle also. His heart almost stopped as he understood what that meant before he looked up to get his first glimpse of the rider. It was the traitor Rocca.

The man who had stolen his horse and pistol and betrayed the Crown Prince Charles John. Craven's right hand instinctively reached for his sword, but he found Timmerman's hand clamp over his before he could draw the blade. It was a sensation he had experienced before, but the last time Timmerman had done this it was in an attempt to kill him. This time there was genuine concern in his eyes as he gave a subtle shake of his head to ask Craven to stop what he was doing. He sighed in frustration as Napoleon called out to the soldiers around them to share a few inspiring words. He received a lukewarm response, which surprised Craven and many of his comrades. They looked around to see that many of the French soldiers were either war weary veterans or fresh-faced recruits with little enthusiasm. Rocca cried out a rallying cry and elicited a slightly better response for their Emperor, but Napoleon rode on, appearing distant and aloof, but still basking in the cries for him and for France.

It was quite the unsettling scene to be surrounded by hundreds, if not thousands of French soldiers and their allies as they cheered for Napoleon, and yet Craven took some relief in how unenthused many of the French soldiers were.

"We will get Rocca. I promise, but not here," whispered Timmerman.

Craven was surprised, for he could hear the sincerity in his old adversary's voice and in his eyes.

"That was him, Sir, it is really him," whispered Paget with excitement as he joined them.

Craven found it most amusing. Paget appeared more excited by the French Emperor than his own people were, but his animation was also drawing curious eyes.

"I think we have outstayed our welcome, don't you?" Craven subtly asked for Paget to take charge and lead them out of the jaws of death.

"Yes, I believe you are correct, Sir," he whispered back and then barked his orders in French to them all. Few understood the words, but all comprehended his meaning. They were all eager to flee to safety before they were inevitably discovered. And yet Craven's eyes were firmly locked on Rocca now, who he wanted to get his hands on even more than Napoleon himself.

CHAPTER 11

Schwarzenberg sighed as he sat back in his grand chair and thought over the news he had received. Before him was Sir Charles, with Craven and Timmerman by his side.

"You are absolutely certain of this?"

"Without any doubt. Leipzig is where Bonaparte commits all of his forces to do battle with us," replied Sir Charles.

Schwarzenberg studied the large map spread out before him. Now that he looked away, Craven shook his head in frustration that the news was not taken seriously when he had delivered it, but at least it was progress.

"Leipzig is nothing but rivers and bridges, a most difficult place to advance upon or concentrate our forces against."

"Yes, it is," agreed Sir Charles, "But this is our chance, our chance to strike Napoleon down once and for all."

Schwarzenberg looked a little excited by the prospect, but also wary of the moves he might now be obliged to take.

"Is this enough? Will you commit the armies of

the Coalition now?" Craven pressed.

"I will do what I deem fit. Now leave me!" Schwarzenberg growled at him.

Craven opened his mouth to speak, but Timmerman jabbed him with a quick short strike to the arm to compel him to stand down. Craven looked to Sir Charles for support, but he found none, and so he said nothing.

"You may leave but remain nearby in case I should call upon you," insisted Schwarzenberg.

"Yes, Sir," declared Sir Charles as they each saluted the Prince before filing out. It gave Craven some hope to know they were not being cast aside just yet.

"We have done all that could be done here, now it is out of our hands," declared Sir Charles.

"Thank you. You risked a lot to come with us, and I cannot thank you enough."

"Not at all. I will do all I can to see us to victory here, and I know that you will do, too. Schwarzenberg will take notice, for he cannot ignore it now. We have set ourselves on a path to the footsteps of Bonaparte himself, intentionally this time."

Craven laughed as he thought back to their surprising encounter with Napoleon.

"You were close enough you could have reached out and touched him," laughed Timmerman.

It was easy to laugh about now that they were out of danger, but as he reflected upon the bizarre interaction, he wondered if it had all been a dream, for it seemed too bizarre to believe.

"Was it really him? Bonaparte?" Craven asked to

confirm whether he could trust his own eyes.

"It was indeed," replied Sir Charles.

"I always imagined the first time we would meet would be upon the battlefield, not amongst his army dressed as their own."

"What a story to tell, ey?" smiled Timmerman.

"Indeed, though I am not sure there are many who would believe it," admitted Craven.

They went on to where the rest of their companions were gathered, once more wearing their own uniforms and looking most relieved to be doing so. Paget had his sword in hand as he practiced solo exercises, cut and thrusting the air as he passed the time, but he came to an abrupt halt when he spotted Craven approaching.

"What did he say, Sir?" he asked excitedly.

"We have done all that we can, but we must wait for news now the same as everyone else," lamented Craven.

A great many senior officers came and went to Schwarzenberg's headquarters over the next two hours, but all Craven could do was wait in the gardens with his comrades in the hope of some news.

"Will it be enough? Will it finally persuade him to march in pursuit of Napoleon?" asked Paget.

"That is what all this has been assembled for. If he trusts the information which we have brought to the table, then, yes."

"And does he? Does he trust you, Sir?"

Craven shrugged.

"I wish I could know, but at some point, a leader

has to trust those around him, and if he cannot trust Sir Charles, then there is no hope for the Coalition."

Paget took a deep breath in as he waited impatiently for any sign of change. Finally, an officer approached them.

"Major Craven?"

"Yes?"

"Please follow me."

He looked over to Paget and could see how desperate he was to come along.

"Alone," insisted the Prussian officer.

Craven nodded in agreement for Paget and the others to stay put before following the officer on. He was led back to the same room where he had delivered the news to Schwarzenberg. A number of officers were already filing out until only two remained by the Prince's side.

"You have gotten what you wished for, Major," he declared.

"I make no attempt to sway your decisions in this war, Sir. I only want to help in any way that I can, whether that means bringing information to you, or marching onto the battlefield under your command."

"Good then, for I have a task for you."

"Yes, Sir?"

"The armies of the Coalition will move quickly now, but we are three armies who must converge on a single location with the perfect timing, for Napoleon will strike at any weakness with ruthless endeavour."

"Yes, Sir," agreed Craven.

"Anything which threatens our advance, which

threatens our flanks, these problems can delay and open such a weakness upon us, but I believe you can help in one such instance."

"In any way that I can, Sir. Command me, and it will be done."

"There is a bridge here." Schwarzenberg pointed to an isolated area between two small towns that lay on the road ahead, "Over this bridge the enemy may harass any advance, and though they would not have the strength to inflict a fatal blow, even a few hours of interference could be severely detrimental to our efforts against Bonaparte. As I understand it, you and your men are experts in raids deep into enemy held territory, and you have a talent for executing the most daring of tasks."

"That is correct, Sir," admitted Craven with pride.

"Destroy that bridge, Major, and it must be by the end of tomorrow, or that bridge will be like an open wound in our side."

"I will see it done."

"These fine men will see that you have what you need, weapons, powder, whatever you require." Schwarzenberg gestured to the men behind him.

"A few barrels of black powder will suffice. Give me that, and I will blow it to pieces."

"Thank you, Major, and good luck."

He saluted before hurrying out to take the news to his comrades. As he arrived, a wagon was being drawn up beside them, loaded with powder kegs, for the Prince had evidently assumed he would take on the task. The two men driving the cart abandoned it beside the Salford Rifles as they hurried on to their next task. Paget smiled as he could sense a mission was afoot.

"Moxy, Ellis, that cart is now your responsibility. Gather your thing. We are moving out immediately."

"Where, Sir? Does the army advance on Leipzig, Sir?" Paget asked impatiently.

"It does, and we advance ahead of it to ensure the passage remains safe."

"That is a lot more powder than we need to supply our rifles," grumbled Moxy as he fished for more information.

"I cannot tell you anything more for now, for remember we never know who is listening in. Our brush with Bonaparte should have been a reminder of that."

"I'm in," smiled Moxy as he marvelled at the massive stash of black powder and the mischief that might be had with it. They rode onwards, yet again not knowing what their destination nor mission was. Finally, as the sun went down, they made camp in a quiet clearing and Craven approached Moxy.

"Yeah, yeah, I know," grumbled the Welshman as he propped his rifle against the wagon and began to unbutton his tunic.

"Not this time." Craven picked Moxy's rifle up and thrust it into his hands.

There was a look of surprise and relief, followed by excitement in his eyes.

"Truly?" he asked as he admired his rifle and the prospect of not having to leave it behind again.

"The time for deceit and trickery is over. It is time to fight now."

Moxy excitedly slung his rifle onto his shoulder, not wanting to let go of his prized weapon before he buttoned up his tunic, relieved to not have to wear a Frenchman's tunic again.

"I know it has not been easy, and I have asked a lot of you, but I would not do it if I had any doubt about your ability to handle it, and the necessity of our work."

"Whatever it takes."

"It is a strange road we have walked these past years, is it not?" smiled Craven.

"It is, and they have been the best of our lives."

"Really?" Craven asked in surprise.

"Come on, look at us before we truly embraced this life. Think back to our time in England. We were lost. We were nothing."

"We were something, but it was not all good."

"What are we doing here. then?" Moxy pressed Craven, leveraging his sentimentality to gain information.

"We're going to find a bridge, and we're going to blow it to hell."

"We are?"

Craven nodded in agreement.

"Perfect," Moxy smiled.

"The catch is we have to do it by end of tomorrow, or before the first light of the next day at least."

"Jumping into trouble without even checking what is on the other side? This mission was made for you," smirked Moxy.

Craven laughed along.

"Come on." He gathered them all about a fire and took out his map to explain what they were doing here. He directed their attention to their destination.

"That is our target. In destroying this bridge, we will protect the flank of our advancing allies so that they may reach their destination in good time and order."

"Then it is finally happening? The Coalition armies finally march to meet Napoleon upon the battlefield?" Paget asked.

It was the moment they had all been waiting for. The Trachenberg plan to avoid Napoleon and only strike at his Marshals was not known to many, but it had become well understood after the events of the past months. But every soldier knew that eventually they would have to meet Napoleon upon the field of battle.

"Yes, we are close now," agreed Timmerman with glee as he imagined the great spectacle of a battle which lay ahead.

"Do we know what enemy presence is in the area?" Matthys asked.

"We know nothing. Only that there is a bridge there and it must be destroyed, quickly."

"By end of tomorrow night," added Moxy.

"Is this true?"

Craven nodded in agreement to Matthys.

"That gives us no time to scout the area and plan such an operation."

"We'll just have to make do," explained Timmerman, who was used to improvising, and thrived on it even.

"What kind of bridge is it?" asked Matthys.

"One which crosses water," replied Craven cheekily.

"But what is it made of? Wood? Stone?"

"Your guess is as good as mine. We were given this mission by Prince Schwarzenberg himself, and that is all I know."

"Does he mean to see you dead?" Ellis asked bluntly.

Craven glared at him, demanding an explanation.

"Are you in the Prince's good graces? For this has the air of a mission you send an enemy to do, not an ally."

"Are you scared?" Craven smiled at Ellis.

"Concerned, I should say, I admit."

"You are?" Craven sounded surprised at his answer.

"A mission like this could be of the utmost importance, or it could be an easy way to get you out of the way."

"Out of the way? But why?"

"You have a habit of ruffling feathers."

"You believe the Prince would send us on a dangerous mission merely to get me out of his sight?"

Ellis shrugged in agreement.

"Perhaps, but both things could be true. He could want rid of me, but the fact is that bridge exists."

"Does it? Are you certain?"

Craven took out his map and studied their destination. There was indeed no bridge listed where they were heading. That fact had not given him cause for concern previously. He was accustomed to old and outdated maps, but Ellis put the seed of doubt in his mind, but Craven did not have to dwell on it for long before shaking his head as he calmed his nerves.

"We must trust those who despatch our orders, for if we do not, there can be no victory here. This coalition is a leap of faith for many, and we must believe in it. For Napoleon has the faith and trust of his armies, and we must have the same if we are to defeat them."

"Spoken like a proper officer," smiled Ellis.

"You would know," Craven snapped back at the man who had reluctantly taken on his officer's commission for the second time after living in secrecy as a common soldier. They sat down by the fire as word quickly spread of what their mission entailed. It soon spurred a hive of activity and conversation.

"Shall we get the singlesticks, Sir?"

Craven shook his head at Paget.

"Not tonight, there will be plenty of time for more training when our work is done."

The young man looked disappointed.

"There is little more I can teach you about the sword, Mr Paget. We have spent years in practice, and I have seen you overcome an army of opponents."

"Then my training is complete?"

"As complete as it can ever be. Now you must work to maintain your skills."

"And yet you will not train this night, Sir?"

"Sometimes knowing when not to fight is just as important as the knowledge of how."

The camp fell silent, for they were words none would ever expect to hear from Craven, who had sought out fight wherever he went for as long as they had all known him.

"Truer words I have never heard, for I was once just like him," Timmerman broke the silence. Laughter erupted amongst them all as they could now look back on the dark days where they battled one another with fond memories.

It was not long before they settled in to get some sleep, maintaining a keen watch throughout the night. At first light they were on their feet, and they needed no persuasion for the mornings were feeling ever cooler each day as winter crept closer. In minutes they were back in the saddle and riding on with their wagon once more. None of them had discussed what would happen if they were attacked along the way, for they could not outrun enemy cavalry with a heavily laden wagon, and the prospect of abandoning all that powder felt like blasphemy, especially to Moxy. Nobody raised any such concerns, but they knew that if push came to shove, they would have to turn tail and flee, leaving the wagon to the enemy. And yet such a possibility was at the back of their minds now, for their gravest concern was the slow pace they were making. They were moving much more slowly with the wagon than Craven would have hoped.

Timmerman rode ahead of them, acting as the

scout which Moxy typically did. It was a role that suited him well, for he had been a guerrilla fighter for years in Spain. Craven meticulously checked his map every time they discovered any signposts along the road, of which there were few. After a day of travelling, the sun was going down and they had still not reached their destination. Craven was about to give up for the night as their horses were tired. It was dangerous to travel over unknown territory after dark, but a whistle rang out from up ahead, and he looked up to see the silhouette of Timmerman on a ridge ahead beckoning for him to come forward.

"Stay here," growled Craven before riding on to discover what Timmerman thought was so valuable. Ferreira and Paget could not help but ride on after him in spite of his orders, for curiosity had gotten the better of them. As they approached, Timmerman waved his hand up and down to call for quiet. They came to a standstill and dismounted, tying their horses to the branch of a tree by the roadside where Timmerman had done the same. Craven shook his head at his two companions who had ignored his orders, and yet he smiled, for he was just as eager for news and did not resent them for it. They approached Timmerman quietly where finally they got their first glimpse at what he had found.

"Well, I'll be damned," declared Ferreira, who had been as doubtful of the bridge's presence as Ellis.

There before there very eyes, was the bridge they had been looking for. Daylight was fading quickly now, but the bridge was lit up by small lamps on either side of the river. It was not enough to light the area around, but enough to cast a gentle silhouette on the bridge itself, and the two soldiers standing guard on either side. The foundations of the bridge were stone and looked ancient, but the rest was entirely made of wood and looked a century old itself. It was clearly strong enough to carry an army across, and yet the sight gave Craven some hope of doing some serious damage to the structure. Had it been a robust stone structure he was not confident about making a dent.

"We found it," marvelled Paget in amazement.

"Did you ever doubt that we would?"

"Well, yes, Sir," replied Paget bluntly.

Ferreira chuckled as Craven studied what was before him. The lamps provided just enough light for him to survey the area with his spyglass, though the light was fading very quickly, and he gazed up to the sky to see the moon was providing very little light, a boon for what he had in mind to do next.

"It must be done before first light, Sir?" Paget asked.

"It must," confirmed Craven.

"Not a bad thing, to do it under the protection of the night," replied Timmerman.

"Except we have no idea what strength the enemy have," Ferreira gestured towards the other side of the river where many campfires were lit. They could make out numerous rows of tents, and yet on this side of the river only two men were standing guard.

"We are lucky. If they had a screen this side of the river, we would never get near them," replied

Timmerman. Paget looked back to the heavily laden cart they had brought with them, which had now almost vanished in the night.

"But the moment we drive that cart forward an entire army will be awoken and sent against us," he lamented.

"Then we won't take the cart anywhere near them," declared Craven as he studied the scene.

"What do you have in mind?" Timmerman asked with great curiosity.

"Once we reach that bridge, we will have no time to waste. We have to destroy it before that army can assemble, or they will be on top of us," said Ferreira.

"Then we must get the powder there quickly and quietly," replied Paget as if it was an impossible task, but Craven smiled. He already had a plan.

"If we can't drive them down there, we'll float them."

"Float, Sir? How is that possible?"

"Look at the current. We go upstream, find a small boat or two, and we ride on down to the bridge."

"And if those in the boats are discovered before they get there? There will be no escape, Sir."

But Craven looked up at the near pitch-black sky as their view range was dropping with every minute which passed.

"I'll do it," declared Timmerman.

"We are still going to need to silence those guards before they can alert the camp," added Ferreira.

Craven nodded in agreement.

"And we cannot fire upon them."

"The only way we can approach without raising the alarm is if we appear as their own," replied Paget.

"We do not have French uniforms anymore."

"No, Sir, but we have one or two of their greatcoats, enough to pass as Frenchmen in the dark."

"Those who go will have to speak French or the deception will be discovered."

"I will go, and Bunce will, too," declared Paget.

"It will be dangerous," replied Craven with concern.

"When did we do anything that is not so?"

Craven groaned in agreement, for in this he could be no help. Only those able to pass as Frenchmen could conduct the mission. Craven looked to the others to see they were all in agreement.

"Timmerman, lead the cart upriver with Moxy and Ellis."

"Three men to guard that powder?" Ferreira asked.

"We have no choice. We will need everyone else here. The rest of you get ready. We will need lookouts along the riverbank to alert us to the boat's approach, for timing will be everything."

"And if they do not find any boats?"

"We will find some," insisted Timmerman.

"We've got all night, so let us not rush, but do this right," ordered Craven.

They all knew what they had to do. Craven took a deep breath as he contemplated how dangerous their mission was, and how many variables existed that could lead to failure. He studied the scene once more as he wondered if there was any other strategy they could employ.

"The plan is sound, Sir," insisted Paget.

"It is as good as any we could arrive at before dawn," added Timmerman.

"Then we are in agreement?"

"It is a reckless plan, but not a bad one," added Ferreira.

"Then let's get the wheels rolling," Craven ordered.

CHAPTER 12

Moxy looked anxious as he gazed around them whilst they drove the cart on in darkness. They could not risk attracting any attention with lamps or torches, not that they carried any with them. With so little moonlight, they could barely see twenty paces in front of the horses, and yet the heavy cart creaked and groaned, which would surely draw the ear of anybody nearby.

"Don't worry. The French won't be out here at this hour," insisted Ellis.

"Because they might be attacked by local guerrillas?"

"Indeed."

"And what is stopping those same men attacking us? How would they even tell us apart from the enemy?" Moxy sounded worried.

"We don't speak French," replied Ellis dryly.

Moxy huffed, for it was not the nerve calming response he had been hoping for. A rider suddenly galloped on through the darkness before them, causing him to almost jump out of his skin until he realised it was Timmerman.

"Have you found anything?" Ellis asked.

"One, but it's in bad shape."

"It might be the best we can hope for. Patch up any holes and hope for the best?" Moxy asked.

"Come on, then," replied Timmerman.

He led them down an old track which looked like it had not been travelled on for some time. The vegetation and grass had grown up to the axles of the cart in some places. They came to a halt beside the hull of a small boat that lay ten paces from the water's edge. It looks dry, the wood cracked in many places, and as Moxy jumped down for a closer look, he could see a narrow branch of a tree had burst through the hull.

"You said bad shape, not a wreck," he protested.

"Can you fix it or not?" Timmerman demanded.

Moxy huffed and sighed further as he stepped into the boat. He reached for the tree branch to see if he might snap it with his hands to assess the damage, but as he placed his left foot beside the hole to get some leverage, the planks beneath burst open. His foot went right through the hull and struck the ground below, causing him to lose his balance and crash down into the base of the hull. Several more planks gave way, but not enough to break his fall. He winced in pain, for his back had landed on the hardwood braces across the hull. Timmerman couldn't help but laugh, but just a moment later a voice called out in French on the far side of the river. Ellis leapt down from the cart and all three men fell silent and went still. Between the trees and the darkness, they could not make out the far side of the riverbank.

"What do we do?" Moxy shrugged off his pain, the present danger putting it to the back of his mind.

"I could speak with them?" Timmerman whispered.

"No, better they do not think anyone is here," pressed Ellis.

Moxy nodded in agreement, for they wore British uniforms and travelled with a mass of black powder. The last thing they needed was a Frenchman prying, as there would be no talking their way out of it. The French voice called out once more, and then a second. It was clear they were soldiers.

"They ask us to identify ourselves."

Ellis shook his head to once again insist they all stayed silent. A few tense moments went by before the Frenchman called out once more. Still the three men remained silent, but there was an almighty crash in the boat beside Moxy as planks splintered, and he leapt for safety as a deer thrashed about in the wreckage. Moxy leapt out from the chaos, and the deer hopped out of the other side, crashing on through the foliage beside them. One of the Frenchmen cried out in panic, thinking it was an attack, but another of them yelled as they spotted the deer. Timmerman nodded in agreement. The animal had masked their presence perfectly, and they listened with relief as the Frenchmen went on, the sound of their conversation soon fading into the distance.

"It will be a miracle if we get through this alive," declared Moxy.

"It won't be a miracle that sees us through this, but pure pig-headed stubbornness," replied Timmerman.

"What is that if not a miracle?" Ellis pointed over to where the deer had run. It had knocked and so disrupted a canvas, which now revealed the bow of a boat. Timmerman rushed to it and ripped the canvas aside to find a fairly robust small boat, the sort which might be used to carry goods along the river. It was certainly sturdy enough for the task.

"A single boat? We really are going to put all our eggs in one basket?" Moxy complained.

"So long as it floats it will do. If we get spotted out there, it won't matter how many boats we have."

"And if the cargo goes overboard? If we get that powder wet, it will be useless."

"Then let's do this right," replied Ellis.

"And if the enemy are to spot us?"

"We hide, low in the bottom of the hull under that sheet. It will look like a boat has come free of its mooring and floated on down the river all by itself," replied Timmerman.

"This is the sort of lunacy only Craven could drum up, and we are all fools for going along with it," grumbled Moxy.

"Let's get this done, shall we?" Ellis got up onto the wagon and tried to lift one of the powder kegs only to find he could barely budge it.

Timmerman leapt up to help as they lowered it over the side onto Ellis who collapsed under its weight. He landed on his back, the barrel landed upon him, winding him before it rolled away.

"On your feet," laughed Timmerman as they lifted the next keg onto the edge of the cart but balanced it this time until he had leapt down to help take the weight. Soon they had the vessel loaded.

"What of the horses?" Moxy asked.

"Let them go. They will find their own way back," replied Timmerman.

Ellis did just that as the other two braced their bodies against the boat and began to push against it, but it was not until Ellis returned to help that they could get it moving. They slid it gently out onto the water, making as little noise as possible. Timmerman leapt aboard and hopped over to the stern to take control of the small tiller, whilst the other two leapt in just as it cleared the bank and floated out onto the water. Moxy looked suspicious, as if they were going to take on water at any moment, and yet to his surprise there was no such drama, and they merely floated out into the middle of the small river with ease. The current soon took control, and Timmerman did not have to do anything as they were swept away at a leisurely pace.

* * *

Craven watched as Paget removed his sword and officer's tunic and put on Joze's greatcoat, which had been taken from the enemy in Spain. He riffled up his hair and smeared some dirt from the ground onto his face.

"Do you have a bottle of liquor, Sir?"

Craven took out a small flask from inside his jacket and handed it over without hesitation, for he could see precisely what Paget had in mind.

"We will be there within a hundred paces, ready to strike," insisted Craven as he hated putting Paget in such danger.

"Do not risk the mission, Sir. Bunce and I can handle it."

Bunce arrived wearing another French coat which belonged to Vicenta.

"Here." Joze passed a dagger to each of them. They could not wear their swords without arising suspicion, for no common infantry soldier wore such long and decadent swords as a British officer did. They stuffed the blades into their waist bands, concealed by the greatcoats they now wore.

"When the moment comes to strike, it will not be a duel nor a gentlemanly affair. You must strike quickly and without hesitation," insisted Craven to the two of them.

"Not exactly honourable work," complained Bunce.

"Do you know what is not honourable? Losing this war. Those Frenchmen down there would happily slit your throat given the chance and remember that when you approach them. If you show mercy, then you risk all of our lives. What is more valuable to you, their lives, or ours?"

"Ours," admitted Bunce solemnly.

"The Major is serious. When the time is right

to strike, we must do so ruthlessly, for if one of us hesitates it might well cost us both our lives and the failure of this mission."

Craven nodded in agreement, welcoming the fact that Paget understood the assignment, but he still resented sending the two young men on their own.

"Remember, you are Frenchmen, but not officers. Act as a common soldier would and talk like a common soldier does."

"But our accents?" Bunce asked.

"Napoleon's armies are vast, encompassing Frenchmen from all across France with as many varied accents as you can find amongst Wellington's army, and many foreigners who have learnt to speak French whilst on the march with Napoleon. Talk simply and act drunk. The act will hold for at least a little while."

"I don't like this spy business."

"Nobody does. It is dirty work, but it is necessary work. Are you willing to do what is necessary for your country and for victory?"

"I am, Sir, always."

"Good, then be ready, for when the time comes you must move quickly."

"And the time to strike?" Paget asked.

"You must use your judgement. All that matters is that the guards upon that bridge cannot raise the alarm."

* * *

Moxy peered out from the bow of the boat, keeping very low in case anybody was watching from the shore. It was an eerily silent time, for the boat made almost no noise at all as it was carried on the current. There was just enough light to make out either shore, but amongst the dense foliage and woods covering much of the ground there could be any number of potential attackers concealed, and they would never know. It made Moxy anxious, for he was not accustomed to being in such a vulnerable spot where he felt powerless. He looked down at his rifle which lay in the boat beside him. It was some relief to have it with him, but even he knew it would be of little use if they came under attack. He looked back at Timmerman who showed no fear at all. He smiled back as though he was enjoying every minute of the experience and embraced the danger. Ellis seemingly showed no emotion at all, but that was not unusual, for he was a most stoic sort.

Ellis pointed ahead and Moxy turned back. He could see a small fire in a field ahead. He could make out ten or more men around it, and it was on the enemy's side where they knew a large camp was situated. The roaring fire lit the scene well, but it was far enough away that the boat remained in darkness. As they drew nearer, Moxy saw they were indeed Frenchmen. Several were asleep whilst others chatted about the fire, and he soon spotted a man on duty with musket in hand, watching over the party as Moxy himself so often had. The man appeared to be looking right at them, and yet as they floated onwards, his gaze did not follow, for they remained in the shadows. Moxy breathed a sigh of relief. On they floated, knowing that they could not be far from the bridge now, which was both a relief but also brought with it an increasing sense of dread. He spotted a glimmer of movement at the bank and instinctively reached for his rifle but then recognised the slight and short figure of Joze in his red tunic. Once more he sighed in relief as he tried to calm his nerves. He watched as Joze gave a signal to the next man along as they spread the word like signal beacons.

* * *

Craven watched as Vicenta waved to their position, the final signal in the chain back to Joze.

"It's time," Craven said to Paget.

He nodded in agreement and set out without a word or any hesitation. Bunce was close by his side. Paget opened Craven's flask and handed it to Bunce.

"Take a sip, just enough so they can smell it on your breath."

Bunce did so before handing it back to Paget who did the same. He took a deep breath as he mentally prepared himself to be in character, for he never fancied himself an actor. He began to sing in a slurred French voice, swaying back and forth and waving the flask in the air as he progressed forward. Bunce laughed along as he joined Paget's song for one word in every five as they staggered on. Craven watched intently as the guards on the bridge began to take notice. At first, they raised their muskets and were about to make them ready when Paget and Bunce hobbled into view. The sight of the two seemingly drunk and disorderly men was immediately disarming to the sentries who lowered their weapons and relaxed. One laughed whilst the other beckoned them on to cross the bridge, without even questioning who they were or performing any such diligence as one would expect of strangers approaching a military encampment.

"Shit," muttered Craven, for he had expected a greater response.

Paget and Bunce hobbled onto the bridge and had gotten almost halfway across it when Craven noticed the shadow of the gunpowder laden boat slowly float into the torch light. He did not know what to do as he watched and hoped that Paget would find a way to keep the guards from noticing. In his drunken sways the young Captain caught a glimpse of the boat himself and could make out his three companions huddling beside the barrels. They were in plain sight now, and if the guards looked out across the water they would be discovered.

"Hit me," Paget whispered to Bunce.

"What?" Bunce said in disbelief.

"Hit me, now, make a scene," he insisted.

Bunce could not bring himself to do it, and so Paget slapped him across the face and laughed. It was enough to set Bunce off who punched him on the nose. Paget staggered back towards the opposite side to which the boat approached to draw all eyes away from it. Bunce was stunned as blood poured from Paget's nose. He came forward to check on him, forgetting where they were and what they were supposed to be doing for a moment, but Paget had not forgotten. He cried out a bitter insult in French before grabbing hold of Bunce with his left hand to keep the two of them in place and out of sight of the boat and began to rain in blows against him. The guards at both sides of the bridge hurried forward to break it up but dared not raise their voices and draw their superiors into the drunken affray. Two of the Frenchmen had put down their muskets to free up their hands whilst another had slung his onto his shoulder. Meanwhile, the fourth and final man held his out before him in both hands to use it to try and control the fighting men.

"Now," ordered Craven as he hurried forward as quickly as he could without making any significant noise. He did not even draw his sword for fear of light reflecting from the blade and held it firm in its scabbard with his left hand.

As Paget felt the musket touch his back, he let go of Bunce and reached in for his knife. He quickly turned around and plunged it into the Frenchman's chest. Paget took hold of the man's musket as he dropped dead with the blade still stuck in his body. He turned to face the other three as Bunce suddenly sprang into action, taking out his weapon as the three Frenchmen looked on in surprise and horror. The one with his musket reached for it, but Paget swung the butt of his captured musket and struck the man across the face, knocking him out, but another of the enemy leapt upon Bunce and overpowered him with his sheer size and strength. He gave the officer a backhanded blow and ripped the blade away from him before turning to Paget, who dared not fire the musket, and had no bayonet affixed either. He stormed forward and grabbed hold of Paget's musket as he drove him over the edge of the bridge, holding the knife to Paget's throat. Paget grabbed hold of the man's knife hand and held on for dear life to stop him from using it, but he could do nothing more against the strength of his attacker as the two leant out over the water, the Frenchman's weight smothering him.

The Frenchman looked furious, but his expression soon turned to horror as Moxy leapt up onto one of the kegs in the boat below and drove the butt of his musket into the man's face. It caused him to stagger back as a blade was thrust through him from Craven who had just arrived with six of his companions. The last Frenchman turned and ran to alert the camp. He had almost reached the camp when Timmerman emerged at the end of the bridge, dripping with river water and covered in mud. He looked a hideous sight. The Frenchman ran right into him, but Timmerman delivered a swift punch to the face which put him out. Craven breathed a sigh of relief. They had come so close to awaking the sleeping dragon which was the French army in camp nearby. They all looked upon one another with amazement that they had achieved the first part of the mission.

Craven leant over to look down upon Moxy.

"Get this job done quickly."

"I will need some help."

"Birback, Holck, Caffy, put your backs into it."

Craven turned back to the bridge to look at the scene of chaos as Matthys helped Bunce to his feet.

"Get these bodies out of sight. I want two guards in place at either end of the bridge as before. Nothing must look out of place to anyone who looks on from afar." He was conscious of how the lanterns lit them up from quite a distance, and they could not extinguish them without arising suspicion.

"Timmerman, you are with me. Matthys and Paget, you have the far end of the bridge. Everyone else get out of sight."

They all sprang into action as the bodies were dragged away into the shadows, and the four men on the bridge took up positions with rifles and muskets, once more playing the parts of Frenchmen, at least from a distance.

"Any problems along the way?" Craven asked Timmerman as they kept watch.

"The whole area is crawling with Frenchmen, at least on this bank. We were lucky, very lucky."

"A little luck is not to be sniffed at."

"I fear we will need a lot more of it in the coming days."

"I thought you feared nothing?" Craven smiled back at him.

"I am no fool. I know what lies in our future."

"Napoleon is just a man, and he can be defeated

like any other."

"How many men have said the same about you?"

Craven shrugged as Timmerman had a valid point.

They could hear the groans of the men below as they heaved the powder kegs into the arches of the bridge, and then the creak of them as Moxy went about lashing them in place. The process only took a few minutes, but it passed very slowly as Craven kept watch over the enemy camp. He could make out some movement still and watched carefully to see if anyone made an approach for the bridge. All was quiet.

"What is that?" Timmerman pointed towards two riders leaving the camp. They turned and started to head for the bridge, "We can't pass as the enemy if they come within sight."

Craven hurried on to the edge of the bridge and hung over it to check on their progress.

"We've got company. How much longer?"

"A few moments," snapped Moxy impatiently.

"Well make it a few moments less, or we'll be swimming with Frenchmen."

Craven hurried back to Timmerman just as the two French riders came into view. Craven and Timmerman's greatcoats provided some disguise for their red tunics, but they knew it would not hold up for much longer.

"What do you want to do?" Timmerman asked as they realised both of the riders approaching were officers.

"If we have to, we will shoot them down."

Timmerman nodded in agreement as he reached for the lock of the French musket he had acquired and made it ready to fire. Craven did the same with his rifle. One of the officers called out, and Timmerman answered him in French, but they kept on coming until they stopped twenty paces short. The look of confusion and suspicion on their faces was immediately apparent. One of them cried out, demanding who they were, and Craven understood that much. He lifted his rifle to the shoulder and fired, shooting the man out of the saddle whilst Timmerman took aim at the other as he tried to draw his sabre. His musket roared to life, but the ball struck the hat from the other man's head and did no harm.

"Shit," snapped Timmerman as he reversed the weapon, ready to batter the rider with the butt of the musket. Craven flung his greatcoat open and drew out his sword from within, giving the Frenchman a full view of his British uniform, who looked past them to see Matthys and Paget hurrying forward to join their comrades. The rider turned and fled. Paget rushed forward to take aim.

"Leave him. We have got bigger problems." Craven pointed to the French camp that had come alive as soldiers hurried from their beds with muskets in hand. He abandoned their position and rushed back to the centre of the bridge to lean out once more and get a look at Moxy's progress.

"I am moving as quickly as I can," insisted the Welshman, knowing exactly what Craven was about to say. They all knew the crack of musket and rifle fire would bring hell raining down upon their heads.

"How long?"

"I am almost there!" Moxy snapped as he tied off a rope to lash the powder kegs down and went to work on the fuses.

"We don't have long," insisted Timmerman as he watched the horde of French soldiers empty from the camp and vanish into the dark void between the well-lit camp and bridge.

"Here!" Moxy tossed a roll of fuse line up and onto the bridge.

"Is it ready?" Craven demanded.

"It is!"

Paget's rifle cracked to life behind him as he took the first shot as an enemy soldier stormed onto the bridge.

"Get the hell out of there!" Craven roared.

Those below leapt from the boat to swim for the shore as Craven unravelled the fuse. He rushed along the bridge as Paget hurried to reload, and more shots rang out from their companions.

"Go!" Craven ordered.

French soldiers stormed onto the bridge, and the mission was now seconds from failure. Timmerman hesitated, wanting to stay and fight, but Craven shook head and nodded for him to go on, which he begrudgingly did. Craven pulled back the cock of his rifle and the frizzen also. He knelt down beside the outstretched fuse as musket fire erupted ahead of him, though many of the Frenchmen rushed their shots as they excitedly ran forward. Lead balls flashed over Craven. He pulled out a cartridge for his rifle and bit the top off before pouring the contents all over the end of the fuse. He then placed his rifle down beside it and pulled the trigger. The weapon was unloaded, but as the flint struck the frizzen, a flash of sparks rained down onto the loose powder. It ignited in a quick puff of firing smoke that singed Craven's eyebrows, causing him to fall as he escaped the flames. He landed on his back, but he could hear the fizz and crackle of the fuse, and he looked down the bridge to see the flame spreading quickly. The Frenchmen quickly realised what was happening. Some turned and fled whilst others raced onwards to try and extinguish the fuse before it could reach the charges they had set. Craven looked back to his comrades to order them to slow the enemy advance, but they were already at it. They fired and reloaded as quickly as they could. One Frenchmen got within three paces of the fuse with a his short briquet sword in hand ready to cut it, only to be shot down. He collapsed over the edge and plunged into the river.

"Come on, Sir!" Paget called out.

Craven leapt to his feet and soared forward in a sprint as quickly as he could, the fuse continuing to burn behind him. The flames reached the edge of the bridge and plunged over, vanishing from view. Moxy paused loading his rifle as he watched and waited with great anticipation to see if his work was about to pay off, knowing if it did not, they were likely all dead men. Hundreds of French soldiers now stormed toward them.

Moxy was frozen and silent for a moment as Craven still sprinted on. An almighty eruption ignited before them. Craven was launched into the air and came crashing down. His companions hunkered down as debris crashed all around them. Moxy got back up to marvel at his work as dust and powder smoke filled the air, completely masking the French soldiers who were now cut off on the far side of the river.

The bridge lay in ruins with a gap at its centre of thirty paces or more, and even part of the stone foundation had been blown into the river. For a moment they had all forgotten about Craven as they gazed upon the bridge, but they were reminded of him when he coughed and spluttered as he got to his feet. He turned back to see the damage and destruction for himself.

"We did it, Sir!"

"Yes, we did, Mr Paget." Craven nodded towards Moxy in appreciation of his efforts. The lanterns that illuminated the bridge had been extinguished by the blast, and so even with the cloud of powder smoke dissipating, they could not see far enough to make out the French soldiers on the far side. Though they could hear the groans and cries of the wounded who had been swept up in the blast.

"Let's not outstay our welcome, shall we?" declared Craven, for he did not want to wait around for any attempt at a reprisal, even if the collapse of the bridge had seemingly made them safe. He knew it would stop an army marching, but it would not stop a smaller force swimming or wading across.

"That's damn fine work," declared Timmerman as he admired the destruction before his eyes for one last time before following the rest as they withdrew from the area.

"I was wrong about this mission, but I was right to have reservations," declared Ellis as he approached Craven.

"Yes, you were," Craven admitted.

CHAPTER 13

"Look at that, Sir," Paget commented as they came out from a wooded road to find a massive army assembling to march before them.

"And it is but one small part of what will be assembled upon the field of battle," remarked Craven as they gazed upon the sea of white uniforms of the Austrian infantry, which composed the corps of the Prince's army. Grenadiers with their intimidating bearskin caps marched onwards, and a squadron of Austrian Cuirassiers nearby were strapping on their armour and plumed helmets. They were equipped in the same fashion as the famous French heavy cavalry, which were always a menacing sight to behold; a mobile and heavily armoured fighting force the likes of which Britain had no equivalent. It was a magnificent sight to experience as they marched on towards the battlefield that would likely determine the legacy of the war. Prince Schwarzenberg and his staff galloped into view, heading right for Craven and his party.

"Well, Major, what of the bridge?" he demanded before his horse had even come to a standstill.

"It is no more, Sir."

Schwarzenberg laughed deep within his belly.

"Then it is true what they say about you, Major."

"And what do they say, Sir?"

"A great many things, but above all that you are a destructive force like no other! My advisors said that bridge could not be destroyed in the time I needed it to be, and I believed them!"

"And yet you sent us anyway, Sir?"

"Something else they say of you, Major. That you are relentless, and relentlessly stubborn. Is that true?"

"I cannot deny it," smiled Craven.

"A man like that can achieve the seemingly impossible, and you have proven that you can. I salute you Major."

"Thank you, Sir, but what more would you have of me?"

"Not a thing. You were attached to Prince John and his Army of the North, and you shall return to his service, but we all march to the same field of battle, Major, and I wish you every luck."

"Thank you, Sir, and you also."

The Prince rode on, shaking his head in disbelief that the mission had been a success.

"What now, Sir?" Paget asked as they watched the vast army march on past them.

"You heard the Prince. We were sent to assist the Rocket Troop, and that is what we will do."

"I thought we were sent to help in any way that we can, Sir?"

"Well, that is true, but would you not join your countrymen who represent England in this great battle that lies on the road ahead?"

"I most certainly would, Sir."

Craven looked out across to the faces of his companions. They had slept only a handful of hours the night before and looked well worn, but nobody complained. Craven led them forward as they moved Northward. It was not long before they stumbled into Blücher's army, which they passed through and continued on towards the Army of the North. It seemed as though every road and every valley were filled with Coalition soldiers who advanced from three directions to close in on Leipzig. The great battle they had all anticipated was finally upon them, and yet they did not reach the Army of the North for some time.

"How will all of these armies arrive at the right moment, Sir?" Paget asked.

It was a thought which was on many minds.

"I do not know, for Schwarzenberg oversees a logistical nightmare. Napoleon has amassed all of his army just where he wants them, and yet we advance across a great many roads, with so many chances for disruption and failure," replied Craven as they advanced towards the marching army. Their horses' hooves squelched in the soft mud, for the autumn rains, combined with the movement of a vast number of soldiers, had turned nearly every road into a swamp. Craven suddenly brought his horse to an abrupt halt.

"What is it, Sir?"

He shook his head for silence as he listened in, but

as they all stopped, it became clear what had drawn his attention. There was a thunderous vibration through the ground beneath them, the sort only a huge body of cavalry could create. Horns blasted in the distance and the sound of musket and pistol fire.

"The battle has already begun, Sir?"

"It must be Schwarzenberg's advance guard," declared Timmerman.

Craven stormed forward with a desperate desire to see for himself. He galloped hard through a wooded track and over several rolling hills as the rest of them struggled to keep up. The echo of battle was drawing near now, and they could smell the powder smoke as it wafted across the area. Craven raced up a steep embankment and finally came to a halt. His face turned to shock and bewilderment, for the sight before him was astonishing.

"My God," declared Paget as he rode up beside him.

Across the open terrain before them a great cavalry battle was being fought. Well over ten thousand cavalrymen battled with one another across the plain. Austrian cuirassiers, Russian Cossacks and hussars, and Prussian dragoons battled it out against French dragoons, Polish lancers, and Saxon Cuirassiers. It was a massive spectacle, which one might assume was a great public display or military pageant before an audience. Except they were trying in earnest to kill one another as sabres clashed and pistols and carbines erupted all across the battlefield. Infantry skirmished on the periphery, but this was a cavalry battle first and foremost. None of them had ever seen anything like it. The scale was difficult to fathom as cavalry formations galloped about and clashed for almost as far as the eye could see. French cannons atop the highest point of the battlefield rained down fire from above. It was a scene of complete and utter chaos.

"This is no mere encounter," declared Paget.

"Perhaps it started as such," replied Craven.

"What do we do, Sir?"

"This is not our fight, and there is little our party can do that a few thousand cavalrymen cannot."

"There can be no victory here," declared Timmerman.

"No, but a battle of attrition only serves to weaken Napoleon, for he cannot afford the losses that our Coalition partners can," replied Craven.

"A grim path to victory, paid for in blood," pondered Bunce.

It was a bloody affair just as the young Captain said, but there was nothing to be done for it.

"Every death and every drop of blood spilt is on Napoleon's hands," declared Matthys.

"Come on, this is merely a skirmish compared to what is to come in the following days, and we cannot fight every part of it."

"A great big fight and James Craven wants no part of it?" Timmerman gasped.

"We will have plenty of chances soon enough," he replied as he led them on, skirting Eastward to move towards the Crown Prince's army. The violent sound of the clash of the immense cavalry battle soon faded away, and after many hours on the road, it was replaced by the equally familiar sound of an army marching. The drone of infantrymen's boots on the ground, the clatter of their canteens, and the creak of heavily laden carts welcomed them back.

They had arrived in good time, as in the distance they could see the Rocket Troop on the road. They were moving steadily along whilst some Prussian gunners struggled to free one of their cannons that had slipped into a ditch, being far heavier than the Rocket Troop's sleds. As they approached, they could see the two elements of the Troop had finally been combined once more. Now at full strength, they had one hundred and forty-two officers and men, over a hundred horses, and four women and two children in their baggage train. Both Captain Bogue and Lieutenant Fox-Strangways rode at the head of their column.

"Major Craven!" Fox-Strangways roared excitedly, for he had felt a great bond with Craven since they had fought alongside one another at the battle of Göhrde; his first taste of combat which no soldier would ever forget. Craven led his small force to converge with the men of the Royal Artillery and took up position by Captain Richard Bogue's side. The clash of Craven's red tunic to Bogue's blue only added yet more to the sparkling array of colour and variety in the Coalition forces.

"Do you ride to battle with us, Sir?" Fox-Strangways asked.

"I wouldn't miss it."

"We have been attached to the Swedish Guard, and so we might indeed see a battle, but I am not sure we will have any part to play in it," lamented Bogue.

"After the Göhrde, how can anyone doubt you?"

"Our rockets make many men nervous, and not just those we aim them at."

"Being led by a French Marshal makes me nervous, and yet still I do it."

"He is a Marshal of France no more, but still many amongst the army doubt his intentions and loyalties, even now," replied Bogue quietly. He gazed around carefully to make sure nobody was listening in as he doubted the Commander of the army they now marched with.

"He is committed to Sweden, that much I am sure, and so long as Sweden is an enemy of France, then I am confident of his loyalty."

Fox-Strangways nodded in agreement, for he would never doubt Craven's word after all they had been through.

"That is good to know, for we put all our lives in the hands of a Frenchman now," replied Bogue.

They struggled on through the mud and watched as several of the infantrymen slipped and fell in it. They dragged themselves back up and had no time to clean themselves off as the clay-like mud clung to their uniforms. Moxy audibly gasped as they saw one of the men drop his musket into the same mud and retrieve it to find the lock was caked with a thick layer of mud.

"Not a good time to march an army, let alone so many. These autumn showers turn all the roads to rivers. There is not enough warmth to harden them in the mornings, and we only make them worse every day," groaned Bogue.

"This is our opportunity to strike the enemy, and we must take it, no matter the hardship," replied Craven.

"Would Wellington do the same, Sir?" asked Fox-Strangways.

"He would and he did. He marched us in the snow and ice of winter so that we might strike at the enemy when the time was right."

"What I'd give for snow instead of this damned mud," he complained.

"Trust me, you would not. When your sword is frozen in its scabbard, the barrel of your rifle sticks to your skin, and your fingers feel like they will break off as your brain wanders into a fever-like state and you wish for death, you would give anything for this autumn weather."

Fox-Strangways said nothing more, for he could not imagine some of the hardships the army had faced in the previous years.

"Will it be tomorrow, do you think?" Bogue asked Craven.

"I cannot say, but this army moves slowly, too slowly," sighed Craven as he looked at the slow progress all around.

"We can only move as quickly as we can move."

"I understand, but if the Coalition armies cannot

amass their strength when it matters most, well..."

"Well, what, Sir?" Fox-Strangways asked.

"Napoleon will attack," added Bogue.

"But he is holding a defensive position, is he not?"

"He is, but just as in a siege, he could sally out at any moment, and if he sees an opportunity to strike before all our armies can combine their strength, he will not hesitate to take it."

They marched onwards, making slow but steady progress until the army was forced to stop by the failing light. Whilst they made camp as best they could, Sir Charles and Mr Solly approached. They did not look surprised to see Craven. In fact, they appeared to be intentionally seeking him out.

"The Prince requests your presence," declared Sir Charles.

"Of course, he does," replied Craven sarcastically.

"May I join you, Sir?" Paget asked.

"Sure," shrugged Craven.

They were led on by the British General who looked ecstatic to see them, for it was not often he encountered any other Englishmen in his duties here in the German states.

"That was a hell of thing, convincing Schwarzenberg like you did," declared Sir Charles.

"I did not convince him of anything. That was your doing."

"Well, true, but I was merely the face of your message," smiled Sir Charles.

"And you loved every minute of it."

"Far from it. I will lead a charge at Napoleon's

cuirassiers before I meddle with such spy craft again."

Craven nodded in agreement.

"It is dirty work, but it gets results."

"They will put that on your headstone, Major."

"It could be worse."

They soon reached the large tent that was Prince Charles John's headquarters for the night. With Sir Charles at their head, they walked inside without issue to find their Commander alone and standing over a map table lit by candles.

"Sir?" Craven asked the Prince as he reported to the Frenchman.

"My dear Major, reports have come to me about an incident with a bridge, blown up right under the nose of the enemy. You wouldn't happen to know anything about that, would you?"

"Prince Schwarzenberg needed it removed and so we saw it done," he replied modestly.

"Just like that? With only your twenty soldiers?"

Craven shrugged and nodded in agreement.

"I suppose I should be angered that you were not by my side, but I honestly do not know who you answer to, Craven. The English Rocket Troop is under my command, but you are merely an observer, and yet like Sir Charles here, you seem to have a difficult time sticking to that role."

"I came here to fight, and that is what I'll do, for anything else is waste of the few talents I do have."

"Oh, you have more than a few talents, Craven. Chief amongst them you are a devil to the French. You should know it is some relief to me that we never had to fight against one another in all these years, for you are a nightmare to your enemies."

"I certainly try to be, Sir."

"You are too modest, for you do a damn sight more than try," added Sir Charles.

"Craven, I brought you here out of courtesy, for you have done a lot for myself and for the Coalition."

"I appreciate it, Sir."

"No more reservations about serving under a Frenchman?"

"I would be a fool to not have any, but I have seen with my own eyes what your intentions are, Sir, and you would not be the first enemy I have made peace with."

"Good, for there will be no room for doubt in the coming days." The Prince directed Craven to the map on his table. It was a far larger map than Craven carried, and the extent of the rivers and bridges around Leipzig and the obstacles which they posed to an advance were now clearer than ever.

"Blücher moves further Northward to the Halle road here, close to our flank as we approach from the North. The Russian and Prussian guards and heavy cavalry will gather here at Rotha in reserve. Austrian grenadiers and cuirassiers will advance between the rivers here. We approach Napoleon from near every angle as we seek to encircle Leipzig and him and his army within it."

"An ambitious plan, indeed."

"You do not approve?"

"The terrain and the timing are in Napoleon's

favour, and our armies lay scattered and uncoordinated. Begging your pardon, Sir, but each army of the Coalition acts on its own, does it not?"

"You could say so, yes."

Craven shook his head.

"Many nations and many armies, and all led by proud men who would not relinquish all that they have to another."

Craven groaned in agreement, for he knew there was no simple answer to it. They could either have an uneasy and cumbersome alliance, or they could be divided and easy to conquer one after another.

"Napoleon fights on the defensive, and so he has the luxury of choosing the location of this battle, but does your Wellington not frequently do the same?"

"He does, and that's what worries me."

"Why?"

"Because Wellington doesn't lose battles."

"Major, we have to go after Napoleon. This is the moment we have been building to, and we cannot hold off now simply because Bonaparte has his pick of the field of battle."

"No, we cannot, but it is a concern."

"Do you fear we reach too far?"

"When Wellington plans a battle, he does so meticulously and with supreme command over every element of his army, and I imagine Napoleon is no different. That level of organisation and planning is vital, and my fear is that we have too many commanders."

The Prince smiled, for he knew he was one of

those such commanders.

"I wish I could give you better news, Major, but this is the situation which we find ourselves in, and we can only do the best with what we have."

"That is the story of my entire career."

The Prince laughed and the rest of them soon joined in.

"How many men does Napoleon have at his command?" Craven asked.

"Perhaps two hundred thousand."

"My God," declared Mr Solly.

"Indeed, combined we might field one hundred thousand or more than he, but we are scattered all around. There is some most pleasant news."

"Oh?" asked Sir Charles in surprise and excitement.

"A week ago, the Kingdom of Bavaria abandoned the Confederation of the Rhine and Napoleon's service, and today they formally declared war on France."

"Then it is happening. The German states continue to turn on Napoleon," marvelled Craven.

"Indeed, but the mission is not complete yet. French armies lay besieged in Dresden, Danzig, and a great many more garrisons across Prussia and Poland. In Hamburg, too, a strong force holds the city. If Napoleon is triumphant against the Coalition army we have assembled, he will be able to draw on a great many of those forces, and the fate of Europe will be sealed under his power. Do not underestimate Napoleon in these coming days. He could just as easily snatch victory from us if we make but a few minor mistakes."

Craven nodded in agreement. To many it would seem that Napoleon had been cornered by a superior force, but he had experienced Wellington survive and even thrive in far worse circumstances. It reminded of him of the days when they were trapped in Lisbon and behind the Lines of Torres Vedras. And the terrain around Leipzig might well provide the same protection now to Napoleon.

"After all these months, the time has finally come," declared Sir Charles with some relief that they were on the eve of battle.

"It will be a tricky affair, and we must be cautious, or we could lose everything," replied the Prince.

"What more can we do?"

"There is nothing more for you to do, Major. By all rights you should not have even been here, but I am glad that you are. It is not lost on me that you have battled for many years in the hope of crossing into France, and now Wellington is on the verge of doing so, and you are not there to bask in the glory that you fought so hard to earn. You may miss that chance because you are here with us, far from Spain, which I imagine feels like home after all these years."

"It does, but my duty is to see to the defeat of Napoleon, and I will see it done if I must pursue him to the end of this Earth."

Mr Solly giggled as he jotted the quote down in his notebook as he imagined how much the London newspapers would enjoy hearing such an anecdote.

"Will you record all that I say?" Craven asked him.

"Just the good bits," smiled Solly.

"Why?"

"For when this is all over, win or lose, London must hear of it as quickly as may be possible. You know as well as I do that everything Lord Wellington does in Spain and hopefully France also now depends on the outcome of this affair which we will witness in the following days."

"I do not intend to witness anything, for I will not watch from the sidelines."

"You will fight in this battle, Major?" Solly was amazed that he would.

"I am a soldier, not an observer," snapped Craven.

"But is that not what you were sent here to do?"

"What my duties are here are not your business, Mr Solly, but if you knew anything about me, you would know that I am a fighter, and nothing will stop me fighting when a fight is a certainty."

"Would you allow myself to ride with you, Major? For I would greatly like to witness the following days through your eyes, and it would be of great benefit for myself to ride with Englishmen."

"Captain Bogue represents the British element in this army, you should ask him."

"I have, but he was not welcoming of my request, but I believe you might be."

"And why is that?"

"Captain Bogue is a strict military man who follows every rule and order he is given, but I know that you do not."

Everyone in the tent burst into laughter besides Craven, but even he could not help but nod in agreement.

"It is done, then," declared Solly.

Finally, the scene settled down, and the Prince looked relieved to have a little humour to cut through the tension. For whilst it was a daunting task for all of them to face Napoleon in battle, he more than any of them knew the challenges and obstacles that lay before them. The Prince took a deep breath as he looked down at his map once more.

"Five armies now descend upon Napoleon. We go at him from all sides, but whether Schwarzenberg can manage them all correctly remains to be seen, and all of his plans must still be approved by the Supreme Commander, Emperor Alexander. All the while he must juggle relations with King of Prussia and Emperor of Austria. It is an unenviable task. For all these leaders of their nations are present at Schwarzenberg's headquarters," he sighed.

CHAPTER 14

On they marched for much of the next day, approaching Leipzig from the Northeast, until stopping to make camp well before dawn.

"We are slowing down, aren't we?" Bunce asked.

"There is not the urgency that one might expect," growled Craven as he looked around for any sign of the Crown Prince and finally spotted his decadent camp being erected.

"Careful." Sir Charles could see the anger on Craven's face, but Craven stormed on.

Charles, Timmerman, and Paget followed on, wanting to know more and perhaps intrigued to see a clash between the two men. Craven rushed up to the Crown Prince who was still in the saddle surveying his surroundings with six of his staff around him.

"Why do we dither?" Craven demanded.

The Crown Prince's staff looked appalled at his rude approach, but they left a response to the Frenchman.

"Dither?"

"All the armies of the Coalition descend upon Napoleon with all haste, but we drag our heels and make camp whilst there are precious hours left in the day that we might progress forward."

The Frenchman calmly got down from his horse and gestured for Craven to follow him to a secluded spot where they might talk privately.

"Major, you command twenty men, all mounted upon fine horses. You may come and go as you please. You marched well into enemy territory and back out again, for that is possible for you. I command an entire army, which is a logistical nightmare, and moreover, one single mistake, and I could lose it all. I will not rush in like a fool. Schwarzenberg commands the largest of the Coalition armies with as many men as Napoleon commands, and until such time as those armies clash, I will not engage against Bonaparte. For he would relish the opportunity to crush all those under my command before we can unite with our allies."

Craven sighed in frustration.

"Perhaps you will one day experience what it is like to command an army of tens of thousands of soldiers, Major, and have the future of your entire country in your hands. But to this day you do not know either of those things."

"Then let me go on, let me join the fight," pleaded Craven.

"Nothing is stopping you from doing so. The Rocket Troop remains under my command and shall march with my army, but you, Major, you are not under my command, and you never were. I appreciate the service you have given to me and to the Coalition, but if you feel you must go forward to join this battle, then so be it."

"I must, for I am not a patient man, and I cannot wait on the edge of a battle not knowing its progress or being able to influence its outcome."

"Go, then, go West to Blücher, for he will charge in without hesitation, for that is his way, and you will find what you are looking for."

"Thank you, Sir," replied Craven with relief.

"Good luck, and may we meet on the battlefield."

"Just don't be so late that you miss it," smirked Craven as a parting shot.

He hurried back Paget and the others and raced passed them, leaving them to hurry to catch up.

"What news, Sir?" Paget asked.

"I won't be late to this battle," growled Craven.

"You are leaving the Army of the North?" Sir Charles asked in disbelief.

"All roads lead to Leipzig, and we shall be reunited soon enough, if Schwarzenberg can hold on long enough."

"Bernadotte drags his heels?" he asked of the French Crown Prince of Sweden.

"He does, and perhaps he is right to in order to protect the kingdom which will one day be his own, but that is none of my concern. We ride for Blücher, for he will show no such restraint."

They reached the others, and Birback groaned, for he could tell they were not intending to rest for the remaining hours of the day.

"May I join you, Major?" Sir Charles asked.

"You can do what you want."

"You should not risk yourself, Sir. You have done enough already, and should any harm come to you, it would fall on our heads," declared Paget.

"Let him come. The greatest battle of all of our lives lies ahead of us, perhaps the greatest battle of all time," insisted Timmerman.

"I could never forgive myself if I was to miss it."

"And if you are killed, Sir?" Bunce was worried.

"Win or lose, my purpose here is complete. Lose, and the Coalition is done for. Win, and we will be on our way to France, and Germany will be only a memory."

"You seem very sure of that?" Ferreira joined in the conversation.

"Come on, gentlemen, this is the clash we have all been waiting for and you all know it. The Coalition has danced around Bonaparte, poking and prodding at his marshals, but it was all a pretext to what we are about to behold. This will truly be the battle of the nations," declared Sir Charles.

"You will have to leave your finery behind, and your tents and campaign equipment also. We ride until dark and then some more. We sleep only whilst we must and then we ride onwards again," insisted Craven.

"You forget I am a cavalryman, Major. I was born to live on the road!"

Craven leapt into the saddle as Sir Charles' associates scrambled to prepare for their departure, grumbling amongst themselves at the sudden upheaval. In just a few minutes Craven was leading his party onwards once more. He took a deep breath of fresh evening air and felt relief at leaving behind the cumbersome army of ninety thousand soldiers. He did precisely what he said he would, leading them on for several hours beyond sundown. They drew the weary and suspicious gazes of Saxon town folk as they rode on, for few could identify who they were and for which side they fought, and yet they made no attempt to obstruct their passage. Finally, when they stopped and set a large fire, most were asleep in record time. They were still exhausted from the long days and nights of their operation against the bridge. Some like Timmerman and Amyn, still recovering from previous wounds.

At first light, Craven was up and readying his horse as Matthys and Ellis awoke the rest of them. They continued Westward, skirting the Northern edge of the outskirts of Leipzig and ensuring they stayed well out of sight to the French army defending it.

Today felt different for all of them, for they could sense it would be the day that the monumental battle would erupt. The time for waiting was over. After an hour on the march, they heard the first thunder of cannons roaring in the distance, and it only confirmed what they all knew. This was the day. On they rode as quickly as they could without exhausting their horses, and at noon they came over a hill to see a sea of dark blue tunics. Blücher was at the head of them spurring his men on. They marched at a pace almost double that of Prince Charles John's men.

Blücher recognised Craven instantly.

"Come to march with us to victory, have you?" he roared enthusiastically.

"We have, Sir."

"Good, then follow me!"

The old Prussian was seventy years old now, but besides his grey hair you would not know it, for he was spry and strong. He had been fighting wars long before most of the soldiers he led were even born. Craven fell in beside the Prussian leader who had just been appointed as a Field Marshal that day.

"Have you ever faced Napoleon upon the battlefield?"

"I have not, Sir."

"It is a difficult thing, for I myself have waged battle against the Emperor three times, and three times he has denied me victory. He will not have a fourth, do you hear me?" he cried out loudly for all to hear, for he was not ashamed of his defeats, but emboldened by them, "You hear those guns?"

"Yes, Sir." It was hard to ignore the salvos of hundreds of cannons roaring in the distance.

"That means Napoleon has engaged Schwarzenberg to the South. I imagine he means to crush the Prince's army before the day is through, and with it crushed he will turn to the rest of us."

"Yes, Sir," agreed Craven once more.

"But we will not let that happen. The enemy believe we are still a day's march away, and so we shall fall upon them with great fury and surprise!"

They rode on over rolling hills, and it was not

long before they came into sight of the enemy. French Marines who wore almost entirely dark blue uniforms that made them look remarkably similar to the Prussian soldiers approached them. A fact that would surely make for a most challenging affair when they came into combat.

Blücher pressed on, following a wide river on their right flank that led Southwesterly all the way to Leipzig which lay ahead. A battered signpost welcomed them to the town of Möckern where the French Marines were dug in, and yet panicked calls echoed out from the town. For just as Blücher had said, his arrival was not expected until the next day. Beyond the rivers to the South, they could see a battle raging at the town directly West of Leipzig, which was the escape route to France should Napoleon need to withdraw. Coalition forces advanced from the South against the town that was connected to Leipzig via two bridges in sequence. It was a target so valuable to both sides that masses of French troops were already marching from the North to strengthen the position.

"Pressure, pressure, that is what we must provide. We must not give Napoleon any room to breathe!"

Blücher drew out his sabre and swung it about his head and cried out in his native tongue as he issued the order to attack. Infantry, cavalry, and cannons all pressed forward to make an assault upon the town. The French guns opened fire first as the Prussian advance spread out and pressed on through the marshy open fields and a forest on their Northern flank. Musket and cannon fire also raged from the

Northeast of their position as an entire Russian Corps stormed towards another French fortified town there held by Polish soldiers. Craven could already see the extent of the battle in the North, but it was but a minor affair compared to vast trade between Napoleon's main army and that commanded by Schwarzenberg.

French cannonballs ripped through the Prussian lines, but there were too few to stop their advance, for most of the French guns raged to the South. Möckern consisted of stone and timber houses and narrow streets, a manor, and palace and walled gardens. The French Marines had fortified key buildings, turning houses and barns and several large stone residences into defensive strong points.

"Marmont stands before us!"

Craven laughed as he remembered fondly the last time he had faced the French Marshal in battle at Salamanca, where he had been so soundly thrashed that his defeat almost lost all French control in Spain. And yet it was a bittersweet memory, for it was the same battle where Gaspard Le Marchant had been shot dead, and the sword he had gifted Craven still being missing only poured salt into the wound.

Blücher cried out in German, and Holck translated for Craven and their fellow Salford Rifles.

"Forward, my children."

Craven smiled, for Blücher was everything the Crown Prince had said he would be. He rode aggressively and angrily forward, fuelling not just on courage, but passion. Craven remained at his side as the Prussians advanced on the town. Devastating volleys ripped out from Möckern, inflicting terrible casualties, and yet onwards the Prussians pressed.

* * *

Schwarzenberg watched nervously on as the vast battle raged before his eyes for as far as he could see and beyond. In every direction the French were attacked, all but from the Northeast. For the Crown Prince's Army of the North's absence did not go unnoticed, and a number of the officers at his headquarters muttered about him in a less than subtle fashion. They doubted his commitment to the cause, and his heart to face his old Commander. In between the cannon salvos he could hear the duel of guns to the Northwest.

"Blücher," he smiled, knowing the old warhorse had taken the fight to the French with the utmost speed and daring.

But the smile soon vanished at two in the afternoon as Napoleon's grand battery opened fire with a blistering salvo from one hundred and eighty cannons. The bombardment was deadly, but it was what it signalled that concerned him most. He cried out to his aides and other officers, demanding reinforcements be brought in from each and every place that they could be found. For just as the cannon salvo came to a close, French formations all across the front line before them began their advance.

Napoleon was going on the offensive, and it was a terrifying prospect. He was attempting to deliver a knockout blow to Schwarzenberg's army before his allies could fully commit their forces. But more concerning than the infantry advance was the immense cavalry force assembling in the middle of the French line. Ten thousand French cavalry rode out from between the grand battery. They formed up in a tremendous formation before pressing forward. Cannon fire struck their positions, but not in nearly enough volume to even slow the immense force, and amongst them was the battering ram that was the gleaming armoured French cuirassiers. The cavalry advance came so quickly and so furiously that none of the Coalition forces could act quickly enough to prevent it. It was an astonishing sight to behold as ten thousand horses thundered across the open ground.

Schwarzenberg watched as the horde of French cavalry smashed into the infantry formations before him, and nothing could stop them. They hacked and thrust down at fleeing infantrymen as the centre of Schwarzenberg's army began to collapse. It was a slaughter, and they were now amongst the guns of the Coalition also. But of far greater concern, the enemy cavalry now had a free run at Schwarzenberg's headquarters where three of the Coalition monarchs watched on in disbelief. A number of the French cuirassiers and others were coming right for them. Many of Schwarzenberg's staff began to panic, as if they had no plan or reserve in place to defend against such an eventuality. Almost a hundred of the French cavalrymen were within a few hundred yards of the headquarters. But for all of the complaints about the endless rain and mud, it was now a saving grace. The soft ground had slowed the French assault and exhausted their horses, and Schwarzenberg could hear a sign at his back that was so beautiful it was like music to his ears. He did not even turn to behold the miracle, for he kept his eyes focused on the enemy as the thunderous hooves of his own cavalry stormed up from the rear.

A great formation of fresh Coalition cavalry stormed past the three monarchs. Austrian Cuirassiers in their fine white tunics which gleamed almost as brightly as their steel breastplates. Their huge straight cleaving swords were drawn and held at the charge. They were joined by Russian Guard cavalry who were equipped in the same fashion. White gleaming cavalrymen galloped forward, mud spraying up and over those fabulous uniforms as they entered the fray and stormed forward in a counter charge against the weary Frenchmen.

They struck the French cavalry with the same force that the enemy had battered the Coalition infantry lines. Smashing through those who had almost reached the Headquarters with ease. The vast force of Austrian and Russian cavalry smashed into what was a ten thousand strong force. The fight descended into a great cavalry melee, just as Craven had witnessed two days earlier. It was a great spectacle to behold, but the tired Frenchmen and their exhausted horses were soon scattered across the fields beyond and driven back to where they had started at Napoleon's Grand Battery. The Coalition infantry that had been scattered soon regrouped and began to reform their lines. The moment of panic was over, but nothing had been gained. Schwarzenberg gazed out upon the villages on the outskirts at the Southern edge of Leipzig ahead, flanking the Grand Battery on both sides to see they were burning as the two sides battled for control.

Worse still, another village immediately before Schwarzenberg's right was still bitterly contested. The ferocious bayonet combat in the narrow streets caused the bodies of the dead and wounded to be piled high as the two sides swept back and forth, neither managing to gain the upper hand. And yet as the stalemate seemed to set in, elite Russian and Prussian Guard regiments, who were still fresh, arrived to renew the assault. They charged in against the fatigued and bloodied French defenders, who could hold on no further. The village fell to the Coalition, but it was but one tiny victory in a vast battle that waged on for miles to Schwarzenberg's left and right.

* * *

"They're getting slaughtered," declared Paget in horror as he watched the Prussian infantry valiantly press forward, but as one battalion reached the edge of the town, they were met by devastating close range cannon fire that devastated the unit. Skirmishers still pressed forward as they duelled with the dug in French Marines. The battle had been raging for almost two hours as Craven and his party watched on, just as the Prussian cavalry beside them did, biding their time and waiting for their moment to strike. Craven was looking increasingly restless, and yet he was not willing to commit his closest friends to the meatgrinder before them. It was a waste of their talents, and yet as they watched, the combined forces of several Prussian regiments regrouped as one mixed force to make yet another advance. He could wait idly by no longer, and he looked to Blücher to see he was of the same mind. He gave the order to his Prussian cavalry who pressed forward.

"Come on then, boys!" Sir Charles roared encouragement.

He knew he had no authority to do so in spite of his rank. For he was merely a hanger on, and yet the excitement brewing in his cavalryman's heart was at boiling point. Craven knew none of the Germans they were now serving besides, and yet it did not matter, for they fought for the same end. A salvo of the guns in the middle of the French defensive line erupted, and even before the powder smoke had settled, the order to advance was cried out from one of the Prussian cavalry officers. They pressed on at a quick pace. Craven drew out his sword and galloped on after them.

"They mean to run down the guns!" Sir Charles called out.

"Only death or victory can come of it!" Paget yelled in disbelief.

As they joined the Prussian formation, they accelerated to a sprint, not worrying about the exhaustion of their horses now, only the necessity of covering the ground before them in record time. If the guns could be loaded once more, they would be obliterated by their next salvo. The infantry who had reformed cried out in support of the charge as they were invigorated, rushing forward against the enemy positions as if they were fresh troops.

"It's going to be close!" Ferreira cried as they could see the French gunners hurrying to reload their guns. They were still ramming home their charges as the cavalrymen reached their positions. They leapt over the earth and rock filled gabions that had been erected to defend the guns. Several of the gunners ran. Others were struck or tramped by the horses as they soared over. Craven directed his horse over the jump and landed amongst the guns, but there was nothing more for him to do as the Prussians scattered the gunners. He turned back to see the Prussian infantry making a valiant charge, many of them were already battered and bloody from hours of combat.

"Come on!" Craven roared.

He galloped on into the town and veered South down the narrow streets until he discovered a mass of French infantrymen behind a barricade on the road in, preparing to unleash a volley into the advancing Prussians. A Frenchman on the street beside them cried out to alert his comrades to Craven's presence, but Timmerman swiftly brought down a backhanded blow with his sabre, silencing the man instantly. Craven hurried on with sword in hand, galloping right for the French infantry position. Their commanding officer sat atop his horse behind them from where he could safely view the battlefield and direct his men. He turned at the last moment as he heard Craven's horse, but it was too late. Craven plunged his sword into the man's body as though it were a lance.

"Retirer!" Timmerman roared in French, pretending to be one of them and ordered a withdrawal.

Many of them turned about to flee, and others gazed upon the British soldiers with amazement and despair, but in that moment of doubt and bewilderment, the Prussian infantry made their final charge. They rushed at the barricade and leapt over it with fixed bayonets, just as Craven's mounted force crashed into the Frenchmen from the rear. Blades and bayonets clashed as the they duked it out for only a few moments before the French infantry turned to flee. Craven looked out beyond the town to see Blücher advancing with the rest of his reserve and soaring into Möckern.

"This way, lads!" Sir Charles shouted over the din.

He galloped onwards, causing Craven and the rest of them to rush on after him, fearful that he might get himself killed. They galloped into two lines of French soldiers who were engulfed in powder smoke, having just fired a volley and now hurrying to reload. Sir Charles rushed in amongst them, hacking back and forth from one side to another. Captain Harris and Mr Solly were right there beside him, both with swords in hand. Craven and the others arrived quickly to their aid as the Frenchmen began to run. The sun was already low in the sky, and the volume of cannon fire had reduced drastically. All around them French soldiers laid down their weapons to surrender amongst the seven thousand casualties they had suffered, though the allied numbers were higher still in large part for the devastating close range artillery fire. It was a hard-won victory, but a victory, nonetheless.

Blücher galloped up beside them as he marvelled at the sight of seeing the backs of the French Marines who fled after a brave resistance. The first day of battle was over. For Craven and Blücher's Army of Silesia in the Northwest it had been a bitter battle for one small town, but the true extent of the vast battle was yet to dawn upon any of them. Both sides had lost more than twenty-five thousand soldiers in the first day of a battle, which would eventually be decided over many more to come, for neither side had made significant gains.

"Where is your Crown Prince?" Blücher asked as he marvelled at their hard fought for gains.

"Where indeed," groaned Craven as they watched Marshal Marmont's Corps flee back for the safety of Leipzig. It was close to six in the evening, and dusk was settling in. The small victories amongst tiny villages were something to celebrate, but neither side could honestly claim victory after a brutal and bloody day with little change in control of the ground.

CHAPTER 15

The second day of the battle was a Sunday, a traditional day of rest, and it certainly was for most of the soldiers on both sides. For they were exhausted, low on ammunition and supplies, and not in any condition to go on to fight. The soldiers of both sides rested in plain view of one another, knowing that the next day the fighting would go on. And yet there was one part of the battlefield which did not rest this day, as the ever fiery and aggressive Field Marshal Blücher pressed onwards with his plans to assault Napoleon's Northern defences. Craven awoke to these scenes as much of the army around them rested, tended to their wounds, and repaired damaged equipment, cleaning their muskets and sharpening their swords. Yet Blücher was enthusiastically riding back and forth, overseeing the assembling of Russian troops ready for an assault. He at least left his valiant but battered Prussian troops in reserve to rest after their difficult previous day.

"Where does he find the energy?" Craven asked in amazement as Blücher seemed to have more reserves and enthusiasm than Paget had when they first met all those years ago.

"He is fuelled by rage and anger at Napoleon, and a love for his people and homeland. For he was handed many defeats at the hands of the French, humiliating defeats that cost Prussia a great deal of land and reputation, and lives, of course," replied Timmerman.

"You used to fight for rage and anger, and it did not provide you with the energy of youth."

"Are you so sure about that? I pursued you from country to country relentlessly. There was nowhere you could hide."

Craven shrugged, as it was true.

"But I was no Blücher. I had no aim nor purpose. Blücher truly loves his people and his country, and I could never be accused of such."

"Even now?"

"My cold heart might no longer be frozen, but I will never be a beacon of heartfelt emotion."

"You're alright," admitted Craven.

They watched as the Russian infantry formed up ready to push on further to the Southwest, and Russian hussars were forming on their flank ready to force a breakthrough, just as the Prussian cavalry had done the day before. They could see the city walls of Leipzig now. It brought hope that victory was a possibility, but also dread in Craven's heart as he remembered the brutal sieges and assaults of such fortified towns and cities that he had lived through.

"Do you believe Schwarzenberg can do it?" he asked Timmerman.

"As I hear it, Napoleon threw everything he had at Schwarzenberg yesterday, and it was not enough.

Time is on our side now, for we shall only grow stronger as Coalition armies continue to arrive with fresh troops to bolster our forces."

They watched as Blücher spurred on the Russian soldiers under his command. Men who were just as eager for revenge against Napoleon as he was, after Napoleon had marched all the way to Moscow and tried to conquer their nation only the year before. This was a coalition united and motivated like never before.

Riders galloped back and forth as news was sent between the Coalition armies, which were spread out in a great perimeter around Leipzig. Craven approached Blücher as he received one such messenger.

"Schwarzenberg writes to inform me that the allied army will take no action this day whilst we bring up reserves and regroup," he explained to Craven with frustration.

"But you will not remain idle this day?" Craven already knew what the Field Marshal's answer would be.

"I will not ease the pressure on Napoleon's army and let them recover all of their strength, not whilst I have fresh men willing and able to take the fight to the enemy."

Craven sighed in agreement. He could not help but feel a little shame for the Army of the North's absence in the face of the second day of the greatest battle he had ever witnessed. And it was only going to grow larger, as more Coalition forces arrived to bolster their numbers.

Blücher barked his orders for the advance to begin, and the Russian generals under his command hurried to see it done with great enthusiasm. It was only nine o'clock in the morning, and his forces were already on the move whilst most of the Coalition armies lay idle. A stream lay between Blücher's forces and the villages that they approached. Gohlis was the most Southern of them and would open up the road to Leipzig of which it lay in the shadow of the city. Gohlis was a small village but with a large palace, revealing its previous status as a Knightly estate. The grandeur remained, but it was now a rural community of Leipzig itself. Four bridges crossed the stream into Gohlis, limiting the bottlenecks. The stream looked relatively easy to cross. However, the near continuous autumn rains meant the embankments were extremely soft and muddy.

Blücher marvelled with glee as he watched the Russian forces advance. Polish soldiers defended the village of Gohlis and its grand palace, but it was not nearly as well fortified as Möckern had been the previous day. Russian infantry and cavalry also advanced on the village of Eutritzsch just one mile to the Northeast of Gohlis. Both lay behind the same stream, but French cavalry formations were positioned between them and on Blücher's side of the water. And yet they seemed paralysed to do anything as Russian infantry stormed past them on either side to attack the two villages. Volley after volley was poured into the defenders of the villages, and still the

French cavalry appeared to just watch on, unwilling to commit to the aid of the battles raging just a few hundred yards either side of them. Their reasoning soon became clear as a horde of Russian hussars stormed on past Blücher and Craven and made a dash at the French, a direct assault.

The two cavalry forces collided, and a great battle of sabres echoed out, but the French cavalry did not hold for long. They turned and fled across the stream to safety with the Russians giving chase and driving them far beyond hope of aiding the Polish infantry they had been sent to assist. Craven watched in amazement as the Russian infantry stormed both villages. Nothing could stop them as the Polish forces there turned and fled, leaving many dead and wounded behind. Blücher cheered for their success as he rode on to cross between the villages where the Russian hussars had taken up position. Craven and his party followed close by. As they crossed the stream, they realised there was only a small strip of land less than a mile long before a narrow river provided the final obstacle between them and the medieval walls of Leipzig city itself.

"You see, Major, a day in rest is a day wasted. Let our weary men rest and let the fresh ones fight, for they do not want to sit idle," insisted Blücher.

"Yes, Sir," agreed Craven as they watched the French forces retreat, some of them across the strip of land they now also occupied, whilst others fled across the river to the Northeast of Leipzig. From this place, Craven could truly understand the complexity of the attack beyond what he knew from studying his map. Three rivers converged on the city, and multiple streams and spurs, marshy fields, and a forest to the West made the approach to the city like a maze. Now that Blücher's work was done, the vicinity fell quiet once again, for the cannons did not fire this day. And yet the advance in the North did not provoke any response or counter, as the enemy appeared content to give up the ground and make the most of the day's rest and relief to prepare themselves for the monumental battle that would soon rage on.

"What is that, Sir?" Paget pointed out to the East where a huge marching column of thousands of French troops approached the city. They were on the other side of the river on the Northeastern approach to the city, the position where the Crown Prince's Army of the North should have been inhabiting.

"There must be ten thousand or more, Sir," gasped Paget.

"Let them come, for we have one hundred thousand more soldiers marching to our aid," replied Blücher.

It sounded like an outrageous statement, which Paget did not know whether to believe, and so he turned to Craven for answers.

"If they ever arrive," groaned Craven in judgement of the former French Marshal's lateness. It was a sentiment being felt far and wide, as the army began to talk amongst themselves and question whether the Frenchman was truly committed to their cause.

"If that is all the reinforcements Napoleon can muster, then they will be crushed like the rest of his army," declared Blücher.

"You seem awfully sure of that fact?" pressed Sir Charles as they watched the winding French column march on before their eyes only a little over a mile from their position. It was close enough that Moxy felt his hands twitch on his rifle, for they were close to entering range.

"Easy, the fighting is done for today, save your energy for tomorrow," insisted Matthys.

"The wait is killing me. We have been waiting for this moment for so many years, and now we are idle whilst Napoleon is right here before us," added Paget.

"He is not going anywhere, not yet," insisted Craven.

"And yet he could, Sir. He could slip out in the night and run back to Paris."

"Not with his army, and if they are destroyed here, then he will be ruined," replied Blücher.

Campfires sprang up all along the lines as the sun began to set. It had been a quiet day compared to the ferocity of the first day of the battle. Cheers suddenly rang out as well as laughter. They looked out to the same road that the French reinforcements had come, for now it was the Crown Prince and the Army of the North who travelled along the same route. Craven sighed in relief, for it was starting to feel embarrassing that his comrades were missing the great battle of their generation.

"Go, then," declared Blücher.

"Thank you, Sir," replied Craven.

"Remind the Frenchman what real soldiering is, Major. For you were there upon the field of battle beside us, and it will not be forgotten."

"I shall see you upon the battlefield, Sir."

He led his party onwards as they headed Eastward and rode within three hundred yards of the Northern tip of the French army dug in at the village of Schönefeld. The enemy watched them pass but posed no threat, as though they feared the repercussions of starting a fight. Even so, Moxy still rode with his rifle across his lap in readiness to give a response at a moment's notice. They passed the final stream at a bridge North of the enemy position and rode onwards as the Army of the North began to make camp. He aimed directly for the Crown Prince, who gazed out at the walled city before them. Craven desperately wanted to ask him the reason for his delayed arrival, and yet he dared not. Timmerman had no such grace.

"You are late to the party," he declared.

"It seems like it has only just gotten started," replied the Crown Prince calmly.

"I am not sure Blücher would agree," replied Craven.

"Of course, he would not, for he is a stubborn old warhorse. It is an uneasy alliance we keep here, but it holds, nonetheless, for look at how far we have come. All our armies here in one place and Napoleon surrounded with half our number. Tomorrow half a million soldiers will do battle for the future of all the world."

"Yes, it will," agreed Craven.

"Make camp, Major, and get some rest, for we will all need it."

"Yes, Sir."

Craven spotted the Rocket Troop making camp only two hundred yards away. He rode on to join them, knowing they would be made welcome as fires were lit and food and water was prepared.

"What did we miss, Sir?" Fox-Strangways asked as he arrived.

"Fifty thousand casualties on the first day all told. That is what they say."

"Today, Sir?"

"Today was the second day of the battle, Lieutenant, and was a pale shadow of what we experienced on the first, but it was in the South where the worst of the fighting was centred, against Schwarzenberg."

"Who is winning, Sir?"

"I believe most men would consider it a draw, but we can take some hope from that, for we have the reinforcements and supplies to outlast the enemy if they continue on at this rate."

"And if this turns to a siege? Double the number of the enemy does not guarantee success, far from it," added Timmerman.

Craven sighed and looked back to the tall looming walls of the city as the fading light cast it into a dark and menacing shadow.

"This is not Badajoz and Rodrigo. The enemy has not had months to prepare a stronghold. It will not be easy, but it will not be another San Sebastien either," insisted Craven as he noticed a messenger galloping quickly towards the Prince.

"Stay here." He strode on towards the Prince to join him and hear the news the rider brought.

Charles John was handed several, notes which he poured over and smiled.

"Napoleon wrote to Francis today."

Craven shrugged as he was not sure what he spoke of.

"Emperor Francis of Austria, Napoleon's father-in-law. He asked for an armistice, and when he got no response, he finally offered concessions."

"Then he fears defeat."

"Indeed. Napoleon feels his empire crumbling all around him, and if even the prospect of defeat plagues his mind, then we have already won."

"I would not assume as such, for he is still extremely dangerous."

"Of course, he is, but he is not the devil which all thought he was. He is but a man, and tomorrow we shall humble the Emperor and take everything from him."

Craven was surprised, for he had started to doubt the Prince's intentions as the rest of the army had, and so it was most surprising to hear him talk in such aggressive terms towards his former leader.

"What was the Coalition response to Napoleon's requests?" Craven enquired.

"They would not hear his terms."

"Good, for he would lie to gain some time in

which to gather his strength. He has done it before."

The Prince nodded in agreement, even if it was a difficult thing to hear.

"Schwarzenberg makes his displeasure with my arrival quite clear, but I will make no apology for it. We each have our reasons for fighting for the Coalition, and I have led Swedish soldiers far from their homes. I would not endanger their future by throwing away their lives early in this affair," declared the Prince stubbornly.

Craven sighed as he sympathised with both sides.

"You do not agree?"

"It doesn't matter now. Nobody will care what an Englishman thought or said upon this battlefield. The presence of British troops at this monumental battle will be but a footnote in the history books."

"It matters to me," replied the Prince honestly.

"Whatever your reasons, they will be forgotten based on your actions tomorrow."

"It brings me no joy to fight against my countrymen, and yet I will do so for my loyalty now remains firmly to my adopted nation."

"I understand, but it is not me you must convince."

"Must?"

"When all of this is over, you will not want any doubt remaining as to your loyalty and commitment to the Coalition."

"One day I will be King of Sweden, and yet this is how you talk to me?" He seemed more curious than angry.

"I do not owe you anything, and you are not my king nor my prince. Wellington did not send me here to assist the Crown Prince of Sweden. He sent me to ensure the success of this coalition," declared Craven unapologetically.

"I admire your courage, Major, for there would be severe consequences for any other man who spoke this way in my presence."

"I only want to see us achieve victory here, and it is important that you know that. For everyone else fighting for this coalition wants it, too, but not all are convinced that you do."

The Prince did not look bothered. In fact, he smiled at Craven's analysis.

"After all this time, and all I have done for the Coalition, still there are those who doubt me? No matter, for tomorrow is a new day, and the complaints and arguments of the day will be forgotten as quickly as they were spoken, but the victors of this engagement will be remembered forever." He looked out to the lights of the city and the tall walls surrounding it.

"I am willing to bet you never expected it to ever come to this?" Craven asked the Prince bluntly in a way that no one else would dare to pry.

"One can never know what the future holds, but it is rarely boring," he admitted.

"That is for sure."

"Leave me now, for I should have some peace to collect my thoughts before bed."

"I will be camped with the Rocket Troop should

you have need of me."

"And what could I possibly need of you, Major, that the tens of thousands of soldiers at my command could not provide."

"An honest answer," smiled Craven.

"I'll keep it in mind."

Craven retired to his new camp where he found his comrades deep in conversation with both the officers and other ranks of the Rocket Troop, many of whom looked relieved to be in the company of British soldiers once more, or at least those who spoke English well enough that they could converse. Spirits were high. The Rocket Troop had arrived upon the battlefield following some successes, or at least not a defeat. For whilst many worried that Napoleon would successfully lash out at the first allied army he faced and grind it to dust, that allied army now had him trapped, and he was seemingly unable to deliver the deadly blow he had been famous for. And yet as Craven looked out at the huge encampment, he realised it was not nearly as large as one might expect for a force of almost one hundred thousand soldiers. An army size he was most accustomed to during the large engagements in the Peninsula campaign, and yet he could see a great many fires in the distance to the North.

"It has been a slow journey, and we became spread thin upon the mucky roads," stated Captain Bogue as he knew precisely what question was on Craven's mind.

"At least you are here," he replied, taking some

relief in the fact that the Prince himself had shown his face upon the battlefield, and had arrived with at least a fair portion of his force.

"Will we get our chance at Napoleon tomorrow, Sir?"

"Undoubtedly, for a reckoning is coming."

"I only pray that I can do right by my country."

"Don't worry about that, for England is far, far away. Worry about the men beside you, and if every man does the same, we shall see our way to victory."

"Victory, Sir? You really believe we will have it?" Bogue asked with a mix of fear and excitement.

"I am sure of it, and I have waited and battled for five years to see it."

"And for me also. I was there at Corunna, when Napoleon chased us out of Spain, and I have never forgiven him. To be there to see the day that Napoleon is well and truly thrashed in open battle, is a dream if it were to come true."

Craven was stunned. He had assumed Bogue's service in Germany was his first campaign, and yet he was merely new to the Rocket Troop, and to command.

"I was at Corunna," replied Craven in a grim tone as he thought back to those dark days.

"Truly, Sir?"

"Truly."

"Then we are old comrades."

"Indeed, we are."

"It will be our shared revenge, then, and for all of England, to bestow a great defeat upon the Emperor of

France," stated Bogue proudly.
"Revenge, indeed."

CHAPTER 16

Craven was awoken by the sound of cannon fire in the distance as the battle opened at first light. It was a sign of what the day was about to bring, for there would be no rest and calm as had been the case for most of both armies the day before. He had slept amongst one of the gunners' tents where they had crammed in side by side, but it was empty now. He rushed out to see troop movements had already begun, particularly to the West with Blücher's army. They already pressed on as they marched from Gohlis towards the Northern gatehouse of Leipzig to attack the city itself. The Crown Prince's camp was quickly being broken down, but they were nearly four miles away from the nearest enemy position. He quickly looked around in every direction to study everything. The Army of the North moved at a leisurely pace as they had now gained a reputation, and yet Craven knew there was nothing he could do to change that. One thing did catch his eye, though. Captain Bogue was striding towards the Crown Prince and his staff with great will and determination. Although it was not the Prince he aimed for, but General Wintzingerode, who commanded the advance of the

Crown Prince. Craven's curiosity got the better of him, and he also felt a little responsibility for the Captain. He rushed to his side just in time to hear his appeal to the German nobleman who he had crossed paths with before.

"Sir, my apologies. I am Captain Richard Bogue. My Rocket Troop was sent here not to parade or for any other reason than to fight. My men are as brave a men as you will ever find. We wish to face the enemy, and as the commanding officer of the Rocket Troop, I humbly request permission to engage with the enemy."

Wintzingerode was an old soldier who had been an officer in many different armies in his twenty years of service. He was only forty-three years old, but his hair was as grey as Blücher's. Craven looked ready to intervene, for he imagined the interruption of a lowly Captain would not go down well, but Wintzingerode was seemingly taken aback by the appeal. Yet he still looked to the Crown Prince for approval before making a decision, but he got it without hesitation from the Frenchman.

"How could such bravery not be rewarded?" Wintzingerode replied.

"Thank you, Sir, my deepest gratitude," replied Bogue humbly and with great excitement.

"For your gallantry and spirit, I will grant you a guard, a squadron of the Crown Prince's finest dragoons, and I order you now to follow your own plans and judgement."

Bogue was stunned, for it was far more than he

could ever have hoped for as Wintzingerode called for an aide to call up the cavalrymen to assist the Rocket Troop.

"Good luck, Captain," declared the Crown Prince.

"Thank you, Sir, and to you also," he replied as he hurried off to see his gunners.

"That is quite the honour you have been bestowed," declared Craven as they hurried back to their own.

"It is, Sir, but would you do me the same and join us?"

"I could not think of a more fitting place for us on this battlefield."

Soon enough a squadron of Swedish dragoons approached to assist them as Wintzingerode had promised. With their blue tunics they looked quite at home with the Royal Artillerymen of the Rocket Troop.

"What are your orders, Captain?" Craven asked as the three parties were assembled and ready to do his bidding. Even General Sir Charles was amongst Craven's mounted force. For a moment Captain Bogue was frozen in shock and disbelief at his situation, but Craven gave out an audibly loud cough to draw his attention, and he snapped into focus.

"Rocket Troop and our fellow allies, we march to face the army of Napoleon! Prepare to march!"

A cheer rang out before they formed into column and began their advance. Craven rode alongside Bogue whilst the Salford Rifles and Swedish dragoons rode ahead as a screen. Like any and all artillery, the Rocket troop and their weapons were a highly prized target to the enemy, who would seize any opportunity to do damage or even requisition enemy artillery at every opportunity. But because of their starting position so far from the front line, it took many hours to close the distance to the French-held positions. It had gone noon before they even got a good glimpse at the enemy, but what drew their attention immediately was a village to the South of Leipzig. It was raging with fire as Schwarzenberg's army battled to seize control, and Napoleon's forces resisted them at every turn.

"It will not be an easy victory, will it, Sir?" Bogue asked Craven.

"No victory is certain until it is achieved, and many a commander has come undone because he thought otherwise," Craven warned him.

"You do not believe we shall have victory here, Sir?"

"I know it can be achieved, but to think it is already a certainty will make a man complacent."

"Yes, Sir."

"You are no stranger to war, Captain, but leadership requires skills I am not sure I ever truly learnt to master, but I try to give it my best."

"What would your advice be, Sir?"

"Trust your instincts. Trust in those under your command, show them that you are willing to give it your all, and that you are willing to do just what you ask of each and every one of them."

"Yes, Sir, I will."

"Good man."

"If I may, Sir?"

"Of course."

"A general and two majors of the British army march with me, and yet I remain in command, should not one of you assume command?"

"You were appointed to this army, Captain. The rest of us are mere advisors."

"Do advisors march to the front line and fight, Sir?" asked Bogue in doubt.

"Well, no, but if you knew anything about me, Captain, you would know I have little respect for the rules of the army and the norms of society. You are in command here, and I will not hear otherwise."

"Yes, Sir!" he replied proudly.

They rode onwards, the village several miles to the South of them raging as an inferno. Blücher's Russians stormed onwards at the Northern gate of the walled city. They had only just entered the afternoon, and the battle raged with such an immense intensity in all directions it felt to many that this would be the decisive day. To their East masses of Russian infantry stormed another village, but these were not the Russians under the command of Blücher. They were men of the Army of the North. The Crown Prince had finally committed himself to the battle, and in no small way. Two whole Corps advanced on the village of Schönefeld just one mile from Blücher's Russians. The French had positioned more than one hundred and thirty cannons, which poured ferocious volleys against the Russians. Entire ranks and columns were swept away by the devastating salvos. Fox-Strangways had never seen anything quite like it and looked a little startled, but to the campaign and battle-hardened veterans beside them, it was nothing new.

And yet the Russian infantry were not alone. Two hundred cannons from the Army of the North were already being drawn up onto a gentle slope opposing the village and being prepared to deliver an even more devastating counter fire. The dead and wounded littered the battlefield, and troops were already struggling to manoeuvre around them. It was still early in the afternoon, and this was just one small part of a vast battle which raged for many miles around the outskirts of the city. Bogue led his party on beside a Prussian Corps supported by Austrian Jägers, who were the equivalent of Ferreira's Caçadores, elite light infantry and skirmishers. And like the Caçadores, they carried a mix of muskets and rifles, for the latter was always in short supply and expensive to equip. They wore dull grey uniforms with grass green facings that provided some camouflage, but they wore peculiar black broad brimmed Corsican hats, with the left side pinned vertically and large hackles. It was a most jovial hat, which seemed at odds with their subtle uniforms.

These were the men once equipped with the marvellous if unreliable Girardoni air rifle, which Craven and his comrades had gotten good service out of whilst they worked. They were long gone from the service of the Austrian Jägers for the same reasons of unreliability, replaced by common muskets and rifles.

Captain Bogue surveyed the scene. He had been given free rein to act as he best saw fit, a most unusual situation, especially for an artilleryman, whose role was so vital and equipment so valuable that they were typically meticulously commandeered and managed by the leaders of an army. And yet few commanders knew what to do with rockets, or how they might best be employed. Bogue knew his weapons well and looked for a target of opportunity as if he were a bird of prey surveying the ground for its next meal.

The village of Paunsdorf lay ahead and was the target of the Prussian Corps, and it seemed as good as any a target. The village was predominately an old knightly estate like so many others surrounding the city. A great manor dominated the landscape and a church also, but rest of the buildings were much more modest affairs and not well-suited to mounting a defence. Four thousand French soldiers of five battalions and supporting elements defended the area with thirty cannons, and they had dug in as best they could. The guns opened fire upon the Prussians as they pressed forward, inflicting significant losses.

"This is our chance!" Bogue roared.

He led them forward into the edge of musket range with the enemy, a tactic no typical gunner would dare. The guns could easily be captured or spiked by counter attacks and the gunners exposed to enemy fire, but the rockets were no typical artillery. They had a short range and were inaccurate over long distances, but Bogue did not intend to stand off from afar and hope for the best. He closed with the enemy where he might direct an accurate and effective fire. He gave the order to deploy his rocket sleds.

The guard of Swedish dragoons and Craven's modest mounted force watched as the well-disciplined gunners quickly unloaded their lightweight wooden sleds and loaded the rockets upon them in remarkably short time. The advantages in weight and handling were clear for all to see, but they waited and watched with anticipation to see if they could be as effective as the guns of the Prussians, who formed up to pour volleys into the defenders of the village. The Austrian Jägers screened their flank as a skirmish force.

"Will this be the day, Sir? Will this be the day that we break Napoleon?" Paget asked.

Craven looked uneasy about making such a claim, for it seemed to do so would be getting ahead of themselves. All around them they could see the vast armies of the Coalition, and yet the French force before them was still a formidable one. Half a million soldiers were now upon the battlefield, either in combat or ready to do so at a moment's notice. Now the allies had pushed the French forces into an ever-smaller perimeter about the city, they could see far more of their allies. Craven had never seen anything like it in terms of scale of the armies, nor the diversity of the participants. Amongst them were the soldiers of France, the Kingdom of Italy, Saxony, Bavaria, Württemberg, Baden, Poland, the Kingdom of Naples, Russia, Austria, Prussia, Sweden, Hesse, Brunswick, Westphalia, Mecklenburg, and Britain. It truly was as many had suggested, the battle of the nations. A great fog of powder smoke swept all across the land, for the third day of battle had already been waging for hours before they had gotten into range with the enemy.

"Prepare to fire!" Bogue ordered.

Excitement was building amongst those watching on.

"Fire!"

The gunners lit the fuses upon the rockets, but it was rather anti-climactic compared to the thunderous roar of the cannons, but that did not dampen the spirits of Craven's party, for they had witnessed the terrifying weapons and their effects with their own eyes. None more so than Holck, and yet he watched with great curiosity to see what Captain Bogue's gunners could achieve. The Congreve rockets suddenly whistled to life and screamed like banshees as they sped from their wooden sleds. Twenty rockets soared out into the sky and whistled as they flew, smashing down into the French positions with incredible and surprising accuracy, striking infantry and gun positions, and killing and wounding many whilst causing panic. The Swedish dragoons could hardly believe their eyes, for they had evidently believed they had been given a futile mission to guard an experimental and ineffective new method of artillery, but the first salvo gained their respect immediately.

Bogue gave the order to re-arm the sleds, a surprisingly quick process. The rockets were light and easily transported, needing none of the complicated preparation which a cannon required in order to fire. He gave the order to fire once again, and the rockets screamed through the air before the Frenchmen could even redress their lines, nor their gun crews complete the loading of their cannons. The comparison reminded Craven of the Girardoni air rifle that had just been on his mind. He watched in disbelief as the Rocket Troop loaded their sleds one after another, unleashing a near continuous salvo. Explosions erupted all around the French positions, causing complete and utter chaos. Not even Holck could look away at the incredible and destructive display.

Some of the French infantrymen returned fire with their muskets, but at the limits of the range of their muskets, they struggled to strike their targets. Only one of Bogue's men was struck by a musket ball which clipped his arm, and yet the gunner bravely shrugged it off as he continued to load one of the sleds. One rocket struck the powder besides a French gun and erupted into a fire ball. An enemy gun opened fire upon them, but the solid cannonball struck the ground between two of the rocket sleds and bounced on harmlessly to the rear. For they were spread out like a skirmish force and difficult to target. Even if they were to be struck, the sleds were merely a simple wooden frame that any man with basic tools could fabricate or repair. There was no significant value in them as there was in iron and brass cannons, which were often worth their weight in gold. More of the infantry fired out at the Rocket Troop, and yet the inaccurate fire landed around them, some musket balls falling short. One struck a rocket sled and sent splinters flying but did not render it unusable. It was a hot combat between the two, but there was no doubt who was getting the upper hand as the rocket salvos continued to explode amongst the enemy positions. It seemed as though they could hardly miss as Bogue directly his gunners with supreme accuracy.

To their right flank the Prussian and Austrian infantry continued to press on against the enemy on the far flank of the village, and allied cavalry waited beside a wood to their left flank. Further back, Russian Cossacks waited in reserve for their moment to be unleashed. The French could provide no counter nor threaten the gunners of the Rocket Troop who continued to rain down hell fire upon them. Fires had broken out across Paunsdorf, and many of the houses had been badly damaged. Even the manor was ablaze. After just a few minutes of combat, the Rocket Troop had unleashed two hundred of their Congreve rockets upon the enemy. It was a startling sight to behold, and their carts carried more ammunition still. The rocket sleds did not overheat like the barrels of the cannons and could go on firing as long as they had ammunition to launch at the enemy.

"They are going to run," whispered Paget.

Captain Bogue had noticed the same himself as the French defenders were in complete disarray and confusion, with some starting to retreat. They could not stand against the horrifying high explosive onslaught any longer.

"Hold fire!" he roared.

He hurried to his horse, which had been tied to one of the ammunition carts at the rear. He leapt into the saddled and gestured towards the Swedish dragoons.

"Follow me!" he cried out as he drew out his sabre.

Like the horse artillery, Bogue carried a light cavalryman's sabre, and their uniform mimicked the British light dragoons, and so he looked right at home as he led the Swedish cavalry forward.

"What do you say, Craven, will you ride with me to victory!" Bogue cried.

He did not wait for a response, but Craven could not refuse such an offer. He drew out his sword and spurred his horse on to lead his party on to join the Swedish cavalry. They were a force of just two hundred horsemen soaring towards defensive positions held by almost three thousand of the enemy, and yet the French were in disarray. Many were already running, and the rest were on the verge of doing so. Craven smiled as he thought back to the leisurely pace that the Crown Prince had marched his army. It was now paying off, as the fresh horses of the Swedish cavalry and Captain Bogue galloped on at lightning speed. They covered the distance to the village in a flash before most of the remaining brazen defenders could load their weapons and form their ranks. None of them could have expected a cavalry charge. The rocket attack had done so much severe damage so quickly the enemy could not react quickly enough to what they were seeing.

Captain Bogue led the charge from the front like a true cavalryman. Sir Charles had a huge smile upon his face in appreciation for the sight.

"That man flies faster than his damned rockets!"

They were just thirty paces from the enemy now, and only a small number had loaded their muskets in time to fire, and yet instead of presenting them, they tossed them away as the cavalry made their final charge. The enemy were so terrified by their approach that many took off their hats and turned about and gave three huzzas. They had given up. Bogue galloped into the Paunsdorf without any resistance as the Frenchmen lay down their weapons. Many sat down in exhaustion from the toll the rockets had taken on them, and not one amongst them put up a fight.

"The victory is yours!" Sir Charles cried to Captain Bogue in great appreciation for his incredible achievement.

"What a thing, Captain, what a thing!" Mr Solly also cried out. He had followed close by Sir Charles' side, despite not wearing a uniform nor carrying a weapon with which to fight. The Swedish dragoons roared triumphantly, for they had achieved a victory without ever having to fight for it, and so the victory went to Captain Bogue and the Rocket Troop. As they gazed at the exhausted battle-weary Frenchmen all around them, the scale of the victory began to set in. Nearly three thousand French soldiers had laid down their arms and surrendered to a force less than one tenth their size. Craven sheathed his sword, astonished that he never had need of it despite what had been achieved.

"I am not sure that is what Wintzingerode had in mind when he gave you a squadron of cavalry for your protection," he declared to Captain Bogue.

"No, I should imagine not, but I saw an opportunity open before my eyes."

"That opportunity did not open. You blasted it open with two hundred rockets!"

Huzzas rang out for the Captain, but not from the defeated Frenchmen this time, but from all who had followed Bogue in the incredible charge.

"We should see to these prisoners before they become rowdy," insisted Sir Charles' aide-de-camp Captain Harris, who looked most at home in the saddle with his sabre in hand, but also wary of the thousands of enemy soldiers that surrounded them. They needn't have worried, as Prussian soldiers rushed in amongst the village and began to round up the enemy and march them from the battlefield. There was little to be done for the dead and wounded who could not make their own way onwards. Bogue rode on to the edge of the village to get a better look across the battlefield for himself. The French forces who had been positioned all about on either flank were in full retreat as they closed their ranks. Napoleon's army was being driven ever closer to Leipzig, a city which would struggle to contain the vast army. Most of the French force in the North were within one mile of the city walls now, and yet to the South they still held on bitterly to the ground against Schwarzenberg's army, which struggled to make much progress against Napoleon's stubborn army.

"This battle is not over, is it?" Bogue asked.

"Far from it, the enemy still think they can win, and they are not wrong to think it. It would not be the first time Napoleon has relied upon a coup de grace to snatch a victory from the jaws of defeat."

Bogue nodded in agreement with Craven. The French army was not in retreat. It merely repositioned to keep up the fight and wait for new opportunities to turn the tables.

"That was an incredible thing you did here."

"Thank you, Sir."

"No, thank you. It was an honour to ride at your side, but you are full of surprises, Captain. I have seen many things in war, but I have never seen an artillery captain lead a cavalry charge, let alone a successful one against ten times his number. This will go down in the history books, and you just ensured that the British presence here at this battle of the nations will not go ignored or forgotten."

"Thank you for saying so, but the Crown Prince should hear of this, not of my achievements, but of our great successes. I would have him tell us what he would have next of us."

"I shall deliver the message myself."

"A major carrying a message for a captain, Sir?" Bogue sounded confused.

"I deliver the message of a hero," replied Craven in appreciation as they heard the creaking of carts. The Rocket Troop was entering the town triumphantly. The Swedish dragoons cheered their arrival and welcomed them as heroes, and the Prussian infantrymen did the same. For they had all witnessed the destructive scenes of Captain Bogue's rockets and his subsequent charge, which had cleared a village they had expected to have had to battle fiercely for at the point of the bayonet and at the cost of a great many casualties.

"You see, Captain, the Rocket Troop are cheered on by our allies. What you did here will not be forgotten, and Wellington and the Prince Regent will surely hear of it."

"Thank you, Sir, but let us save the celebrations for when victory is ours, if it yet may be."

"I shall return shortly."

CHAPTER 17

"Major Craven, a fine display!" roared the Crown Prince as he approached.

"Sir, Captain Bogue would have me inform you of the successful capture of Paunsdorf."

"We saw it without own eyes," replied Wintzingerode.

"Three thousand of the enemy captured, Sir," added Craven.

"Three thousand?" Wintzingerode asked in disbelief.

"Taken by the hand of Captain Bogue himself at the head of your dragoons, Sir."

"It would seem the English for having the smallest contribution upon the field are making every effort to have an impact far greater than their number," replied the Crown Prince.

"Yes, Sir, and I would like to say it is of my doing, for that is why I was sent here, but I was merely an observer to Captain Bogue's fine work."

"Please inform the Captain of my gratitude for his eminent services, and that I request he continue his exertions in the same fine manner which he began," declared the Prince.

"I will, Sir."

But he did not depart as if wanting to ask a question.

"What is it?"

"Sir, you told me you would not risk all that you had unless victory was possible, do you now believe that it is?"

"With bravery like we have witnessed from men like Captain Bogue, it is a certainty."

"I will ensure the Captain hears of it."

"Good luck, Major."

Craven galloped on back towards Paunsdorf where the Rocket Troop and their cavalry escort had paused to take a breather. Craven found Bogue in the same place he had left him, peering out towards the enemy positions where they were reforming in a huge unbroken line from the Eastern edge of Leipzig and stretching for more than a mile. The fighting outside the North gate and of the Army of the North's soldiers immediately on their left flank at the village of Schönefeld continued to rage with horrific losses, but there was more than half a mile between the Prussians and those opposing them on Napoleon's Northeastern flank. The lull in the action had allowed both sides to regroup and redress their ranks.

"The walls are closing in on Napoleon, are they not?"

"It would seem so," replied Craven as he looked out across the battlefield beyond. The fighting still raged on, especially in the South, "The longer this goes on the worse it is for Napoleon. He does not have the reserves or the supplies to keep this up forever."

"Then we shall have our victory, but at a great price."

"Defeating Napoleon was never going to come cheaply or easily, but you already know that, for no man who served in Portugal and Spain could not."

"Indeed."

"The Crown Prince would have me convey his deepest gratitude and appreciation for your efforts here. He requests that you continue in your exertions."

"And we shall, for as soon as the Prussians begin their advance, we shall be right there beside them," promised Bogue.

It was a welcome rest in the midst of the battle, but a cheer rang out before them. They looked over to see thousands of Saxon soldiers at the corner of Napoleon's line cry out, but it was not a battle cry, but something else as they gazed over at something near Bogue's position. He looked across to see the Crown Prince himself and his staff had arrived just two hundred yards away to survey the scenes themselves. The Saxon soldiers amongst the French line were greatly excited by his presence.

"What on Earth do they jeer for?" Bogue asked.

"Those men once served under Bernadotte, now the Crown Prince of Sweden," declared Sir Charles as he arrived beside them.

They watched in disbelief as three thousand Saxon soldiers turned their tunics inside out and put them back on before dashing forward, and yet they were not making an attack on the Army of the North. They were crossing over to join them and turn against Napoleon. Cheers rang out along the Prussian lines as the Saxon men came to join their fellow Germans in the battle against Napoleon. The Crown Prince stood up tall in his stirrups and took off his hat, which he waved enthusiastically towards the Saxon soldiers as they came over to his side. Their departure left a gaping hole in the French line. It could not be exploited by the Army of the North, but it was a massive morale boost, and an equally devastating loss for Napoleon's army. The shocking scene elevated the spirits of the Prussians so severely they immediately advanced towards the enemy before any orders had even been given. There was a revitalised sense that victory was near now, and the allied lines all across the North pressed on in a huge wave attack.

"Forward!" Bogue cried.

* * *

Schwarzenberg gazed out upon the vast battlefield beyond. For several miles along his front line his army took the fight to the enemy as they battled over the Southern villages which skirted about Leipzig. Progress was painfully slow, and the enemy fought desperately for every inch. Emperors Alexander and Francis watched on at the dreadful losses beyond, hoping and praying for victory, whilst doing all that they could to present a confident and strong demeanour, even though the battle seemed to hang in the balance. Neither side could seemingly take the upper hand, and nowhere was that fact so prevalent as at the village of Probstheida at the centre of the French line. The enemy had turned the place into a fortress, and even though fires raged from nearly every building, including a grand stone church, the enemy ruthlessly defended it. Some Prussian regiments that had been sent to assault it retreated back towards Schwarzenberg's headquarters with only half the men they had set out with. The losses were horrifying.

* * *

Captain Bogue led his Rocket Troop on in support of the Prussian attack, which was now directed at the nearest village to their right, named Sellerhausen. Sir Charles cried out enthusiastically as he rode onwards with the Salford Rifles and Swedish dragoons. It was a magnificent scene as the enemy were pressed all along the Northern French lines. Bogue led his gunners on towards the village to place them in range of the enemy musketry once more, putting his own life in the line of fire to ensure they could provide the best fire support possible to the Prussian advance. They watched as the hole in the French line caused by the Saxon defection was soon plugged by Guard cavalry, but that did not cause concern for the allied soldiers. They knew it signified the final reserves having to be deployed by Napoleon, whilst the Coalition reserves were amassed in all directions.

A fierce battle broke out between the Prussian infantry and the French defenders of Sellerhausen, whilst the Russians to their right continued to battle it out across Schönefeld as they had all day. The village was now a burning husk of ruins as fires burned all over, and yet still the French defended it. Bogue gave the orders for his gunners to deploy their rocket sleds as Craven and the rest of the cavalry watched over them in reserve, just fifty paces from the artillerymen.

"Fire!" Bogue roared.

The first salvo was unleashed, the screaming rockets almost drowning out the sounds of battle all around. Explosions erupted amongst the enemy troops, inflicting significant damage, but it also drew attention to the dangerous new threat Bogue had brought against them. Enemy sharpshooters opened fire upon the gunners. One was struck in the leg. Moxy leapt from his horse and hurried forward to take a kneeling position near the line of rocket sleds. He took aim at one of the enemy who had targeted them, who were sharpshooters, but equipped not with rifles but only ordinary muskets. They were shooting far beyond their accurate range, which was only one hundred yards to hit a man-sized target, and yet the weight of skirmish fire was enough to keep heads down. Ferreira quickly joined him, and soon enough all the Salford Riflemen were spread out as a skirmish line laying fire down upon the enemy, whilst Timmerman, Sir Charles, and his few comrades watched on, for they were of no use in a ranged duel.

Bogue barked his orders as he kept up the

rocket salvos, knowing they could turn the tide at Sellerhausen just as they had at Paunsdorf. Another salvo of rockets was unleashed, but as they hurried to load the sleds, three of the gunners were shot down, one killed instantly and two others badly wounded. One man dropped the Congreve rocket he had been carrying. His companions hurried to his aid whilst Bogue took up the rocket himself and carried it to the sled ready to fire. Yet as he rested it into position, a musket ball struck his head, causing his Tarleton helmet to be catapulted from his head as he collapsed lifelessly to the ground.

    Craven hurried to his side, reaching the Captain before his own men could, as they struggled with the wounded and continued to work their rocket sleds. Craven found Bogue face down and not moving. He turned him over, hoping to give some care to his wounds, but now that he could see the wound for himself, he realised the Captain was already dead. A musket ball had entered below his eye and passed all the way through his head. It had been a quick and painless death at least. The gunners nearby stopped in dismay and disillusionment as they looked down at the dead body of their commanding officer in the arms of Craven. It seemed unthinkable to them that the hero who had been unscathed in the most daring charge against three thousand enemy soldiers had now been struck and killed before their very eyes. Nobody had any words, until Fox-Strangways noticed what has happened and rushed to Craven's side, only to realise his Captain was dead. He cried out in pain, and yet his despair lasted only a few seconds as the sounds of the battle raging all around him caused him to snap into action.

"Take the Captain to the rear!" he roared to several of his men who watched on, having abandoned their duties in disbelief at the gruelling sight. They did as they were ordered as Fox-Strangways drew out his sword and held it aloft.

"For Captain Bogue and in his honour, fire at will!" he roared as the twenty-three-year-old assumed command, tears streaming down his face.

Craven was in awe of the young man, who was several years Paget's junior, and who did not have even an ounce of the battle and campaign experience of the thirty-year-old Bogue whose shoes he had been forced to step into.

"By God, we will give them hell, Sir," Fox-Strangways said to Craven even as Bogue's body was carried away.

"With men like Captain Bogue and yourself, Napoleon never had a chance," declared Sir Charles as he rode up to provide some assistance, or at least to show his support in the face of such loss and hardship.

Mr Solly was with him also. "What can I do?"

"You are an Englishman, aren't you? Pick up a sword and use it," snapped Fox-Strangways.

One of the wounded Rocket troop men who had been shot in the arm but remained at his post to ferry rockets back and forth, drew out his sabre and passed it up to Solly. The look of despair was on all the faces of the Rocket Troop, for they had been very fond of their Captain. And yet they went about their duties with stubborn efficiency even whilst the French sharpshooters continued to target them. The sun was fading quickly now, but a cheer rang out across the line as they looked to the West to see the French finally fleeing from Schönefeld, which they had bitterly contested all day. The victory and sight of the fleeing French forces running from the burning ruins of the village caused a great boost to morale for the allied line. Prussian troops suddenly stormed forward to put those in Sellerhausen to the bayonet as they charged upon French positions without a care for what fire came back at them. To their west Prussian and Russian cavalry descended upon the Guard cavalry who had replaced the Saxon defectors, and further to their South more Russian infantry swarmed in against Napoleon's Eastern flank.

"Hold your fire!" Fox-Strangways ordered as they watched their allies storm in against the village. He turned back to find his horse and leapt into the saddle with a look of grim determination. Craven and Sir Charles rushed up to his side, just as the Crown Prince and General Wintzingerode and their staff advanced into their sight to see two of the Rocket Troop men lift Captain Bogue's body onto one of the Rocket Troop carts.

"You cannot stop me," Fox-Strangways growled as he looked out at the French positions in Sellerhausen.

"Wintzingerode and the Crown Prince gave this Troop the order to advance and follow its commander's judgement. You have command,

Lieutenant. Command us," declared Craven.

Fox-Strangways was stunned as he looked to Sir Charles, expecting a contrary argument, but the cavalryman made no protest.

"Onwards, onwards to victory!" roared the Crown Prince in English.

Fox-Strangways needed no more confirmation. Not that he intended to listen to any naysayers, but it hardened his resolve even further to know he had the support of every soldier around him. He drew out his sword, and Craven, Timmerman, and Sir Charles followed suit as the Swedish dragoons formed up at their side. Captain Bogue had gained their unwavering respect, and they would follow his successor all the way to Napoleon himself.

"Charge!" Fox-Strangways cried.

The squadron galloped past the Salford Rifles who continued to skirmish, except for Paget who quickly mounted Augustus and galloped on to catch up with them. They soon caught up with the Prussian infantry as they made their final rush into the village. Bayonets and blades clashed as Fox-Strangways slashed an enemy officer dead in a single swing. Craven leapt a barricade and landed amongst a gun crew who reached for their weapons to defend themselves. But before they could, Timmerman's horse leapt over into the position and trampled one man dead as he hacked at the sword arm of another, cleaving it off with weapon still in hand. Craven thrust at another man, but he turned and fled with the rest of his gun crew. Paget jumped in beside them, for once being late to the party as he struggled to catch up.

"Shall we spike the guns, Sir?"

"Most certainly not, those are our guns now!" Craven had no intention of losing an inch of ground that they had now taken. A line of Prussian infantry formed up beside them and gave a withering volley at French infantry who attempted to counter charge.

"Drive them out!" Fox-Strangways roared.

The cavalry formed alongside him as Prussian infantry poured down a parallel road to them. A mounted French colonel and his staff turned the bend ahead as they tried to rally their troops. Upon sight of the Swedish cavalry they charged at them, along with two-dozen men that had rallied and a dozen artillery drivers who were in the saddle also. Fox-Strangways did not even need to give the order as his entire party launched forward to go directly at the enemy. He went straight at the French colonel, their blades clashing as they came to a standstill, locked in a duel whilst the battle raged all around them. There was no space for the horses to move, and the combat descended into a static melee. Mr Solly found himself at the front, hacking wildly back and forth as he struggled to fend off bayonets, his civilian attire seemingly drawing the enemy to him as if he was someone of importance.

Captain Harris pushed up beside him and drove his horse into one of Solly's attackers before thrusting his sabre into another. Solly seized his opportunity to smash his sabre down onto the head of another of the infantrymen. The attack had no finesse at all, but the power and weight of the blow cleaved the man's shako in half before cutting deeply into his skull. He pried the blade from the man's head, causing him to drop down dead.

"We will make a soldier of you yet!" Captain Harris shouted.

Sir Charles laughed at the scene before driving on against another opponent. Holck reached down and seized the barrel of a musket in the hands of one of the enemy, ripping it from his grasp. The terrified Frenchman turned and fled in horror. Fox-Strangways continued to rain down blows against the French colonel with such fury as if the man was personally responsible for the death of his Captain. The colonel thrust his sword into Fox-Strangways arm, and though he initially cried out in pain, he grabbed hold the blade with his left hand and held it firmly in place, plunging his sword into the colonel's chest. The Frenchman collapsed forward and fell dead from his horse. Fox-Strangways ripped the blade from his arm and cast it down onto the ground beside his vanquished opponent. Paget rode up beside him to assist and parried off a bayonet that was aimed at him before Charlie hacked down at the same infantryman, slashed at his neck and causing him to drop his weapon and flee. A great cry rang out from the allied infantry all around them as they made one final push. The roar alone seemed to be the final nail in the French coffin as they abandoned the fight and began to flee in the fading light.

Fox-Strangways took one more deep breath as he gathered his strength and tried to fight through the pain. Blood was seeping into his shirt and tunic sleeve from the open wound.

"To victory, it is yours," insisted Craven as he rode up beside the Lieutenant.

Fox-Strangways looked around to his friends and comrades. They were filthy dirty, exhausted, and bloodied, but they looked to him with joy now. Joy that victory was in sight.

"We are with you, Lieutenant," Mr Solly declared, holding up the sabre he had been loaned.

Fox-Strangways nodded in agreement and appreciation before driving his horse at a steady pace as they rode on to sweep the enemy from Sellerhausen. Soon enough they were on the edge of the village where they came to a standstill as they watched the whole of the French Northern line flee back towards the city. A great cheer rang out from the allied forces, for they had achieved an unquestionable victory this day.

* * *

Schwarzenberg watched from his headquarters as the sun went down on the bloody and powder fog covered field of battle. Napoleon's army still held firm, but they had lost significant ground throughout the day. The fields all around lay scattered with the dead. Twenty-five thousand losses on each side. It was a horrific figure, but it was Napoleon who could not replace those losses, whilst fresh troops remained all around the Prince's position.

He looked to the Emperors and rest of his staff to see there was some relief and belief in victory now. The third day of the Battle of the Nations had come to an end, and there was a sense that it was all coming to a close. The defeat of Napoleon was in sight, and yet much to Schwarzenberg's chagrin, Probstheida had held out. He could see the French fleeing in the North where Prince Charles John and Field Marshal Blücher had achieved great successes, but in front of his eyes the French lines remained firm, mostly where they had been all day. He shook his head in frustration as he swore to himself that the next day would draw a conclusion to the affair.

* * *

Craven watched as the wood was thrown upon the burning ruins of Sellerhausen as the Rocket Troop made camp amongst the ashes, their carts of explosive Congreve rockets moved to safety on the Northern outskirts of the ruined village. Prussian and Austrian troops had made themselves comfortable there also as they made merry, celebrating their survival and success against the French. Matthys was busy working to sew up the wound in Fox-Strangways's arm. He winced with pain, and so Craven passed him a flask of liquor.

"No, I would be fresh for the morning," protested the Lieutenant.

"There will be nothing fresh upon this battlefield come first light. Take it."

He did so and took a large mouthful before nodding in appreciation. He rested back against the half-collapsed wall he sat against.

"What a day," he marvelled.

"Indeed," agreed Craven.

"Thank you, thank you all for following me today."

"It is our duty."

"You could have assumed command any time, from Captain Bogue or from myself."

"The glory was in the hands of the Rocket Troop today, and I would not rob you of it."

"Captain Bogue's loss will be felt far and wide."

"Yes, it will, but his bravery will also be known."

Matthys finished his work and tied off the stitches.

"Let me have your tunic, Sir, and I will patch it up as best as I can," offered Matthys.

The Lieutenant nodded in agreement. He leant forward and let Matthys help him out of it before Craven hauled him to his feet so they could go and warm themselves beside one of the fires. In spite of the vast number of dead strewn across the fields, the makeshift camps all along the line were alive with conversation as the soldiers reminisced about the three days of battle, or the one in the case of the Army of the North. In spite of their late arrival, nobody held it against them now. They had made up for their lost time with a tumultuous day of combat. More than anything there was a rising hope amongst the army that the end was in sight.

"Captain Bogue's loss is so much to bear," declared Fox-Strangways quietly.

"There is no shame in it," replied Craven.

"There is not?"

"A cold and heartless man might be able to shrug off such a loss, but not a good one," insisted Craven.

"Lieutenant Fox-Strangways, is it?"

They turned about to find the Crown Prince himself standing before them.

"Yes, Sir!" Fox-Strangways snapped to attention, but the Frenchman waved him off as he continued in a familiar manner.

"I saw what Captain Bogue did today, and you also."

"Yes, Sir, Captain Bogue's heroic efforts…"

"They will be rewarded, I can assure you, and you have my deepest sympathies. For this army lost a great soldier here today."

"One of a great many."

"You are a fine man, Lieutenant, and you do credit to your Rocket Troop, to your country, and to your fallen Captain."

"Thank you, Sir."

"Nobody would think less of you for stepping back from your duties tomorrow. That wound should have time to heal."

"I beg of you not to order it of me, Sir. A gunner needs not an arm to command, only his legs."

"I will do no such thing. I wish you every luck tomorrow, Lieutenant. Are you ready for victory?"

"I am, Sir, I am ready and willing to see it done."

"Good luck and good night, gentlemen." The Prince left them be as he walked amongst the army.

"We made a difference today, didn't we, Sir? Our rockets made a difference?" the Lieutenant asked Craven.

"Most certainly, you have ensured the British contribution here was ten times what its number might suggest. It was damned fine work."

"Yes, it was, and I will make sure that news of your deeds are heard far and wide," insisted Sir Charles.

"You yourself were a part of that success, Sir."

"I was merely an observer, just like Captain Harris and Mr Solly," smiled the General.

"I am not sure anyone will believe that, but for the sake of us all, you will report it as so," ordered Craven to the Lieutenant.

CHAPTER 18

Craven slept well atop a pile of rubble with only his blanket to keep him warm. It was a cold morning. A thick fog had not allowed the sun to penetrate the sky. A fire still burnt brightly in front of him, having been fed all night. Fox-Strangways gazed out into the distance towards Leipzig, but he could not make out the walls for the fog. And yet they could hear the clatter of men and equipment and the creak of heavily laden carts. The city was alive, and that surely meant one thing. Craven threw off his blanket and joined the Lieutenant, and whilst they could not see as far as the city walls, it was evident that the enemy they had driven out from Sellerhausen the day before had not retreated further still. A gust of wind swept a cloud of fog into the sky, and they could see all the way to the Russian Cossacks to the East and South down to the ruins of Probstheida, which was still smouldering and belching black smoke into the sky. Everywhere they looked there was no sign of the enemy formations, only the dead.

"They have withdrawn back into the city, Sir."

"So, it would seem."

The soldiers around them gazed out upon the

abandoned positions with glee, but then as the fog lifted above the medieval walls of Leipzig, they remembered that the fortress was yet to fall. For three days the allied armies had battled and suffered to take the open ground, and the prospect of a siege to follow it was repulsive. The fog began to lift further, and with it the revelation that French soldiers poured out Westward to escape.

"This is not a siege. It is merely a rearguard," declared Craven.

Allied Guns roared to life as they bombarded the city.

"It's begun, Sir. It's begun, the beginning of the end!" Paget cried excitedly.

Craven hurried to find his horse. Joze was already fixing his saddle, anticipating his need of a mount. Craven leapt on the horse and wheeled about as he rushed back to the front of the ruins of the village. Coalition armies were forming up everywhere he looked, as the guns continue to roar.

"This is it."

"What, Sir? What is it?"

"The battle is won, but now the Coalition marches to cut off Napoleon's army and ruin him!"

Schwarzenberg was at the centre of the Coalition armies and had assumed command of them all. He directed the columns forward. Five columns descended upon the city of Leipzig from the North, East, and South. It was a general advance of monstrous proportions. Paget could hardly believe what he was hearing. Not only did they have a chance to defeat Napoleon, for that had already been achieved, but now they had a chance to cripple him also.

"Come on!" Craven roared as infantry formations stormed on past them on either side of the village. The Salford Rifles hurried to form up in a loose formation, leaving their horses behind in the town. Fox-Strangways vanished for a few moments before reappearing with the men of his Rocket Troop, but without their rockets and sleds. They formed up beside Craven as an infantry force. Many carried muskets, which typically they only used for the defence of their equipment. Others had only their swords in hand, but there was a look of dogged determination on their faces. They were ready to make the assault, no matter the risks or the cost.

"This is not your fight today."

"The Rocket Troop has no orders, but today we are not the Rocket Troop, we are with you, Major."

The Swedish cavalry who had been assigned to guard the Rocket Troop then strolled forward to do the same. They were dismounted and carrying their carbines ready to fight on foot. Combined the mixed force numbered almost three hundred soldiers.

"Who is in command?" Craven asked.

"You are, Sir. You supported our gunners, now let us support your infantry," declared Fox-Strangways.

A cheer rang out in support of Craven taking command, for the time for rockets was over. It was now time for cold steel.

"Today we defeated Napoleon but let us go forth

now so that the world might remember that we did not just defeat Napoleon, we thrashed Napoleon!" Craven roared.

An excited cry rang out from the combined force who were champing at the bit as if they were fresh and not battle hardened and weary. The chance of inflicting such a humiliating defeat upon the man who had plagued them for so many years seemed to invigorate each and every soldier. The feeling was felt far and wide as the soldiers advancing across the plain cried out excitedly. Craven ripped his sword from its scabbard and held it before him, pointing to the walls of Leipzig.

"Follow me!"

They hurried forward, not in formation or in any order whatsoever, but as a horde, just as the Germanic peoples had done to the Roman armies centuries before across the same land of Saxony, at the Battle of the Teutoburg Forest. The allied army stormed forward to do just the same as had been done to those Roman invaders. It was a poetic mirror of those events, considering Napoleon harkened back to the Roman Empire and had modelled his trademark standards upon that ancient culture.

Cannon volleys flashed over the heads of the advancing armies and smashed into the walls of the city. The defenders of Leipzig soon opened fire, but they could not stop the vast assault as battering rams were carried to the gates and ladders to the walls. Russian and Prussian soldiers clambered over onto the walls, eager for revenge after the horrifying losses of the past three days. Skirmishers fired at those atop the walls, peppering them as they tried to resist the assault. Cries rang out from inside the city as panicked soldiers desperately tried to flee, and yet there was only one road out from the city, and it crossed a single bridge. All the allies knew this, and as they had done upon the first day of battle, once more they pressed onwards to envelop the road and trap Napoleon's army for good. A tremendous fire rang out as the frenzied assault progressed. A battery ram thundered at the gatehouse beside Craven's position, but he was impatient and shoved his way through the lines to reach a ladder and come within striking distance of the enemy.

He soon got his wish as his comrades struggled to keep up. The Major was so invigorated by the determination of the whole army that he almost ran up the ladder. He leapt on to the rampart beyond to find Russian soldiers storming up and over everywhere he looked, and many of the defenders were already abandoning the walls. Timmerman leapt over beside him.

"The gatehouse!" he roared.

They ran onwards. Craven slashed a bayonet aside and plunged his sword into the man wielding it, barely slowly his stride as he spun about and tossed the man from the walls as he hurried on. He stormed on down a stone stairway to the rear of the gatehouse, only to find fifty French infantrymen formed up ready to fire if and when the gate failed. Timmerman hauled him back out of the way. The timing of the breach could not have been better, as the gate cracked beside them and was thrown open. A cry rang out as the attackers stormed forward. The French force unleashed a volley upon them, but it barely slowed the assault as allied soldiers stormed on over their dead and wounded. Craven rushed out to assist, storming in against the infantry. They were crammed in tightly with the assaulters who were all back-to-back, there was no room to swing a sword or use the butt of a musket. The two sides battled it out as if it was a barbaric medieval contest with spears, and yet without shields to protect themselves, it was an even more bloodthirsty affair.

Craven took hold of the blade of a bayonet, knowing it was only sharp at the point. He thrust into the lead arm of the man wielding it, causing him to lose control of the weapon and drop it. Craven seized his opportunity and leapt in to where the man had been standing. He took the end of his sword in his left hand and held the sword vertically before running the line of bayonets, smashing them aside and exposing those holding them to the assaulting force. Timmerman leapt in first and thrust his sword home into one man, as the soldiers beside him seized their opportunity to butcher their enemy. They did so without mercy, for all they had lost was fresh in their minds. They stormed forward with such ferocity that many lost their footing as they collapsed upon the French soldiers, pinning them to the ground with their bodyweight as their companions stabbed the stricken soldiers.

Some of the enemy soldiers tried to run, but every street was littered with both laden and empty carts, cannons, and the wounded. On three sides of the city walls allied troops poured into Leipzig, savage street fighting erupting in every street. Some of Napoleon's remaining rearguard locked themselves in houses to fight from strong points, but it would do them no good. Grenades were tossed into some, and others were set alight. Craven led a charge forward against another wall of infantry who were a rag tag force wearing eight different uniforms. This was quickly a desperate rearguard action as Napoleon tried to save as much of his army as he could. The Swedish cavalry soared forward beside Craven, though they had no bayonets and so used their carbines as clubs or charged with sabre in hand.

"Craven!"

He stopped just in time to see Lieutenant Fox-Strangways beside two of his Rocket Troop men who carried a Congreve rocket across their shoulders. They had rested their blankets over their shoulders and sides of their heads to shield themselves from the blast. Fox-Strangways held up a shard of wood to the fuse and it flashed to life. Craven leapt to the side of the street and turned away just in time, as the rocket screamed to life. It soared though the street just a few feet and parallel with the ground. He watched in disbelief as the projectile crashed into the French line before him and erupted in a flash. He turned away to save his eyes, but he looked back to see a scene of complete and utter carnage. Many of the enemy who had survived simply threw down their weapons, speechless at the horror that had been unleashed upon them.

The blankets of the two Rocket Troop men who had manhandled the weapon were on fire, but they cast them aside, their uniforms singed as they patted themselves down and coughed out the smoke they had inhaled. It had been a highly dangerous use of the rocket, but it had paid off. Panic was setting in all throughout the city as the allied armies swarmed through into seemingly every street. Craven could hear the sound of a horse approaching along the street ahead, and the rider came to a standstill fifty yards ahead of them. Both man and animal were unmistakable.

"Rocca!" Craven cried out angrily, for it was the turncoat who had betrayed them all. A Frenchman who the Crown Prince had trusted in only to be betrayed, and he was riding the horse he had stolen from him. Moxy rushed forward and lifted his rifle to the shoulder to take aim at the man.

"No, he's mine," growled Craven.

"I can have him now."

"You will not!"

Rocca rode on. Moxy huffed angrily at losing his opportunity, but Craven led them onwards. All across the city they could hear the battle wage on. Leipzig itself was in remarkably good shape, for it had not been subject to artillery bombardment until this morning, but the streets were littered with French equipment. They hurried on after the traitor, who was a hulking man and had proven a formidable opponent. He galloped on towards the Western gatehouse, which was crammed with Napoleon's troops as they struggled to make their escape. But they were bottlenecked not just by the gatehouse, but the lone bridge that led from the city out Westward to the only escape route the French army had left open to them. Rocca cried out angrily as he tried to bully his way through. He even cracked his riding whip down on the heads of several men, but they would not budge, nor could they, for they were wall-to-wall and back-to-back. Some turned in horror at the sight of Craven's force. The city echoed with the sound of musket fire and the clatter of cold steel. The enemy were as cornered rats, but instead of fighting back, many at the front tried to press on to escape, whilst those at the rear threw down their weapons and gave up all resistance.

Rocca cried out in fury as he dismounted and abandoned the horse he had taken from Craven. He drew out the Major's double-barrelled pistol that he had gained with the horse. He hurried on down a side street as Craven darted on after him. Craven pursued the huge Frenchman down two narrow streets. He stopped briefly as Rocca stopped to fire at him. The pistol ball struck the wooden frame of a house and sent splinters on Craven's face, but his quick reactions had saved him from death or blindness. He wiped the blood from his face with his sleeve and continued the pursuit.

On they ran, and Craven soon reached some stone

steps, much like the ones he had descended at the gatehouse after breaching the city. He looked up just in time to see Rocca fire the second barrel of the stolen pistol. He ducked to the side, but the shot still struck his right arm, blasting through and out the back of his tunic sleeve. He winced in pain, and Rocca smirked as he tossed the pistol down at Craven. He cut it away with his sword only to groan in pain once again, the impact of the cut causing pain to surge through his arm.

Timmerman rushed to his side, and many of the others were not far behind, but two-dozen French soldiers raced forward along the edge of the walls with bayonets in hand. Timmerman tackled him onto the stairs to save them both from a volley of the enemy.

"We've got this," insisted Paget as he led their companions on to engage the enemy.

"He's mine." Craven angrily pushed Timmerman off him.

"Don't be such a stubborn bastard. We are in this together." Timmerman held out his hand to Craven.

He sighed in frustration as he took it and was hauled to his feet, but he struggled to lift his sword, and so had to take it into his left hand. He was well skilled with his offhand, but not nearly as much as his dominant one, and so he nodded in agreement to accept Timmerman's help against the giant Frenchman.

"Let's get this bastard," insisted Timmerman.

They stormed up the steps and onto the rampart.

It was empty except for Rocca, who desperately looked for any way to escape from the walls. From this elevated position they could see the chaos which ensued all across the city. Tens of thousands of French soldiers had been trapped inside the walls, the loss of which would be as great as those killed in the desperate and bloody battle the day before. Their time was running out, for thousands of allied soldiers poured into the city from three directions every minute that went by.

"Rocca!" Craven roared as the two men approached him.

He gave up his search and turned to face them finally.

"Not man enough to face me alone?" he smirked.

The only one who is alone is you. Your Emperor and your armies have abandoned you," snarled Timmerman.

"You're a dead man, Rocca, and when we are through with you, we are coming for France," added Craven.

"You will never step one foot into my country!"

"Not one of you can stop us."

Rocca let out an angry war cry before storming forwards to attack them. He swung a huge blow for Craven, whose weaker left arm could not stop the blow, and his sword was knocked aside, his hand barely maintaining his grip of the weapon. The Frenchman swung a mighty blow over at Timmerman who parried it but staggered a few paces from the weight of the impact. He stopped just short of the edge where he could see the melee being fought by their companions below. Rocca lifted his leg to kick Timmerman over the ledge, but Craven brought down a cut against his boot that knocked it back down. Rocca quickly responded with a backhanded blow from his sword hand. The ward iron of his sabre smashed into the side of Craven's face, opening a deep cut and disorientating him as he fell against the rampart. Rocca followed it with a quick punch to Craven's bloody arm wound. He cried out in pain as the thunderous punch struck the wound inflicted by his own pistol.

But Timmerman slashed a cut across the Frenchman's face. He staggered back, his nose cleaved open and blood streamed down his face. But Timmerman did not pursue him and instead went to Craven's aid, helping him to his feet.

"You still with me?" he roared in Craven's face.

He nodded in agreement, but he was still disorientated.

"You Englishmen should have stayed in England, for you will die here today!"

"Craven, are you still with me?" Timmerman pressed, as his old adversary seemed out on his feet. Timmerman slapped him hard across the face, "I didn't live this long to see you die at the hands of a Frenchman. Fight Craven, fight!" he screamed into his face, but he seemingly could not get through.

"Your time is up." Rocca stormed forward.

Timmerman had no choice but to oppose him alone. He rushed forward and delivered a flurry of blows to confuse his giant opponent, preventing him from having the time and space to deliver another devastating blow. Rocca parried each and every one of them before kicking one of Timmerman's legs out from under him. Rocca hacked down at Timmerman's head as he knelt on one knee. He took his sword in two hands and parried above him as if he was using a pole arm. The attack was stopped dead, but Rocca kept applying pressure, and with both his height and strength advantage, Timmerman was powerless to stop him. Both his own blade and Rocca's were pushed down against his throat. It felt like his time was up as both blades sliced into his neck, and he was barely able to slow them down.

"So be it," he declared defiantly.

But a sword blade whistled over his head, and the point plunged into Rocca's chest. Timmerman would recognise that blade anywhere, for he had battled against it countless times. He could make out the engravings of Andrew Ferrara in the fuller, the old, treasured blade of James Craven. Rocca staggered back, losing his hold over Timmerman as he pulled himself off of Craven's blade.

"On your feet," growled Craven, who had seemingly awoken from his dazed state, even if he looked like a dead man walking, and yet he would not give up.

"Let's finish this," demanded Timmerman.

Rocca held up his sword ready to go on fighting, but he was struggling to breathe. All three of them looked like they had walked through hell, and all were leaking blood from fresh wounds. Craven went first, pushing a thrust and following it with two cuts. His form was ragged, and his blows had only half the power he intended, but Rocca was weakening also, and his blade was being knocked aside by even Craven's lighter blows. Timmerman rushed forward with a flurry of cuts. Rocca parried each of them until he was back up against a wall. He pushed off from it and shoved Timmerman back, swinging a wild horizontal cut for Craven, who ducked under it. Timmerman immediately went on the attack again, and Rocca turned to face him, but Craven leapt up from his crouching position. He launched himself forward from his legs with all the energy he could muster, plunging the point of his sword into the Frenchman's heart.

Rocca froze upon the impact and looked down to see that he was finished. He had just enough energy to pull Craven's blade from his body before stumbling several paces and falling over the edge of the battlement. He crashed down upon his countrymen below, flattening three of those who battled with Paget and the others. They looked down at the brutal display and merely threw down their arms and surrendered. Paget looked up at his two comrades in disbelief at their bloody state. He hurried for the steps to reach them, but as he reached the top step, he tripped and fell forward onto the battlements that looked out Westward to where Napoleon's army fled in a huge snaking column. What mostly caught his eye was the wooden bridge that had bottlenecked the entire army.

To his amazement he could see stacks of materials for bridge building nearby, and the enemy had no shortage of manpower and skills with which to build them. Yet seemingly nobody had bothered, perhaps because the prospect of defeat had never crossed their minds.

"Sir, Sir!" Paget beckoned for the two bloodied officers to join him.

They staggered over to his position to see that he pointed down to towards the single wooden bridge that was the escape route from Leipzig. It was crowded with French troops with thousands more waiting to cross.

"What of it?" Craven asked wearily.

"Look, Sir, look!" Paget cried impatiently.

He was pointing to a large boat moored beneath the bridge, which was a peculiar sight, but it reminded Craven of their daring mission to blow up a bridge for Prince Schwarzenberg. As he looked more closely, he could see that this boat too was heavily laden with barrels and that could well hold powder. Moxy rushed up beside them and Ferreira, too, who carried Craven's double-barrelled pistol which he returned to him. Craven had neither the energy nor the words to reply, despite how important the weapon was to him. He took it and stuffed it into his officer's sash about his waist.

"They mean to blow it for sure," declared Moxy as he carefully studied the scene.

The wooden bridge spanned the Elster River,

which ran North to South along the Western edge of the city. It was of sturdy construction designed for heavy traffic in and out of the city, including laden wagons and artillery as well as armies on the march. It was wide enough for supply carts to pass one another in either direction but was currently filled with Napoleon's soldiers as they shuffled onwards to escape the wave of the allied army which gave chase.

"You are sure?" Craven began to come to his senses and realised the significance of what they were looking at.

"They have rigged it to blow." Moxy looked at the fuses and pointed to a man who had been given the duty of igniting the charges, a mere lowly corporal who looked unsettled and uneasy with his task and all that he was seeing.

"If that bridge blows, it will cost Napoleon as much or more than this entire battle," declared Timmerman with glee as he tied off a neckerchief about his bleeding neck. Craven looked back into the city to see hordes of French soldiers still flooding towards the gatehouse below them. He went back to the wall to survey the bridge once more. Unlike the one they had blown in their night attack, this one was occupied by a vast force.

"What would it take to make them blow it?"

"Make them blow it?" Paget asked in surprise.

"That corporal is waiting for his moment to blow the only bridge out of this city, what would convince him to do so?"

"Put him under fire and then have an officer of his

own army demand he ignites the fuse?" Timmerman said with a great smile upon his face as if he had a plan.

He hurried back down to the body of Rocca and stripped off his tunic before pulling it on over his own, which made it fit at least somewhat better than it did. For its previous owner was a man of beastly proportions. He vanished into a tower nearby and returned with a roll of rope.

"What are you doing?" Craven groaned.

"Completing the mission." Timmerman tied off the rope around one of the battlements, tossing it up and over the wall. His impression of a French officer was barely half believable, and yet in the chaos of the situation it might just work.

"Once I am on the ground, open fire upon the corporal, but do not kill him. Unnerve the man, strike down those nearby, and strike the ground beside his feet. Rattle him."

He did not wait for their response as he climbed over the battlement and onto the rope, but Craven grabbed hold of him to share a few final words.

"Don't die out there. You are a bastard, Timmerman, but you are our bastard, and you deserve to live to enjoy this victory."

"Look at them run. I am quite safe." Timmerman smiled and shrugged him off. He quickly descended to the ground below. In the chaos before them, nobody paid him any attention, especially as more of Napoleon's army poured out from the city any way that they could. More ropes and ladders had been thrown against the Western walls as others in the Frenchmen's army did the same.

"Do it, but don't kill the poor lad," insisted Craven as he looked to the timid corporal who had been delegated the duty of destroying the crossing when the time was right.

Moxy fired first, shooting dead a lieutenant who was only a few paces from the corporal. Ferreira was next, shooting a veteran sergeant who might pay more attention than most to the goings on. Paget took aim with his long rifle and shot at the corporal, landing just a yard from his feet. The Frenchman flinched and looked out at the soldiers dropping with alarm, before looking to the walls where they were being fired upon. He cried out for those around him to take notice, and just as they did, a mass of Russian infantry surged out onto the rampart to the South of Craven's position. It sold the narrative they wanted the man to believe even better than they could have hoped, as panic set in amongst those on the bridge and many more who were waiting to cross.

The Russians opened fire, shooting the enemy like fish in a barrel and with little care for who they targeted, which was of grave concern to Craven and the plan Timmerman had devised, and yet the musket fire was inaccurate. Soldiers all around the French corporal were struck, and finally, he himself was clipped in the left arm.

Timmerman was watching the scene unfold carefully from both sides as he reached the water's edge. Finally, as the corporal reached breaking point, and his hands began to shake with fear, Timmerman called out to him. He cried out orders in French, demanding that the corporal blow the bridge for the sake of Napoleon, to save his life even.

The Frenchman looked deeply uneasy, but another volley ripped out from the Russians, as well as more accurate fire from Craven's comrades, and a dozen soldiers fell all around him. He lit the fuse and hobbled away to save his own skin. The fuse burnt tall and bright as the mass of French soldiers on the bridge realised what was happening. They cried out as they tried to hurry those before them on, but it was too late. The fuse reached the boat below the bridge and the barrels of powder inside it, igniting with a deafening eruption. The bridge vanished in a fireball as Craven and his comrades ducked down for cover. Timmerman hunkered down by the riverside as debris was blasted high into the sky. The French soldiers on the bridge were launched into the sky and river, many of them killed instantly. The eruption reached high into the sky for all to behold across the entire battlefield. Every soldier amongst the allied army knew of the bridge's location and significance. Triumphant cries rang out from hundreds of thousands of soldiers as the debris began to settle, for with the destruction of the bridge the fate of most of those trapped at Leipzig was sealed. Craven looked out into the city to see French soldiers all over abandon their positions and lay down their weapons. The rout was vast and devastating to the enemy. Craven then turned back to the West. Many of those waiting to cross plunged into the river to try and make it to safety.

They watched as the Polish General Poniatowski, veteran of the Russian campaign and many others, galloped into the river and tried to cross. His horse reached the muddy embankment on the far side of the river, but struggled to climb out and toppled over, crashing down over the Polish French general, subsequently drowning him. Many more tried to make the crossing, and plenty drowned as he did. Marshal Macdonald, the son of a Jacobite army veteran, struggled to cross two logs that had been thrown cross the river, one leg astride each. He had almost made it across when several of more fleeing soldiers leapt onto the logs and unsettled them. Macdonald tumbled into the water, causing a great laughter and mockery to arise from Craven and the allied soldiers who watched from the walls of Leipzig. He was pulled to safety through the thick mud, only to flee with his tail between his legs like the last remnants of Napoleon's army.

The battle was over, and the gunfire soon died down as all those of Napoleon's grand army trapped in Leipzig having surrendered. There was no energy left to pursue Napoleon, but his army was shattered and unable to turn back and provide any resistance as they continued to flee. Ecstatic cries rang out across the allied army as they celebrated the triumph, for it was in no doubt now. Napoleon had lost twice the number of the Coalition armies in dead, wounded, and captured.

It was a devastating loss for the French Emperor. The Battle of the Nations was over, and the victors were not in doubt. Napoleon's campaign in Germany, to which many of his opponents called the War of Liberation, were rapidly coming to a close as he fled back to France in defeat and disgrace. Craven wiped blood from his face as he gazed out upon the fleeing French army, taking great delight in seeing their backs.

Timmerman tore off his French tunic as he struggled back through the French soldiers who did not obstruct his movement now. He hopped along with a great enthusiasm at his work as he joined Craven and the others upon the wall once more.

"What a day, Sir," declared Fox-Strangways as they marvelled at the sight Napoleon's army fleeing from their presence.

"What a day, indeed. This battle shall be remembered for many years to come, and in England it will be remembered for the bravery of Captain Richard Bogue," declared Craven.

"To Captain Bogue!" Fox-Strangways roared.

The battle for the German lands seemed all but over as Craven looked Westward now with envious eyes as he dreamed of their advance into France.

"Victory is ours," declared Timmerman.

"Yes, it is, to all of us. To Victory!" Craven cried.

"To victory!" roared his comrades.

THE END

Printed in Dunstable, United Kingdom